Praise for
The Queen of Sands

"Mona Tebyanian's debut novel provides readers with an escape into two parallel narratives set three hundred years apart. One focuses on a young woman seeking her destiny in a harsh environment, and the other depicts romance, adventure, betrayal, and court intrigue. The two together contain all of the elements that readers look for in a young adult fantasy novel."
—Noelle Brada-Williams, chair of English and comparative literature at San Jose State University

"This is a charming novel adorned with all the trappings of a medieval romance: castles, knights and ladies, court intrigue, a damsel in distress rescued by a handsome prince, and revelatory dreams. It also has the psychological interests of medieval romance, as its protagonist undertakes a journey that is both geographical and spiritual, a journey across time and desert toward greater self-knowledge. It will engage, intrigue, and delight you, and it will transport you to the ancient Middle East. I highly recommend it."
—Robert Bjork, foundation professor of English at Arizona State University

"*The Queen of Sands* takes the reader to a land of dreams, royalty, love, and betrayal. A rollicking fable and absorbing, engrossing novel."
—Mark Mustian, internationally bestselling author of *The Gendarme* and *Boy With Wings*

"*The Queen of Sands* sweeps you into a world of desert myths, royal drama, and unforgettable characters you can't help but root for. It's packed with adventure, mystery, and heart—the kind of story that makes you want to read 'just one more chapter' until you've devoured the whole thing."

—Jake Stehman, author of *A Battle For Fire* and *A Game as Old as Time*

"Drawing from her extensive knowledge of Persian culture and folklore, Ms. Tebyanian has created a vast world from an unforgiving desert and the romantic adventures of an intrepid young woman. Guided by visions, she experiences nobility, love, betrayal, and tragedy on her journey to realize her destiny. A thoroughly engaging tale for the young adult or mature reading audience."

—Raymond Hutson, author of *Topeka ma'shuge*, and *To Slaughter a Camel*

"*The Queen of Sands* will sweep you away! An assured and ambitious debut."

—Erin Nieto, author of *Love and Conductivity*

The Queen of Sands
by Mona Tebyanian

© Copyright 2025 Mona Tebyanian

ISBN 979-8-88824-861-4

All rights reserved. No part of this publication may be reproduced, stored in a retrieval system, or transmitted in any form or by any means—electronic, mechanical, photocopy, recording, or any other—except for brief quotations in printed reviews, without the prior written permission of the author.

This is a work of fiction. All the characters in this book are fictitious, and any resemblance to actual persons, living or dead, is purely coincidental. The names, incidents, dialogue, and opinions expressed are products of the author's imagination and are not to be construed as real.

Edited by Miranda Dillon
Cover design by Catherine Herold

Published by

3705 Shore Drive
Virginia Beach, VA 23455
800-435-4811
www.koehlerbooks.com

THE QUEEN OF SANDS

MONA TEBYANIAN

VIRGINIA BEACH
CAPE CHARLES

To my partner in life, Arzhang Naderi,
Your presence has been my greatest source of inspiration.
This journey would not have been possible without you.

AUTHOR'S NOTE

Creating *The Queen of Sands* has been an immersive journey that was inspired by the endless deserts and rich cultural histories of the Middle East. The plot of this story includes love, fate, and sacrifice and follows the lives of a prince who goes against the grain and a young woman who is pursued by the spirits of the past. The characters navigate choices that transcend time, revealing how the consequences of the past shape the present. Their journeys are driven by courage, ambition, and the pursuit of truth, challenging the boundaries between memory and reality.

While the kingdoms and landscapes are imagined, they are created with a lot of respect for the histories and cultures of the regions that inspired them. Through this tale, I aimed to convey the agelessness of love and the might of destiny. This narrative calls for you to embark on a journey through the ancient sands and solve mysteries that link the present with the past. I hope that within these pages you will find adventure, intrigue, and connection.

CHAPTER ONE

Esther had lived in the desert her whole life. It was both a blessing and a curse to see the sun shining in the middle of the sky every day. She lived in Aseeta, a modest village where people hunted and traded with other villages. Aseeta was barren, and all Esther had ever seen in her life was just sand and the blue sky, but she knew, after about a day's ride toward the South, a turquoise-blue sea connected to the desert; however, she had never gone that far. The houses in Aseeta were humble, and people did not expect much from life. They worshipped the goddess of sand, and each year on the seventh day of winter, they gathered in the Herna temple to pray and ask for forgiveness so that the goddess had mercy on them. Aseeta was once vibrant and full of life, but after what happened centuries ago, people changed. Everyone in Aseeta believed in a myth that went back to 300 years ago when the goddess of sand rose out of the desert in the middle of a gigantic sandstorm and turned everyone into sand.

After the sandstorm, many people died, and those who survived told the story of what had happened to the next generations. It all started with a sandstorm. Then, in the middle of the storm, the figure of a woman was shaped in front of everyone's eyes, a woman made of sand and astonishingly huge. According to the myth, she was the goddess of sand, and she was very angry with her people. She roared with rage as she destroyed everything and turned everyone into sand. People in Aseeta worshipped the goddess of sand for thousands of years, and her name was mentioned in all the ancient books of the South. Before the goddess of sand destroyed Aseeta, the city had a powerful kingdom. Aseeta was huge, with so many buildings. People were rich and had a decent life, and their kingdom was powerful and stable, but everything changed in one day. A great empire fell, the palace and all the buildings got destroyed, people turned into sand, and nothing remained of the city and their civilization. Years later, those who survived the incident found a new place to settle down and called it home. The goddess of sand was holy, yet terrifying to the people of Aseeta, and to keep her pleased, they gathered on the exact day the sandstorm had happened, in a temple they had built to pray and repent of their sins so nothing like that occurrence ever happened again. Everyone wanted to erase the memory of the sandstorm, yet they could not resist the urge to tell their children about the goddess and her power, and somehow every child in Aseeta knew about the myth.

When Esther was a child, her mother told her the story too. She could close her eyes and imagine the goddess of sand destroying the whole city with her giant sand hands. If there was one thing Esther was good at, it was harnessing the power of imagination.

Esther was nineteen. She was quiet, sweet, and charming. She had a slim figure compared to other girls in the village, and her big brown eyes made her attractive. She was mysterious and unique, and even her mother could not sometimes tell what she had on her mind. She had lost her father years ago, and all she had in the world was her mother.

"Make sure to return home before the ritual starts tonight," Illashka, Esther's mother, said.

"Why do I have to be in the ritual, Mother? No one cares if I am there or not." Esther's voice was barely above a whisper.

"You do not attend because of others. You attend because you have to, so the goddess of sand protects you throughout the year," Illashka said.

"I already feel protected by her. I can even sometimes talk to her." Esther looked down, kicking at a loose stone.

"Do not say that, my child. Only the chief of the village can communicate with the goddess. Do you know what these people will do to you if they hear you?" Illashka asked.

"I am not afraid of them," Esther said.

"But I fear for your life. You are all I have in this world," Illashka said.

"If you fear for my life, then we shall leave this place behind and start a new life somewhere else. There is nothing for us here in Aseeta," Esther said.

"It is not that simple. I have lived here my whole life, and we may not be welcomed in other villages. Besides, it takes days, maybe weeks, to see another village in the desert. It is dangerous to travel," Illashka said.

"But you know I will do it one day, whether you come with me or not. I cannot live in Aseeta my whole life," Esther said.

"Perhaps after I die, because I will not let you leave as long as I am alive," Illashka said with a sad voice.

"How can you say that, Mother? Even if I leave, I will come back to get you, and you will live for a very long time," Esther said while holding her mother's hands.

"Fine, let's not talk about this subject anymore. Do you want to go to the ruins again?" Illashka asked.

"Yes, but I promise to be back for the ritual," Esther said.

She wished her mother could understand her and let her live as she wanted, but Illashka had never tried to see the world through her daughter's eyes. She was too afraid of the goddess of sand and the chief of the village that no matter what Esther said, she was not willing to listen.

Esther finally arrived at the ruins of the abandoned palace in the desert, which the goddess had destroyed. It was mystical and peaceful. It was so quiet that she could stay there for hours, even days, without being bothered. It was her routine to leave the village and go to the ruins, the only place she felt at peace since the people of Aseeta believed the palace was cursed, and so no one dared to go there. She usually escaped the village at night and hid in the ruins of the palace, away from everyone's eyes, lying down on the soft sands and watching the stars. The palace was massive, with beautiful carvings on the stones, but after its destruction, only a few pieces of the columns and a half-ruined roof remained of it. There were also several stone inscriptions with years of ancient knowledge that belonged to the library of the palace and somehow had miraculously survived the fire and the sandstorm centuries ago, but the people of Aseeta believed it was dark knowledge, and so no one read them or tried to preserve them, but Esther was different from the people of her village. She spent hours in the ruins, reading the inscriptions, learning about her ancestors, and meditating in the silence.

The serenity at the ruins was breathtaking. Esther started walking around, touching all the columns on her way. Although nothing much remained of the palace, it was still magnificent and dreamy. She sat in a corner, resting her head on one of the columns, and closed her eyes. She was gradually sinking into the sands, and she could no longer feel her body. She was free; she could be anywhere she wanted. Hours passed and everything was still until she suddenly felt a whoosh of wind in the air. It was slight at first but soon started blowing harder, until she could hardly open her eyes.

This is not a good sign on the night of the ritual, she thought.

It was almost midnight, the time for the ritual to start. Esther started running toward the village. The wind was strong, and sands were everywhere. The temple was almost invisible, but she knew she was close. When she got to the temple, the ritual had already started. Everyone in the village was there, and the sound of the people chanting prayers was so loud that the echo of the wind outside the temple could hardly be heard. A storm could start at any second, and she could feel the fear in the people's voices. She knelt like others and bowed for the statue of the goddess of sand that was in the center of the temple. Right under the statue's feet was a big pile of sand, and after the chanting was over, everyone started circling the statue and filled the small bowls they had in their hands with the sacred sand so that the goddess kept them safe throughout the year, but unlike everyone in the village, Esther did not believe in the goddess's power. She believed that the legend of the goddess of sand was merely a bedtime story for children, and those who believed in her power were crazy.

CHAPTER TWO

WHEN ESTHER WAS a little girl, she wanted to mix with other girls her age, but she was never accepted, and when she grew older, she was the one who didn't want to socialize or befriend anyone. They all seemed simpleminded to her, and all they cared about in life was how to survive and see the next dawn. Since her childhood, everyone in the village thought she was crazy, and they all knew about her weird dreams. The people had tried to banish her from the village because they believed she was cursed and would bring calamity to the community, but her mother had begged them to leave her daughter alone and assured them that she would not cause any issues. Esther was always terrified of sleeping because she had the same dream every night, over and over. She saw a woman in her dreams who was beautiful but scary at the same time. The woman glowed with light, and she only said one thing to Esther in her dreams: "Set me free, please." And as soon as she wanted to ask her who she was and how to set her free, the woman disappeared, and she woke up. There was a horror in her voice and a plea in her eyes that haunted Esther every night, and she was confident her dreams meant something, but she had not found an answer for them for years, and she blamed the village for that. She wanted to flee the desert to experience a new world, and maybe then she could figure out the reason for her dreams.

One hot summer night, Esther went to the palace again. She had explored every corner of the palace, and she had one favorite spot for herself. She lay down on the sands and closed her eyes. The heat of the sands on her back was pleasant, and she could stay there for hours. *I wish I could have seen this place before its destruction. It was probably glorious and majestic, with so many fountains and gardens*, she thought. She always felt at peace in the palace, and the silence in the desert had created a glorious night. She was almost falling asleep when she suddenly heard a loud noise and saw a very bright light. She could barely open her eyes, but when she could finally open them, she saw a woman standing in front of her, glowing with light. She was the same woman she saw in her dreams every night. The woman had long hair and incisive black eyes. She was tall, and her body was glowing in the darkness of the night. Although she was beautiful, something was frightening about her face, and for a few seconds, Esther thought the woman was going to kill her. She could not think of anything at that moment. She could not move, and it was like time had stopped. The woman looked into her eyes and said, "Set me free, please." She said the same thing she always said in her dreams, but it was even scarier in reality. Esther wanted to ask her how, but she could not even open her mouth; the presence of the woman had paralyzed her. She just stared at her, and within a few seconds, the woman disappeared into the thickness of the night, and everything went back to how it was: the desert, the silence, the darkness.

Her hands were trembling, and her heart was beating fast. She had not dreamed it. The woman in her dreams was real. *Maybe a sorcerer has cast a spell over her, and she has been trapped for years, or maybe she is the sorcerer herself, dead for centuries, and needs a human sacrifice to return to life*, Esther thought, and she was eager more than ever to leave Aseeta and look for the woman, so no power in the world could keep her in the village anymore. She could feel something extraordinary waiting for her, and all she had to do was open the gate and step inside.

She was so excited that night that she could barely sleep. What happened to her in the deserted palace was the most exhilarating incident of her whole life, and she could not stop thinking about it. She went to the ruins several times after that night, hoping to see the woman again, but she did not show up. She had so many questions to ask her, and she had promised herself to stay strong and not be intimidated by her presence anymore. Esther had to know who she was and why she showed up in her dreams every night. One night, when she was in the ruins again, lying on the sands and watching the stars, something extraordinary happened. The stars were moving around fast, and in just a few seconds, the face of a woman was shaped in the sky. Everything was magical. It was the most beautiful thing Esther had ever seen in her life. The stars were bright and shiny and the whole area was lit up. She did not know who that face belonged to, but it was peaceful, and it resonated with her. She was certain it was the goddess of sand, sending her signs and assuring her that leaving Aseeta was the right thing to do. She was determined in her decision, but she did not want to tell her mother about it. She would disagree and stop her, and she would watch out for her every minute of every day if she knew what she had in mind. Esther decided to wait and tolerate the boring life in Aseeta for a bit longer until it was the perfect time to leave. Besides, she did not want to leave in the extreme heat of summer. She would not survive even a day in the desert in the middle of summer, so she waited until it got cooler. Even in the fall, the desert was still harsh, and the chance of survival was slim, but she could not wait any longer.

The day of departure finally came, and she knew her mother was busy that day. It was the day all the women in the village gathered together and baked traditional bread. It was a gesture of welcoming fall and thanking the goddess of sand for the summer to end. She felt guilty for leaving her mother, but she was certain she would forgive her someday. Life could be so simple in Aseeta, but she was not the type of girl to settle for a normal life. She could marry a young man in the village, have children, and have a life like her mother and other women in the village, but that was not what she wanted in life. Above all, how could she ignore her dreams and forget about that woman? She was calling on her, and she had no choice but to follow.

When she left, it was just getting dark, and she walked the whole night because she knew the day's extreme heat would make it almost impossible to walk. When the first rays of sun touched her face, she knew she had to stop. She was exhausted, and she had no energy to continue, so she decided to make a small refuge to keep herself safe from the heat.

Five days passed without seeing a single soul, and her stash of food was running out. She was thirsty and tired, she could hardly move her feet, and she constantly rubbed her cracked lips together. She was unsure if she could continue anymore; she needed to rest for a while, but it was too hot, and as her eyes were being closed, she saw a pond in the distance, or maybe it was a mirage. *It would be a shame to die out of thirst so close to a pond*, she thought, so she pulled together all the strength in her body and moved her feet, one step at a time, until she got closer. Luckily for her, it was not a mirage. There was a pond there in the middle of the desert, and a tree. She quenched her thirst and decided to lie down under the shade. Soon, her eyes closed, and there was another dream again. She was in a place she had never seen in her life before. There were giant trees everywhere, and everything was green and lush. Birds were singing, and the sound of the river flowing was soothing, but everything changed in a second. The sky became dark, the leaves of the trees started falling, and she heard a screech in the distance. When she woke up, she was wet with sweat. It was only a dream, but it felt so real to Esther. When she was in Aseeta, she had only one dream, and that was of the woman who asked for her help. It was the first time she had a different dream, and she was sure it was somehow related to her journey.

She took off her clothes to take a bath in the pond. She needed to relax after that horrific dream and all she had gone through in the past several days. She missed her mother and the touch of her hand on her hair. However, despite all the hardships, she had no intention of going back, and she was even more persistent. As she was swimming in the pond, she heard someone behind her.

"So, you are finally here, Esther," a man said.

Esther turned back and saw a dwarf in torn and filthy clothes staring at her. She submerged her body into the water, trying to hide away.

"Who are you? How do you know my name?" Esther asked.

"I am the keeper of the pond. My name is Zelmata," he replied.

"Keeper of the pond? What does it mean?" she asked.

"It means I am in charge of protecting this pond," he said.

"Why does a pond need protection?" she asked.

Zelmata stepped closer, his voice dropping to a hush. "This is no ordinary pond, Esther. The tears of your three guardian angels created this pond, and they knew you would come here one day. They asked me to protect it with my life. Bathing in this water opens the gates of your heart to a divine knowledge that only you will see. I have been waiting for you for so long."

"I do not understand anything. How can you be waiting for me when I do not even know you?" she asked.

"You do not need to understand everything you see or experience. Tell me! Have you understood yet what your dreams mean? Sometimes, you just need to have faith. Is it that hard?"

"How do you know about my dreams?" she asked with curiosity.

"Enough asking why and how! Hurry up and get dressed! We do not have much time," he said.

This old man must be crazy. He has certainly lost his mind being all alone in this desert, but how does he know about my dreams? she thought as she got dressed.

"Do you know where you are, Esther?" he asked.

"No. I left my village five days ago, and I do not know where I am now," she replied.

He spread his arms wide. "You are in Azhtar, the land of angels. This place is sacred, and only the chosen souls by the goddess of sand are allowed to enter, and you are a special soul."

"Does it have anything to do with my dreams?" she asked.

"It does, and I have been waiting here to show you the path. You have a long journey ahead of you, and you are just at the beginning. Take this book! You will need this in the future. Whenever you feel lost and do not know what to do, ask the book. It will guide you," he said.

Esther opened the book and said, "But there is nothing written in this book."

"You cannot see it yet. You will see it when you need it. Keep it with you and guard it with your life. It will save you during hard times," he said.

"I do not know where I have to go. I just knew I had to leave my village," she said.

"Go to the North, Esther! You need to find the pine tree by the river. Only there will you find the answers to your questions. I did what I had to do. Now it is time for me to leave."

"Do not leave me, please. You cannot just show up to me and tell me things that I do not understand and leave. I started this journey to find an answer to my dreams, but what you told me about the pond, this book, and my guardian angels is like a fairy tale. I do not believe in magic," she said.

"This is no magic, and you do not have to force yourself to believe anything. All you need to do is follow your heart without reasoning, and it will get you to your answers."

"Do you know who the woman in my dreams is?" she asked.

"It does not matter whether I know her or not. Unlocking the mystery of your dreams is your responsibility, and only you can help yourself. I am just a messenger, Esther," he replied.

"Fine! I will figure out everything all by myself. At least tell me which way is north," she said.

"That way is north," he said while pointing out with his fingers.

Esther turned her head to look at where Zelmata had pointed, but a few seconds later, when she looked back, he was gone, and she was all alone in the desert again. She went back to the pond and looked at her reflection in the water. If everything Zelmata had told her was true, she was in a fairyland that no ordinary man could enter. She pressed the book tight to her chest and lay down by the pond. It was almost getting dark, and there was a slight chill in the air.

She felt so peaceful the whole night, and she slept more than she should have. When she woke up, the sun was in the middle of the sky, and it was blazing hot. Although she did not want to leave the pond and the shade, she had to continue her journey. Everything seemed brighter that day, like a miracle was going to happen. Something magnificent was in her destiny, and she had no intention of giving up, but all she could see was desert and sand. The first day after leaving the pond passed peacefully, and she told herself that her guardian angels were looking after her, so there was no need to be scared. She tried to eat and drink as little as possible, but she finally ran out of food and water. She had been walking for six days without seeing a single soul, and it felt like the world was empty. She was exhausted, and she could barely move her feet. It was dead quiet, and the only thing she could hear was the screech of the devil in the desert, longing to take her soul. It was pointless fighting to live, and she finally gave up and let her body collapse on the sands. The second her body touched the sand grains, her soul started roaming around, and Esther dreamed again. She dreamed of something that felt familiar yet unknown. Esther was dreaming of a woman she had never seen in her life before. However, the connection she felt with her was so strong that it made Esther want nothing more than to know her. The woman's face was kind and calm, and she felt like she knew her from another world.

CHAPTER THREE

CENTURIES BEFORE ESTHER, there was Aphra and Jasper. They were best friends, and they lived in a land far away from Aseeta. They had known each other since they were little, and they spent most of their time together. They played and laughed, they cried, and they explored the forest together. When Jasper was only six, the rebellions killed his father, and his mother raised him alone. When he grew older and realized how his father had died, all he wanted was to become a knight and protect his people. Aphra was five when she first met him, and although he was only one year older than her, he always felt protective of her. He cared about Aphra, and as they grew older, he gradually started having feelings for her. There was nothing and no one in the world that Jasper loved more than Aphra. He adored her. She was the definition of love for him. To Jasper's eyes, no other girl was as beautiful as Aphra, and there was nothing he would not do to make her happy or impress her.

Aphra was from a decent family. They were neither wealthy nor poor. Her father was a merchant, and they were happy with what they had. She was her parents' only child and loved them very much. Life was pretty simple for Aphra. She had all she needed in life: her loving parents, a house to live in, and the whole wilderness of Kalastra to explore. Kalastra was enchanting, and its beauty made everyone fall in love with it. It was a vast land, with breathtaking nature. It was green, with majestic mountains. The forest was thick with pine and oak trees, and the lakes were light blue like the sky. Aphra loved the beauty of Kalastra.

One day, when they were still very young, Jasper fifteen and Aphra fourteen, they went to the forest together so Aphra could pick some rare wildflowers, but along the way, when Aphra fell off her horse and twisted her ankle, they had to stay in the forest until she felt better.

"What happened, Aphra? Are you hurt?" Jasper asked.

"I think my ankle is twisted. It hurts," Aphra replied.

"Let me see," he said as he examined her ankle. "It is twisted, but it is not awful. If I find some herbs to put on it, you will feel much better in a few hours."

"My horse is gone, Jasper! What do I do without a horse?" she asked.

"The stupid horse was useless. Do not worry. It will find its way home. Wait here for me and do not move! I will be back soon," he said.

When Jasper got back, Aphra had already passed out. He smashed the herbs and bandaged her ankle. It was nothing serious, and he was confident she would recover soon, but they could not stay in the middle of the forest, so he touched her forehead gently and woke her up.

"I bandaged your ankle. You will be as good as new tomorrow," he said.

"Thank you, Jasper. I do not know what I would do without you. I cannot even ride a horse," she said.

"It was not your fault. The horse bolted suddenly. It does not matter now. We should find shelter for the night. We only have one horse, and you are injured. We cannot make it back to the city before sunset," he said.

"My parents are expecting me to be back. They will be worried," she said.

"I know, but we have no choice. It is dangerous to leave now. Believe me!" he said.

"Okay, where should we stay for the night?" she asked.

"When I was looking for herbs, I found a cave not so far from here. It is the perfect shelter for the night," he said.

Aphra could hardly walk, so Jasper carried her in his arms. She was so tiny and fragile to Jasper. It was the first time he'd gotten that close to her and was able to touch her. Her eyes were so close to his heart that he thought she could read it aloud. *What if Aphra realizes everything and does not want to see me anymore? I will die. I will die if I do not see her,* Jasper thought.

"What are you thinking about? You seem so sad," Aphra said.

"I am just worried about you. Does it still hurt?" he said and lied to her.

"The herbs are working. I will be fine. I can try to walk if you are tired," she said.

"You are not heavy at all, lighter than a feather," he said with a smile.

"I can see how strong and muscled you are. You do not need to tease me," she replied with a smirk.

"Look! The cave is there, just a little farther ahead," he said.

When they entered the cave, it was nothing like they expected. It was not an ordinary cave. It was ancient, and it was shaped more than a thousand years ago, or maybe even more.

"It is so magical in here. Look! There are so many blue crystals in the cave," she said.

"What is this place? How come we have never found it before?" he asked.

"We had never come this deep into the forest. I am so happy we found it today," she said.

"We should give it a name. Do you not think so?" he said.

"You are right. This cave should be our hiding place. No one should know about this cave, no one, not even our parents. Promise me, Jasper!" she said.

"Okay, girl. I promise you. What do you want to name it now?" he asked.

"I think we should name it the Crystal Cave. What do you think?" Aphra said while giggling with excitement.

"The Crystal Cave sounds good. Okay, come and sit here! You need to rest!" he said.

"I am so excited that I do not feel any pain now. Maybe everything that happened today was to lead us to this cave. I feel so ancient and wise in here," she said.

"You are funny, Aphra, and I like how you always find a reason to smile in every situation. I wish I could be more like you," he said.

"You are better than you think. You always make me happy. Look! It was you who found this cave today. Promise me we will never stop being friends!" she said.

"I promise you, Aphra, if there is one thing you do not need to worry about in this world, it is to have me as your friend for eternity," he said.

"Even when you become a knight and go to the court?" she asked.

"Even then, but if you do not want me to become a knight, I will forget it," he said.

"Being a knight is the only thing you truly want in your life. How can you forget it?" she asked.

He wanted to say, *Because I love you more than being a knight, having you is the only dream that keeps me awake at night, and the thought of losing you is the only nightmare in my life*, but instead, he said, "It is raining. We were lucky to find this cave. I should make a fire for the night."

"What can I do to help?" she asked.

"Just relax and watch the rain. I need to collect firewood, but I will be back soon."

Jasper knew Aphra loved the rain, and he wanted to create a memorable night for her. The rain was soft, and the weather was brisk. He was alone with Aphra, and life could not get any better. When Jasper came back, it was almost dark. He made a fire, and they both warmed themselves up.

"It would be a beautiful night sleeping in this cave and watching the rain if I had not twisted my ankle," she said.

"We would not be here in this cave if you had not twisted your ankle," he replied.

"You are right. Then promise me we will come back here again, especially if it rains," she said.

"I promise you, Aphra. Now close your eyes! You seem tired. I am here with you. Everything is fine," he said, laying his jacket on her shoulder.

"Can you talk to me until I fall asleep?" she asked.

"What do you want me to say?" he said.

"When will you enter the tournament?" she asked.

"I do not know. I am not ready yet. I only have one chance, and I do not want to ruin it. Once I become a knight, so many things will change for me. I will tell you my secret then, the one you always beg me to tell you. I sometimes see it in my dreams, that I say it to you, and you stare at me without any emotion on your face. I am scared of what you would say." He looked at Aphra, but she was already in a deep sleep. He lay next to her, and it was like time had stopped for him. He looked at her face like he had never seen it before. He wanted to memorize the details of her face. She had the most beautiful eyebrows, lips, and her tiny chin, and her soft, silky hair drove him crazy. He even dared to touch her hair. He did not want to sleep that night. How could he sleep and miss the chance of watching her? If there was one thing in the world worth waiting and fighting for, it was Aphra.

The next morning everything was different for both Jasper and Aphra. Jasper had spent a memorable night watching his love sleep for the first time in his life, and Aphra had made an important decision in her life.

"Thank you for the herbs. I do not feel pain anymore." Aphra stretched out her leg and flexed her ankle gently.

"You are welcome. It was not so hard to find the herbs," he said.

"But if you were injured, I would not even know what herbs to collect, or if I were alone, I would not know what to do," she said.

"Well, maybe I should teach you a few things," he said.

"I want to do even better," she said.

"What do you have in mind this time?" he asked.

"I should be able not just to help myself but others too. I want to learn how to become a healer. My uncle is the court's physician, and he needs an assistant," she said.

Jasper shifted uncomfortably, rubbing the back of his neck. "But you're a woman. Only men can be physicians."

"There is no such rule, and if there is, I want to be the first female physician in the city."

"That is not a game, Aphra. So many people will not like it," he said.

"Good thing I do not care about those people. I have made my decision, and no one can stop me," she said.

Aphra was a stubborn girl, and no one could persuade her to do things against her will, especially not Jasper. Aphra's personality was strong. Although she seemed to be a soft girl who could be easily broken, she was exactly the opposite, and Jasper knew that better than anybody.

Days and months passed, winters and springs came one after another, and Jasper and Aphra were no longer kids. Aphra was twenty, a young, beautiful, talented girl whom many young men in the city wanted to marry. She was passionate about helping people, and that was the driving reason for her to learn medicine from her uncle. She was loved by everyone, and her parents were proud of her. She was the only woman in the city practicing medicine, a role model for many young girls who looked up to her. However, she had haters too. Men who believed the only responsibility of a woman was to marry and bear children could not tolerate seeing a young, successful woman, so they occasionally caused problems for her, but each time, Jasper was there to help her out.

Being a skilled physician was not the only quality Aphra possessed. She had a beautiful voice too, and it was mesmerizing when she played the lute and sang along. She was kind and softhearted, she was beautiful inside and out, she was a dreamer, and, unlike other girls, she liked to spend most of her time in the forest. She was a great rider, and she loved to paint, which was her new passion.

Jasper was twenty-one, and he was a great fighter. He was excellent with the sword, and he spent hours in the forest, practicing swordsmanship. He had a muscled body, and his dark wavy hair, combined with his green eyes, made him somehow attractive. He wanted to impress Aphra, and he always wondered what she thought of him, but she was tough to read. Jasper always told her that she was a complicated girl, and he was right. He sometimes thought that Aphra could read his heart, terrified of what she would find out, but unlike him, Aphra was mysterious, and Jasper was always scared of losing her, like she would go to a faraway land one day and leave him behind forever. He wanted to confess his love to her many times, but he never dared to say anything, so he kept quiet for years, waiting for the best opportunity.

CHAPTER FOUR

IT WAS CUSTOMARY in Kalastra to hold a tournament each year to give young men a chance to prove their abilities and military skills to the kingdom to become a knight. Every eligible young man, whether noble or not, was welcome to enter the tournament, and it consisted of two important sections: The first was the joust, which was a one-on-one duel between mounted men, using wooden lances, and the second was also a one-on-one battle, but without horses and using swords. Out of hundreds of men who attended the tournament, only the ten best fighters who had won both competitions against their rivals were chosen as the Kalastra knights.

Jasper had planned to attend the tournament that year, and he wanted to celebrate his success later by confessing his love to Aphra. He was the best fighter in Kalastra, and he was ready to show his abilities to the king and prince, but most importantly, he wanted to impress Aphra by becoming a knight. The tournament lasted for four days, and he asked Aphra to meet him in the Crystal Cave after the tournament was over, and Aphra accepted. At the end of the fourth day, Jasper finally became a knight, and one of his dreams came true. He felt he was unstoppable, and he could achieve anything. *I am no longer an ordinary man. I am the knight of Kalastra. I am powerful, and she cannot resist me*, he thought as he rode toward the cave. When he got to the cave, she was not there yet, so he started practicing how to tell her everything. He wanted to say that he fell in love with her from the first day he saw her, when they were only kids. He wanted her to know that he had been hiding her love in his heart for so long and that he would do anything for her. He would make the impossible possible, and he would move mountains for her.

She finally came, and as she approached him, his heart started beating fast, and his palms started sweating.

"I heard everything from the people in the city. I am proud of you. You are finally a knight," Aphra said.

"I still think I have been dreaming everything. I wish my mother was alive to see this day," Jasper said.

"She has been watching you from heaven. She is proud of you. I am certain," she said.

"There is something I need to tell you, Aphra, something I have been keeping to myself for a long time, but I need to tell you now," he said.

"What is it? Why are you so worried?" she asked.

"I do not know how to start. It is not easy to say. I have been practicing so many nights how to tell you, but I cannot find any words right now," he said.

"Then just say it!" she said, looking at him, confused and curious.

He waited for a few seconds and finally said, "I love you, Aphra. I have always loved you. You are the reason I wake up in the morning every day and the one I see in my dreams every night. I have loved you for years, and I can no longer live without you. Come to the court with me! Marry me! You will be my lady, and I will cherish you for the rest of our lives together."

Aphra was silent. She was looking for words, but she knew no matter how she said it, he would be heartbroken. She'd been aware of Jasper's feelings for a while, and she tried her best to keep him away because he was just a friend to her, like a brother. How could she love him? They were raised together, and she always thought Jasper saw her the same way too.

"Say something! Tell me you love me too!" he said.

"You have always been by my side, and you have protected me ever since I can remember, and we have spent so many years together, but you were always my friend, and you will always be. I do not love you, and I cannot marry you," she said.

"But you have feelings for me. I know you do. I have seen it in your eyes. You cannot deny it. Do not do this to us!" he said.

"I like you as a friend, as someone I trust and have known my whole life, but that is not love. I am certain. I am not in love with you," she said.

"We belong to each other. Do not tell me you never felt anything for me. You are mine. You have always been mine," he said.

"I belong to no one. What is wrong with you, Jasper?" she said.

"I cannot believe you. All the time we spent together, the songs we wrote together, all the good memories we made together—are they all meaningless to you? Is it that easy for you to forget?" Jasper asked with rage.

"Those memories are so precious to me, and you are still the most important person in my life," she said.

He shouted, "Stop saying that!"

"I am sorry, Jasper, but I cannot lie to you. I do not love you, and I feel horrible right now," she said as she wept.

"Do not pity me! Hate me if you want, but I will not let you pity me," he said.

"I never pretended to love you. I was always honest with you," she said.

Jasper left, hurt and heartbroken. He had kept Aphra's love in his heart for so long, but she had destroyed everything in just a few seconds. The thing he was always afraid of was true. She did not love him. She did not want him. What was he supposed to do without her? He even wished, for a second, he had not said anything; he could at least see her then, but everything was over, so he promised himself to erase her from his mind and to never think of her again, but he could not keep his promise for even one night.

CHAPTER FIVE

ONE YEAR HAD passed since Jasper became a knight and moved to the court, one complete year that he had not seen Aphra. He was heartbroken, unable to forget her, but life continued for both of them. Aphra still helped her uncle as the physician's assistant, and she sometimes spent time in the forest playing the lute and painting. She loved painting nature. One day, when she was sitting by the lake, doing her painting like usual, she heard several men galloping toward her. She was terrified, there was no time, and the sound was getting closer each second. Before she could do anything, four men surrounded her. Her father had always warned her about not being alone in the forest, but she never listened.

Things in Kalastra had become very hard in the past few years, and the insurgents loyal to Lord Henry were everywhere. Lord Henry was constantly at odds with King Alger, who was the king of Kalastra, and he was banished to the northern borders of Kalastra when the king was still young and at the beginning of his reign. After twenty years of exile, Lord Henry had finally gathered enough men loyal to him who all hated King Alger and wanted him overthrown.

Lord Henry believed he was the true heir to the throne of Kalastra, and King Alger had stolen the kingship from him. When young, King Alger and Lord Henry were two of the best knights in Kalastra. At that time, the king who ruled over Kalastra was a cruel and bloodthirsty man who believed everyone in the court was planning treason against him, including his wife and son. He doubted everyone, and in the end, he finally killed his only son because he thought he had allied with his enemy, and not long after, his wife killed him with poison and ended her life right after. With the king dead and no heir to the throne, Lord Henry, the queen's nephew, believed he was the legitimate, true king of Kalastra. After the king's death, there was no central government in Kalastra, and there was chaos everywhere in the country. Alger, who was more popular and praised by the people of Kalastra than Lord Henry, could finally win the throne with the help of Lord Dougal, whose daughter he married right before his coronation and who was one of the most powerful lords in the kingdom. Lord Henry never accepted Alger as the king of Kalastra, and he rose against him several times until the king finally exiled him.

Aphra would have died that day in the forest if it were not for Prince Larko, King Alger's son. When the men approached her, she started screaming, and luckily for her, Prince Larko heard her scream. He was hunting in the forest that day, with two of his knights somewhere close to that area. It was only a matter of minutes for Larko and his two knights to kill those men and rescue her, but Aphra had passed out from anxiety, and when she opened her eyes, she saw Larko sitting next to her, holding her head with a worried look in his eyes. As she tried to get up, Larko said, "Hey, easy! How are you feeling?"

"I'm better now. Thank you, sir. You saved my life." Aphra's voice quivered as she brushed the dirt from her skirt.

The man adjusted the strap of his armor, eyes kind yet searching. "Anyone would've done the same. But what were you doing here alone? These woods aren't safe at all, especially for a lady."

"I was reckless. My father keeps telling me not to come to the forest alone, but it is so peaceful here. Nothing like this had ever happened before," she said.

"There is a first time for everything. You could be dead if we had not heard your scream," he said.

Aphra looked at their armor and cloaks and realized they must be knights of Kalastra.

"I was lucky you were around. Thank you, my lord. My best friend and I used to come to the forest a lot, but I suppose it is not safe anymore. He is also a knight," she said.

The man raised a brow, a faint smile tugging at his lips. "I'm not a knight. I'm Larko, the prince of Kalastra."

"Please forgive me, Your Highness, for not knowing you," Aphra said with a shaky voice as she bowed to Larko.

"Do not worry. I am a normal person like everybody else. You seem tired, and it will get dark soon. Pack your things! We will get you home," he said.

"Thank you, Your Highness, but I do not want to be a burden. I think I will be fine going home alone," she said.

"Of course you will, but this makes me feel better. You will be riding with me," he said.

Aphra got on the horse with Larko. He was handsome, kind, and caring. She was still shivering, remembering everything that had happened. If it were not for Prince Larko, she could be dead. As everyone said, he was truly gallant, and there was something peaceful about him that made him attractive no matter what he said or did. She held on tight to him and tried to enjoy the ride.

"What is your name?" he asked.

"Aphra, Your Highness," she replied.

"Are you a painter, Aphra?" he asked.

"Yes, Your Highness, but I am not professional. I rarely paint, and I just do it as a hobby whenever I am not helping my uncle," she said.

"What does your uncle do?" he asked.

"He is the court physician, and I am his assistant," she said.

"You must be a brave young lady, pursuing a profession not accepted by society," he said.

"I think people have finally accepted me as a healer," she said.

"How come I never saw you at the court?" he asked.

"I do not go to the court often. I usually prepare the medicine my uncle needs at home, and I accompany him on his visits to see the sick people in the city," she said.

"Do you not like the court?" he asked.

"My uncle is a great physician, and he does a great job at the court. I do not think I am needed there. I would like to help the people in the city, people who cannot afford to pay a physician, and I would like to be there for them," she said.

"I admire you. You have a kind heart," he said, then waited for a few seconds. "Tell me about your painting! What do you usually paint?"

"Trees, flowers, houses in the village, and anything that does not move," she said.

"Can you paint a portrait of me? I promise not to move," he said with a smile.

Aphra liked his sense of humor. She smiled and said, "I will try, but I have never done a portrait before. I do not think I am fit to paint you, Your Highness."

"Then learn how to do it! You seem to be a talented girl," he said.

"Of course, Your Highness, if that is what you want me to do," she said.

"If you are passionate about learning painting, I will command the painter at the court to teach you," he said.

"You are very kind to me, Your Highness. I do not know how to thank you," she said.

"Thank me later by painting a fine portrait of me when you are good enough," he said with a smirk.

Aphra smiled into the fading light. "As you wish, Your Highness."

CHAPTER SIX

WHEN LAMIA WAS a little girl, she always felt lonely. She only had one brother, who had died at an early age from sickness, and after what happened to him, her mother was never the same. The queen of Sinkaba was never on good terms with her husband. She had not married with love, and all she had in the world was her children. When her son died, her soul died too, and nothing was important to her anymore. King Malik of Sinkaba was cruel and a tyrant. His father had ruled over Sinkaba for decades, and everything was peaceful during his reign, but after his death, Malik killed his older brother and took over the crown. He was a warrior, and he expanded the realm of Sinkaba with each battle.

After his coronation, he married the daughter of one of his ministers, Farah, whose beauty and charm were well known among everyone in the palace. Not only was she beautiful, but she was also one of the best riders in Sinkaba. She used to go hunting with King Malik, and she was better than everyone in the hunting squad, even the king himself. Farah was never in love with King Malik, and her father had forced her to marry him. She was scared of the king and never felt safe as the queen of Sinkaba. She was sure a man who had killed his brother for power was capable of doing anything, and she was right. Malik had married Farah for her beauty, and he was never in love with her either. When Lamia was born, things changed for Farah a little. She became more interested in her marriage with King Malik and tried her best to build a family, and everything was normal until her son, Nadeem, was born. When Nadeem was only two months old, he got sick, and he never recovered. When he died, part of Malik's heart, which had just softened, died too. He lost his prince, and Lamia was all he had. He no longer cared about Farah, and they got more separated with each passing day. Farah's haters in the palace started making rumors about her, convincing the king that she was plotting treason and planning to kill him. King Malik first resisted believing anyone who accused his wife of treason, but after Farah completely detached herself from him, he started to doubt her. He finally imprisoned and killed her in cold blood in front of his daughter's eyes. Lamia was only six when her father killed her mother, and she could never forget the horrific scene of her father's executioners butchering her mother. She cried for days and nights, and she saw nightmares for years. She had lost her mother and her little brother, and she was terrified of her father. She was always alone, and her nanny had raised her in solitude and fear. She hated her father for what he had done to her mother, and she could never forgive him. She was deprived of a fatherly figure all her life and hated all men until she saw Larko when she was only fifteen.

King Alger of Kalastra had invited King Malik to visit his realm and celebrate his son's birthday in Kalastra. In the royal visit, Lamia was taken to Kalastra too, and for the first time in her life, she was leaving Sinkaba. Although Lamia was a princess, she always felt like a prisoner in her father's palace, and she was never allowed to leave the city by herself. When Lamia passed Mount Zaka and saw the first glimpse of Kalastra, she knew she would love everything about it. Kalastra was so different from Sinkaba, and she had never seen so much greenery all at the same time. The weather was perfect, and the rivers were boisterous. Everything was alive, and Lamia felt she was born again. When King Malik and Princess Lamia arrived at the Kalastra castle, King Alger and Prince Larko welcomed them warmly. Larko was only a few years older than Lamia, and he was so handsome that he took Lamia's breath away at the first sight. When he helped her get off her horse, she looked into his eyes, and she knew she belonged to him. At court, everyone was excited to see the people from Sinkaba, and all the young knights in the castle were fascinated by Lamia's beauty, trying to get her attention somehow, but Lamia's eyes only saw Larko. He was gentle and sweet, and they sat next to each other at the feast King Alger had arranged for his son's birthday and his guests.

"Are you enjoying the feast, Your Highness?" Larko leaned closer so Lamia could hear him over the music and laughter echoing through the hall.

A warm glow lit her eyes as she turned to him. "Very much. Everything in Kalastra is better than I imagined."

"What did you imagine?" he asked.

"When I was in Sinkaba, everyone told me that Kalastra was beautiful and green, so I pictured it in my mind, but it is so much better than what I thought. When I saw Kalastra with my own eyes, I realized it is a completely different world. I am in love with the forest, the river, the lakes, and the gigantic, sky-piercing mountains," she said.

"Then I shall take you for a ride in the forest tomorrow, and I will show you all my favorite spots. What do you think?" he asked.

"I would love that, Your Highness," she replied.

"Tell me about Sinkaba! How is life over there?" he asked.

"Nothing like here. Sinkaba is all desert, and that is all I can say about it since I spend most of my time in the palace," she said.

"Why? I thought you enjoy spending time in nature," he said.

"I do, but my father does not allow me to leave the palace much, and when I do, his guards follow me everywhere. It is a long story, and I do not want to bore you tonight," she said.

"You can tell me all about it tomorrow on our way to the forest, but for tonight, we shall enjoy the feast," he said.

Everyone in the castle was at the feast: the knights, the lords, the ministers, and King Malik's guards. They ate, drank, laughed, and danced until midnight, and it was every young man's wish that night to talk and dance with Princess Lamia. Her beauty had mesmerized everyone, and she had rejected every dance request, hoping to be asked by Larko. Unlike all the young men at the feast, Larko was calm and composed, and he was not much impressed by Lamia's beauty; however, he did not know what his father and King Malik had planned for him and Princess Lamia. That night, King Malik offered his daughter as Prince Larko's bride, the future queen of Kalastra, and King Alger agreed to unite their nations and secure their alliance with Sinkaba. Both Prince Larko and Princess Lamia were unaware of what their fathers had planned for them, and the day after the feast, Larko took Lamia to the forest for a ride simply out of courtesy and hospitality. Lamia had barely slept the night before, and all she had thought about was Prince Larko. She was in love with him without even noticing how it had happened. Larko was handsome, caring, gallant, and precisely the type of man every girl dreamed of having. He was excellent with a sword and far better than any knight in the kingdom. Lamia had thought of him the whole night, and when she woke up in the morning, she knew it would be a fantastic day.

She had dreamed about waking up in Kalastra before, and it had finally happened. She was excited for the day, and despite not sleeping enough the night before, she felt energized. Her maid, Aesha, helped her get dressed, and she wore the best dress she had brought with her. Aesha could see how truly happy she was, and she could see the light in her eyes for the first time in her life. The weather was perfect, and the trees had just started to bloom. Lamia was riding next to Larko in the forest, and life was beautiful that day. She saw things that she had never seen in her life before in Sinkaba, and everything was enchanting.

"Look! What is that funny small animal climbing up the tree so fast?" Lamia asked with excitement.

Larko followed her gaze and chuckled. "That's a squirrel. I suppose you're seeing one for the first time."

She let out a soft laugh, still watching the creature leap from branch to branch. "I am. It looks so funny. Most of the things I see here don't exist in Sinkaba."

"Will you tell me more about Sinkaba, and why you do not leave the palace much?" he asked.

"I will, but it is not a pleasant story," she said.

"It is fine. I will listen if you want to share it," he said.

"I lost my mother when I was a child, just like you, and my life changed in so many ways after her death. I was happy when she was alive. She was the only person who really loved me, and I still remember how she stroked my hair before going to bed. I wish I could go back in time and see her face just one more time," she said as she wiped a tear off her face.

"I am sorry, Lamia. You do not need to say anything if it bothers you. I should not have asked," he said.

"It is all right. I like to talk about my mother because I cannot talk about her with anyone except my maid, Aesha. I feel so lonely in Sinkaba," she said.

"What happened with your mother?" he asked.

"My father killed her. He thought she was plotting treason against him, but she was innocent. She did not care about politics, and she was the most innocent person I knew. He killed her in front of my eyes, and I still see nightmares when I close my eyes at night. I hate my father, and I want nothing except to see him take his last breath," she said with hatred in her voice.

"He will pay for what he did to your mother someday, but you should let go of your hatred so you can live in peace," he said.

"I cannot let go of my anger and hatred for him. He does not care about me, and he does not love me either. I do not remember a single happy time with him. I have been scared of him all my life, even before he killed my mother," she said.

"Why has he imprisoned you in the palace?" he asked.

"He married two times after killing my mother. The first woman gave him no child, so he married again, and I had two younger brothers, until they both died in the battle last year. So, I am his only successor, the continuation of his dynasty, and that is all I am to him. I do not care about his throne, and he knows it. He thinks I will run away someday, and he will not find me anymore; that is why he imprisons me in the palace," she replied.

"Time will heal everything, even the worst wounds. I was lonely and depressed after the loss of my mother too, but I overcame it. I am the only heir to Kalastra's throne, and my father and the whole kingdom expect a lot from me, and I feel responsible for my people. So if your father is as cruel as you say he is, you have a responsibility toward your people, and you cannot just leave Sinkaba," he said.

"Talking to you makes me feel better, Your Highness. Thank you for listening to me," she said.

"I think we have talked enough about depressing matters. Let's ride faster. There is a beautiful lake that I want to show you," he said, kicking on his horse.

They spent the whole day in the forest, and Lamia followed him wherever he went. Her heart was racing, and she could not stop thinking about him. The thought of taking his hand and sleeping in his arms drove her crazy. All she knew was that she did not want to leave Kalastra. She wanted days to drag and nights to shorten so she could see him every day, all day. Before seeing Larko, she thought all men were scary, like her father, but Larko was different. He changed everything in her mind. He was gentle and kind and not only to Lamia but to everyone he knew.

After getting back from the forest, Aesha told Lamia that her father had summoned her to his chamber. She never had a pleasant conversation with her father, and she was terrified of what he would say to her. She knocked on the door gently and entered the room.

"Did you want to see me, Father?" Lamia asked.

Her father was standing by the window, looking outside, and without turning his back, he said, "Kalastra is beautiful and full of potential, but a stupid king governs it. Neither Alger nor Larko deserves to rule this vast land. I do not know how much longer I will live, but you are everything I have in this world. You should be the queen of Sinkaba and Kalastra both."

"Do you want to attack Kalastra, Father?" she asked.

"No. Why should I attack when I can have it peacefully?" he said.

"How is that possible?" she asked.

"I have decided that you marry Prince Larko, and King Alger has agreed with me. This union benefits us in many ways. We will expand our realm, and you will become the queen of both nations. I have made the decision, and I will not change my mind," he said as he walked toward her.

Lamia could not believe what she had just heard. Finally, the goddess of sand had heard her prayers, and she was going to grant her wish through someone she least expected.

"Why are you staring at me? Do not tell me that you do not like Larko, for it does not change my mind. On the contrary, be nice to him and try to steal his heart. He is only a man, after all," he said.

Lamia wanted to scream with happiness and hug her father, but instead, she said, "I will do as you want, Father, but does the prince want to marry me too?" she asked, trying to hide the joy and curiosity in her voice.

"I do not know. King Alger must be talking to him as we speak. Use your femininity and do what other women do! You are not a little girl anymore. With your rare beauty, you do not need to do much," he said.

Her pulse quickened at his crude encouragement, but she forced a respectful nod. "I won't disappoint you, Father."

"That is what I expect to hear from you. You are my girl. You are strong, and you can have anything you want in this life. Always remember that!" he said.

For the first time in her life, Lamia liked what she had heard from her father. She went back to her chamber and looked at herself in the mirror for hours. She was magnificent, a different beauty that she had not seen in any other woman, but that was all she had. She looked at the details of her face, and she could not find courage and wisdom in it. She knew she was not a strong woman. She'd feared her father and everyone else in the palace for as long as she remembered. She was the princess of Sinkaba, but she lived like a hostage. The more she looked at herself, the more pitiful the woman in the mirror looked to her. She did not want to be weak anymore. She had wings to fly, but she had trapped herself in the mud. She was the future of Sinkaba, the only heir to the throne, and the only child of great King Malik, but she had let her fears hold her back. She wanted to change. She wanted everything in her life to be different, and above all, she wanted Larko. She only had a few days left to steal his heart, and she was going to do anything to have him. The supper was in a few hours, and she wanted to look her best for Larko. She called for Aesha.

"I have to tell you something, Aesha. I have never hidden anything from you," she said.

"Please do, Your Highness. Your secrets are always safe with me," she said.

"My father wants me to marry Prince Larko. He has already talked with King Alger, and he has agreed with the union," she said.

"How about you, Your Highness? Do you want to marry Prince Larko?" she asked.

"I do not know, Aesha. He is handsome and charming, and he will be the king of Kalastra someday, and if I marry him, I will be the queen of Sinkaba and Kalastra both," she replied.

"King Malik has made an excellent choice, Your Highness. Prince Larko will be a great husband, and we need to make sure this union happens," she said.

"Can you prepare my lavender silk dress for tonight? I want to look my best," she said.

"As you wish, Your Highness," she said.

Lamia had never hidden anything from Aesha. She was not just a maid to her. She was her friend, and she trusted her with her life, but when she asked her if she loved Larko or not, Lamia could not tell the truth. She was afraid of even admitting it to herself, let alone talking about it with someone else. It was her little secret, and she did not want anyone to know.

Unlike Princess Lamia, Larko was not so excited to hear the news from his father. He was young, and all he cared about was expanding the realm of Kalastra.

"What do you think about King Malik and his daughter?" King Alger asked Larko.

"He makes me angry. He is a bastard, and if it were not for you and his daughter, I would punch him in the face and send him back to his desert and not allow him ever to set his feet in Kalastra again," he replied.

"I agree with you. Unfortunately, he is not a likable person," he said.

"Then why did you invite him to Kalastra?" he asked.

"He is our powerful ally in the South, and we cannot afford to lose him. We need to tighten our bond with him and Sinkaba," he replied.

"What do you mean by that?" he asked.

"King Malik and I have decided that you marry Princess Lamia. She is a beautiful girl, and she will be a good wife to you, not to mention the union will benefit us in so many ways," he replied.

"You cannot decide who I marry, Father. I will make that decision for myself when the time is right. I will not marry Princess

Lamia," he replied.

"Why not? She is beautiful, and she is the daughter of a powerful man. What better choice can you have?" he asked.

Larko took a step closer, voice rising. "Is that all that matters? Beauty? Power? What about love?"

"No one marries for love, my son," he replied.

"I will, and I do not care about your arrangements with King Malik. I will not marry his daughter," he said.

"Think again, Larko! You are making a big mistake. Rejecting his daughter will make him furious. Think about the consequences of your decision! The future of Kalastra relies on you," he said.

"No, Father. You cannot do this to me. You cannot make me feel guilty because I choose love. Kalastra is everything to me, but I cannot sacrifice my happiness. I cannot marry without love," he said.

"You are the prince of Kalastra. You are the only heir to the throne. The burden is on your shoulders whether I talk about it or not. You cannot evade your responsibilities. You must make a wise choice when it comes to marriage. Love might happen later, when you are married, or it may never happen, but when you are a king, you can have any woman you want," he said.

"I will marry for love, and when I do, I will never betray my wife. I will not do what you did to my mother, so keep your advice to yourself. I will not ask King Malik for his daughter's hand, and the best I can do for you is to say nothing and not reject her in public," he said and left the room.

Lamia was looking her best at the supper, and she was so excited to see Larko that she thought she would pass out at any second. Her beauty was dazzling, and everyone in the room was staring at her except Larko. He did not know what Lamia felt for him, but he did not want to do anything to give her false hope. He evaded looking into her eyes the whole night, and he left the feast earlier than usual. Lamia could feel something was wrong. Larko was not the same man she had gone riding with in the morning. They had spent hours in the forest, and they had talked about so many things, but he was silent suddenly, at the supper, and he did not even look at her. Being in Kalastra with Larko was like a dream to her. However, just like every dream ends, at last, hers had ended as well. She had only a few more days left in Kalastra, and she did not know how to find Larko alone. She dressed up every morning, hoping to see him, but he was nowhere in the castle.

It was finally the day of departure, and all Lamia cared about was saying goodbye to Larko. She wanted to tell him that she loved him, and if he did not love her back, she would wait for him until he finally saw her as a lover. It was raining that day, and everyone in the castle was present in the courtyard. King Alger said goodbye to King Malik and Princess Lamia. Larko hated King Malik after realizing what he had done to his wife and how he treated his daughter, so he said goodbye to him, hoping not to see him again, and when it came to Lamia, he felt guilty. He did not love her, and he could see in her eyes how desperately she begged for his love and affection.

He kissed her hand and said, "I hope you enjoyed your time in Kalastra, Your Highness."

Lamia's eyes softened as she looked at him, warmth flickering in her gaze. "I did. Thank you for taking me for a ride and showing me Kalastra. The good memories I made here with you will stay with me forever."

A faint smile tugged at the corners of his mouth. "I'm glad you liked Kalastra. I hope to visit Sinkaba someday too."

"I hope so. Goodbye, Larko," she said.

She got on her horse, and King Malik commanded everyone to move. She wanted to turn back and look at him one more time, but her pride did not let her. They got farther and farther away, and she knew he was not looking at her anymore. She loved him, but she could not confess her love to anyone, not even to Larko. She had found meaning in her life after so long, and she was happy for the first time. She promised herself to be a strong woman and deserving of Sinkaba's throne.

She had hidden in her chamber for years, but she decided to change. She wanted to forget the past and give her father a chance. She felt naive for not caring about Sinkaba before, and she promised herself to be worthy of the title she carried, but at the end of the day, what kept her awake at night and made her cry was the thought of Larko. Days and months passed, and she did not receive any message from the prince. All she wanted was a day alone with him to tell him how she felt about him. Lamia was no longer ashamed of confessing her love to Larko. In her eyes, he was the perfect man, courageous and honest. He was the beginning and end of love. It was going to be either him or no one. As she grew older and the reputation of her beauty spread worldwide, many kings and princes asked for her hand in marriage. Finally, one year after King Malik and Princess Lamia returned to Sinkaba, a messenger from Kalastra came to Sinkaba. The letter was from King Alger to King Malik, confirming the marriage between Larko and Lamia, asking for a time, and suggesting the wedding happen in a few years. King Malik was happy with the suggestion because, whether or not the wedding happened, he had a chance to take over Kalastra. If Lamia was going to marry Larko, she would become the queen of Kalastra and Sinkaba both, and if they called off the wedding, he had an excuse to attack Kalastra, and he liked both options.

CHAPTER SEVEN

"MOTHER, MOTHER, COME here! Hurry! She is awake," the boy said.

The woman rushed to the tent where Esther was sleeping. She was panting with fear and drenched with sweat. She did not know where she was or how she had gotten there. For a second, she thought she was back in her village. Her head was spinning, and her heart was beating fast. The woman was talking to her, but she was too confused to understand anything. Finally, she screamed as hard as she could and ran out of the tent, throwing up on the sands.

"Calm down, my child! You are safe here. Do not be scared!" Hila said, holding her tight.

"Where am I? Who are you?" Esther asked.

"Eke, go and bring some water!" Hila told her son.

"Try not to talk, my child. I know you must be scared, but trust me. I want to help you. My son found you in the desert on the sands. If we had not brought you here, you could have died," Hila said.

"Mother! Where is my mother?" Esther asked.

"Drink this water! We can talk after you feel better," Hila said.

Esther swallowed all the water at once. She was unconscious for two days and had not eaten or drunk anything. The woman took her back to the tent and told her to lie down. She was still too feeble to talk or move.

It was finally nighttime. Owls were hooting, and lizards were out of their hiding places. There was a nice breeze in the air, and stars were crystal clear in the sky. Esther slowly opened her eyes and tried to sit up; she had slept the whole day. She then remembered her dream: She had seen a beautiful woman who lived in a vast green land. There was no desert where she lived. There were mountains and rivers, and birds were chirping all the time. Everything she had seen was new to her, but somehow, she felt connected to that place, like she knew it very well. Not only the city and the forest, but she also felt she knew the woman and the prince. Esther could feel whatever Aphra had felt: her joy, sorrow, and fear. Somehow, she knew all the details of her life without even seeing her in real life. *How could a dream be so powerful?* she thought.

"Do not move so quickly, my child! You are still weak," the woman said.

"Thank you for saving me. I owe you my life," Esther said.

"My pleasure, young lady. Tell me! What is your name?" the woman asked.

"Esther," she replied.

"Where are you from, and what were you doing all alone in the desert?"

"I am from the South, and I am traveling north," Esther said.

"Where in the North exactly?" the woman asked.

"Kalastra, I suppose," Esther replied.

"It has been long since I have heard the name Kalastra from anyone," the woman said.

"Why? Does no one ever travel to Kalastra from here?" Esther asked.

"Not really. Kalastra was a great country that once existed a long time ago, but when the Dejovian kingdom fell, Kalastra lost its glory too; it is nothing like what existed before, and no one travels from here to there anymore," the woman said.

"How long ago was it?" Esther asked.

"Three hundred years ago. I suppose people have forgotten about Kalastra and its glory now," the woman replied.

"How can I get there?" Esther asked.

"Why do you want to go to Kalastra? People are not so welcoming over there. Where is your family? You are very young to travel on your own," the woman said.

"I have no one except my mother, who lives in Aseeta. Look! It is a long story, and I cannot tell you everything because I still do not understand it myself, but I need to go to Kalastra. Can you please help me?" Esther asked.

"I will help you, but you should know that it is dangerous. It is about ten days from here, and you cannot make it on foot. You need a horse," the woman said. "Eat your food now! You must be famished. You need to take a bath too. I have brought you clean clothes."

Esther gave her a warm smile. "Thank you. I still do not know your name."

"My name is Hila," the woman replied.

Esther then looked at the boy sleeping in the tent and asked, "Is he your son?"

"Yes. He is all I have. My husband died last year," Hila replied.

"I have lost my father too. I have no one in this world except my mother," Esther said.

"She must be very worried about you," Hila said.

"I am sure she is, but I had no choice. I had to leave my village," Esther said.

"What is it that you are looking for?" Hila asked.

"Myself. My past and future. I need to find answers to my dreams," Esther replied.

"Dreams or nightmares?" Hila asked.

"Both. When I was in Aseeta, I had a nightmare every night for as long as I can remember, and it terrorized me each time, so one night, I decided to end it. I left my village, and as soon as I left Aseeta, I started having dreams about Kalastra," Esther replied.

"And you heard the name of Kalastra in your dream?" Hila asked.

Esther nodded and said, "It was beautiful, green, and lush, nothing like my village."

"I cannot say that I understand you, but I will help you as much as I can," Hila said.

"You are so kind, Hila. How can I repay you?" she asked.

"You are a strong girl, and I want you to succeed and find what you are looking for, whatever it is. I want nothing from you, dear," Hila said; then she put her finger in the water of the tub that was in the corner of the tent and said, "The water is not so hot now. Take a bath and try to sleep again. You will feel much better tomorrow."

For once, Esther was not scared of sleeping and dreaming. Aphra and Kalastra were fascinating to her, and she wanted to know more. After taking the soothing bath, she wore the clean clothes Hila had prepared for her and slept like a baby until morning. She had never slept that great in her life before. Finally, she opened her eyes and looked around the tent, still lying down. The tent was humble but beautifully decorated. The sunrays had penetrated the tent and formed a star on the sands. She placed her hand on the soft grains and felt their silkiness, smiling at the tiny hedgehog looking at her curiously. She closed her eyes again and tried to enjoy the serenity surrounding her, but the peaceful feeling she was experiencing did not last for long. When she heard people talking about her outside the tent, she decided to step outside and introduce herself. After all, she was a stranger who had entered their village, and people were curious to know who she was. As soon as she got out of the tent, everyone stopped talking, and they all stared at her like she was a superhuman or a creature from another planet; then she saw Hila coming toward her, saying, "Come inside the tent, Esther! We need to talk."

"Why was everyone staring at me? I know I am a stranger here, but the way they all looked at me was so weird," Esther said.

"I should have told you this last night, but I did not even know where to begin," Hila said.

"What are you hiding from me?" Esther asked.

"What I am about to tell you might seem strange to you, but the people in this village strongly believe in it, and they have been waiting for so long," Hila said.

"I am listening, Hila," she said.

"Your story matches the legend we believe in, and our ancestors, years and years ago, had told us about your arrival to our village someday," Hila said.

"I do not understand. How could your ancestors know about me?" Esther asked.

"It is simple: Because you are special. You must have known it by now. We believe you might be the promised queen, and we are excited and scared at the same time," Hila said.

"What do you mean by 'the promised queen'?" Esther asked.

"According to the legend, one day, a young girl from the deep South, who possesses the book of knowledge and is traveling north, will come to the village, and she will be the promised queen who will unite North and South and build a glorious kingdom," Hila said.

"How can that girl be me? I am sure I am not, and how do they even know I have a book with me?" Esther asked; then she rushed to find the book in her backpack.

"No one has taken your book, but I think someone might have come into the tent last night," Hila said.

"I need to leave. Thank you for all you did for me, but it is time for me to leave now," Esther said.

"Do not rush, and do not be angry with us. There is someone who wants to see you before you leave," Hila said.

"I do not want to. I just want to leave this place. I thought the people in my village were crazy, but now I see superstitions are inseparable parts of the lives of the people who live in the South," Esther said.

"How do you know the people in the North are different?" Hila asked.

"I have seen them in my dreams. They are very different," Esther said.

"I am not sure what you saw in your dreams, but whatever it was belonged to three hundred years ago. Wait and see the chief of our village. You will not regret it," Hila replied.

"Fine, I will see him, but I will leave after that. I am no one's queen, and I am not special. I cannot even save myself, let alone unite the people of North and South. I want to run away from this desert," Esther said.

"You cannot escape your destiny. Life is a mystery, my child. Embrace it!" Hila said.

Esther felt everything was becoming more confusing as she moved forward in her journey, and she had no control over what would happen to her. First, it was the old dwarf who told her about her guardian angels and how he had waited so long to see her, and now it was these people who thought she was their promised queen. She did not understand what was happening, but she was determined to find all the answers. Finally, Esther entered the chief's tent. The tent was completely dark, and she could smell fragrant herbs burning in the fire. She walked slowly toward the center of the tent and saw an old man sitting there by the fire.

"Why did you want to see me?" she asked.

"Sit down! Do not be afraid of me," the chief replied.

"I am not afraid of you. I am in a hurry. I should leave soon," she said.

"You are not late for anything, Esther. You are exactly where you are supposed to be," he said.

"How do you know that? Is it because you all believe in a legend that your ancestors told you? This is absurd. I am not a queen. I am just trying to find answers for my dreams," she said.

"You will find the answers you are looking for when you remember everything, and when you do, you will unite the lands of North and South," he said.

"What should I remember?" she asked.

"The book you carry with you will help you. So guard it with your life. It is ancient, and it carries the knowledge of the world," he said.

"Is that the book of knowledge?" she asked.

"Yes, it is, and only a few people in the world can read the book. You might think the book is blank, but it is not. The book itself chooses who can see its contents, and when the time is right, the words will reveal themselves to you," he said.

"What should I do now? I do not know what I should remember," she said.

"Go to the North and ask for guidance along the way. Look for the signs the universe gives you. Your journey is hard, and you have to endure so many hardships, but the reward is big," he said.

"Why did you want to see me? I am certain it was not to tell me about the book of knowledge," she said.

"I ask you to have mercy on the people of the South once you become the queen."

"Why would I not be merciful? I have never harmed anyone in my life, and I never will. That is the only thing I can say with certainty," she said.

"Then farewell, Esther. There is a fine horse ready for you, with food and drink," he said.

"Is that all you wanted to say?" she asked.

"Yes, that is all. Now I can embrace death with open arms, knowing that I saw the promised queen in this life," he replied.

"I cannot say I understand or believe you, but I thank you for your hospitality, and I hope we meet again," she said and left his tent.

Esther stepped outside the tent, and what she saw was beyond her expectations. Everyone in the village was present there, and when they saw her, they all knelt.

"Please get up! You do not need to do this. I am not who you think I am. I am not a queen," she said to the people.

"They respect you. They know you are their savior," Hila said softly, watching Esther with kind eyes.

"I wish I could say the same thing about myself, but whatever my destiny is, even if I am not the queen you are all waiting for, I promise to repay your kindness one day," Esther said.

"You owe us nothing, Esther. This horse is yours. I hope we meet again," she said.

"I hope we do too," Esther said; then she hugged Hila tight.

CHAPTER EIGHT

ESTHER GOT ON her horse and rode as fast as she could. All she cared about was getting to Kalastra. She was sure she could find the answers to all her questions there. Maybe a new life was awaiting her in Kalastra, and all she had to do was leave the desert behind. The old man's voice was still ringing in her ears. He had told her she was the promised queen. *Could that be the reason for all my dreams? How can I be the queen of a land I have never seen in my life before?* she thought. The old man asked her to have mercy on the people of the South, but why? They had never done her any harm. It was true that the people of her village did not like her much, and they thought she was crazy, but they had never hurt her. There were still many things that she did not know, and she was eager to figure them out.

After riding for one whole day, she could see the scenery was changing gradually, and the weather was getting milder. She camped for the night, made a fire, and ate the bread and cheese Hila had given her. *If one day I become a queen, I will repay her favors,* she thought as she stared at the fire. The flames were beautifully dancing before her eyes, swaying from side to side, changing colors.

She reached out for the fire and let the flames turn her skin color into light blue. The fire had hypnotized her. As she looked deeper into the fire, she saw Aphra in the flames; she was crying quietly, and she was alone. Why was it that she could feel her pain? "How can I help you?" she asked Aphra, but there was no answer. She disappeared from the flames. "No! Please, do not leave. Help me! Why do I dream about you? Why do I see you everywhere? Why do I feel your pain?" Esther asked while sobbing. "What happened to you? What do you want me to do?"

Then, suddenly, as if lightning had struck her, she remembered the book. The dwarf and the chief had both told her that the book would help her in her time of need. *It is the book of knowledge, and I feel lost; it is the perfect time to ask for guidance,* she thought. She grabbed the book and stared at it for a few minutes. It had to work; she had no other choice. She looked up at the sky; it was a beautiful night, and the stars were shining. "Dear goddess of sand, please help me find out what I need to know. Reveal the unknown to me. Tell me how I can help Aphra. Who is the woman I have seen in my dreams all my life? I feel so lost. Help me, please!" she said, then closed her eyes and opened the book. She expected a miracle to happen, and luckily for her, it did. Words started appearing on the blank page before her eyes. *The tree sprouts each spring and gains a new life, but the root never dies. Search for your roots!* appeared on the page. Esther started laughing with immense joy. It was all real; the book had magic. Whatever the old dwarf and the chief had told her was true. It was the book of knowledge; then she read it again because she had not understood what it meant the first time. *How can I search for my roots?* she thought. She wished she could talk to her mother. Maybe she knew something from the past that no one had told her. She then lay down and closed her eyes. All she wanted was to see Aphra again. Aphra was lonely and sad when she saw her in the flames, and Esther had to help her out.

Soon, her eyes grew heavy, and she fell into a deep sleep. She saw Aphra again, but this time she was not in Kalastra. Her hands were tied, and she was hurt. She could feel her pain. It was a scary scene, and she wanted to wake up, but she had no control over her dream; she was supposed to see everything. Esther woke up to the sound of her scream. She was panting and crying. It was a horrible dream, but she knew it was not simply a dream; it was real. It had all happened three hundred years ago, but she did not understand why she was dreaming about her after so long. She could not sleep anymore that night. It was still dark, but the dawn was close. Based on the map the chief had given her, Mount Zaka was just a little farther away. After passing through the mountain, there would be no desert anymore, and she could see the land of Kalastra. On the other side of Mount Zaka, she could finally see trees, flowers, and lakes. She had never felt such excitement in her life before.

"Come on, boy! We have a long day ahead of us today, but the payoff is amazing. Are you excited like me?" Esther asked the horse. "Okay, fine! You do not need to answer me," she said with a smile. She then hopped on her horse and started galloping; the faster she could get through the mountain, the better. After riding for a few hours, she got to Mount Zaka finally. It was huge and majestic. Esther could feel the chill in the air; she was not used to cold weather. She rubbed her hands together and said, "We have to pass through this mountain together. You are a good boy, right? I know you will not fail me," she said, then looked at the mountain for a few seconds. "Let me confess something to you. I have never been this excited in my life before. I have lived in the desert all my life. Now I am about to see a place that I have only been seeing in my dreams recently."

Mount Zaka was a challenging mountain to pass. The passage was narrow, and the valleys were deep. Esther had to overcome her fear of heights first to pass through the mountain. In the beginning, everything seemed easy. The passage was wide, and she was riding her horse gently, but after a while, the passage got so narrow that she preferred to hop off her horse and walk. She was afraid of heights, and she was terrified of falling off her horse and into the valley. She clung desperately to the rocks and was not able to look up or down. Her horse was moving ahead of her and looked back occasionally to check on her. "Great! I can see you are teasing me, but it is fine," she said to the horse, then raised her head. "Dear goddess of sand, please give me the courage to pass through this mountain. I cannot do it without your help." She moved as slowly as she could, one step at a time. She was in no rush anymore. She closed her eyes for a moment and remembered her mother's face. *She must be so worried about me, but if she knew what I am about to do, she would be so proud of me,* Esther thought. It took her longer than she expected, but she finally passed through the most challenging part of the mountain, and as soon as she reached a flat area, she stopped to rest.

There were no mountains in Aseeta, and the best she had done was lie down on top of the dunes. She was exhausted after climbing for the whole day, and since it was getting dark, she decided to make camp for the night. She grabbed a piece of bread and took a big bite out of it; she was starving, and her fear of heights had made her even hungrier. A cold wind started blowing, and she only had a small blanket to cover herself. She lay down on the cold stones and looked up at the stars. She felt closer to them, and they were even brighter than other nights. She grabbed the book and pressed it hard to her chest.

Everything she had seen in her dream last night was still fresh in her mind. It did not take her long to fall asleep; she was exhausted, and even the hard stone felt like a cushion. Not long after she fell asleep, in the middle of the night, she heard a loud noise, like a rumble. Esther ignored it at first; she was so tired that she could not even open her eyes, but then it got so loud that she could not ignore it anymore. She opened her eyes, and there she was again, the woman she had seen before in Aseeta when she was in the deserted palace. She was the woman she always saw in her dreams, and it was the second time she had appeared to her. This time, however, she looked more pitiful than scary. She was glowing with light, and her presence had lit up the whole mountain. Esther wanted to talk to her and know who she was, so she gathered all her strength and asked, "Who are you? Tell me your name!"

The woman moved forward and looked into her eyes with desperation, saying, "I am truly sorry. Please forgive me and end this torture."

"What have you done? Who have you harmed?" Esther asked.

"An innocent person," the woman replied.

"Then why do you ask me for forgiveness?" Esther asked. She was puzzled.

"Please forgive me so I can be set free," the woman said.

"I need you to answer me. Do you understand?" Esther said.

Then, before Esther could do anything, the woman vanished in the blink of an eye, and the mountain was all dark again. Esther was angry. She needed to communicate with her, but all she kept doing was asking for forgiveness. She was sure this woman was not Aphra, because she had seen her in her dreams before. Aphra was beautiful, but innocent and peaceful at the same time. Esther felt like this woman was the key to unlocking all the mysteries, but she could not make anything out of the mess that was in her mind. She closed her eyes and tried to sleep, but it was pointless. How could she sleep with everything that was happening to her? Her world was upside down in a short period. When she was in Aseeta, the only thing that bothered her was seeing that woman in her dreams, and she was determined to find her, but as soon as she started her journey, the mystery became more complicated, and she felt drowned by each passing day. In just a few weeks, everything had completely changed for her. She was not the same girl she was before. She was more determined, and her goals in life had changed. The woman in her dreams had appeared to her two times in reality, and she was no longer imaginary, and on top of that dream, ever since she had started her journey, she kept seeing people in her dream who used to live three hundred years ago.

However, what was more interesting than her dreams was the old dwarf waiting for her for years to give her an ancient, magical book and an old man who believed she was the promised queen uniting the people of North and South. What was she supposed to do? How could she put all the pieces of the puzzle together? There was still a lot she did not know, and she knew the green land of Kalastra could help her figure out everything.

As soon as the first rays of the sun hit the stones, Esther started moving. She still had a few more days to get to the land that was marked on her map: Kalastra. It was a beautiful day; the sun was shining, and it was a pleasant sensation to feel the sun's warmth on her back. The silence in the mountain was scary, and the occasional sound of gravel falling into the valley added more depth to her fear, so she started talking to herself and her horse to maintain her sanity and overcome her fear of heights. She was walking for hours, and it was almost midday when the sun suddenly disappeared, and the sky turned tar-black. She could see big clouds in the sky moving toward her, and the sound of rumbling was getting closer rapidly. Esther could not move for a few seconds.

Is it the sound of rain? she thought. When she was in Aseeta, it used to rain two or three times a year, but it was very short and quiet. Everything was happening so fast that Esther could not even move to find shelter. In just a few seconds, the heavy drops of rain started pouring on her face, and she was completely soaked. She hid under a rock and watched how the crazy rain was washing the debris off the rocks. The scent of rain on the dirt had filled the air, and it was the best thing she had smelled in her life. The occasional lightning in the sky and the majestic sound of thunder had fascinated her. She never thought rain could be so beautiful. She closed her eyes and stretched her arms out to feel the rain; it was heavy and cold. *So, this is how it rains in green lands! It turns day into night,* she thought.

The harmonic sound of rain had hypnotized her, but it finally stopped raining after a few hours, and the sun came out and started casting rays of light at everything. The air was brisk, and the sky was a perfect blue again, without any clouds in the picture. She stretched her body and crawled out from under the rock. Everything felt fresh and clean, like it had been polished. She only had a few more hours left in the mountain, and if she was lucky, she could get to the meadow before dusk. Although she had lived her whole life in Aseeta, she somehow felt a connection with Kalastra, and the closer she got, the more excited she became.

"We are almost there, boy! Can you believe it? After this mountain, it is all green, no more desert," she said to her horse. "Are you also excited like me? I think you should be. You have lived in the desert your whole life, just like me."

After walking for a few more hours, it was finally over. She had passed through the mountain, and as the sun was setting, she saw the first glimpse of the green meadow. She watched the sunset at the horizon as the orange and blue rays of light laid down on the grass, finally resting and welcoming the night; it was an epic view. She could not take her eyes off the vast green land that was turning into orange, soon becoming completely black. She burst into tears uncontrollably. How could she feel so close to a place she had never seen in her life before? What was it about Kalastra that attracted her to itself more and more every day? She felt like she had seen that sunset before, but she could not recall anything. The sunset was so beautiful that nothing mattered to her at that moment. She was where she wanted to be. She tried to absorb the full beauty of the sunset and the meadow. She wanted to fill her lungs with clean air, breathing every particle she could. She knelt to touch the grass; it felt fresh, a shade of green she had never seen before. Her horse was grazing in the meadow already. He seemed as happy as her. She did not have much left to eat, but it was fine; she was not in the desert anymore, and she could easily find food. She made a small fire to keep herself warm and bit into the last piece of bread she had with her. What a beautiful night it was. She felt calm and at ease after years. She lay down on the grass and looked at the stars in the sky. She could see the same stars she'd seen in Aseeta's sky. Everything was vibrating with life and energy—the earth, the sky, and the grass—as if Kalastra was welcoming her. She wished her mother was there with her, and she could see that she was right. She was always certain there was a reason for all her dreams, and now she could feel it. *What is this feeling I have in here? Why do I feel so powerful suddenly, like I can do anything I want?* she thought. She then wrapped herself tightly with the blanket she had, and despite the chilly night, she fell asleep in a few seconds.

When the first rays of sun hit her sleepy eyes, she barely opened them and rubbed them as hard as she could. The sun was graciously casting its light on everything. The grass was shimmering, moving from side to side, the birds were chirping, singing happy songs, and a turquoise-blue river was flowing not far from where she had slept. If heaven existed on earth, it was here. Everything was so dreamy that she thought she was still sleeping, but she was awake, and for once in her life, reality was way more magnificent than her dreams. She washed her face in the river; the water was freezing cold and refreshing. Everything was so perfect that Esther did not want to leave this place, but she had to move. She looked at her map and saw it was just a few more days to get to the city.

"Come on, boy, we should leave. I know there is plenty of food for you here, but you cannot eat all day," she said to her horse, then jumped on him gently and started petting his mane. "Thank you for accompanying me on this journey. We will witness many great things together," she whispered into his ear.

CHAPTER NINE

AFTER MEETING PRINCE Larko in the forest, all Aphra cared about was the next time she could see him. She had never felt that way before, and she was scared of what would happen in the future. She saw Prince Larko several times after that day, and each time, her feelings grew stronger for him. She used to go to the court for her painting class, but she only cared about meeting Prince Larko. Soon, she became famous at the court. The girls started envying her, and people began gossiping. They all thought Prince Larko was having fun with Aphra, and obviously, nothing serious could happen between them since Prince Larko was supposed to marry Queen Lamia of Sinkaba. King Malik died a few years after visiting Kalastra, and he never got to see his daughter marry Prince Larko. After his death, Lamia took over Sinkaba's throne, and unlike her father, she was loved and respected by the people of Sinkaba, and they all saw her as their savior. The marriage between Larko and Lamia was significant to the kingdom of Kalastra, and King Alger had arranged it years ago when Larko was still very young.

Aphra was nothing like Queen Lamia. She was a young and

beautiful girl from a decent family, but no queen or princess. Kalastra was a powerful kingdom, but they still needed good allies, and calling off the wedding with Queen Lamia would jeopardize the kingdom's future. Even if Prince Larko was not going to marry Queen Lamia, he could marry the daughter of one of the lords instead of marrying a commoner. Every lord and lady at the court wished to bond with the king, not to mention every girl's dream was to marry Prince Larko. Aphra could feel the heavy looks of other girls when she went to the court and knew no one welcomed her there except Prince Larko. She was not a quitter, but the things she had heard about herself and Prince Larko broke her heart, and she decided to tell him that she no longer needed to come to the court and could practice at home.

"How was the class today?" Larko asked.

"It was good, Your Highness. I believe I am getting better. I have learned so many things from the master," she said.

"I am sure you will become an excellent artist, and once you get there, you should paint a fine portrait of me. You owe me that," he said with a smile.

Larko hoped to see a smile on Aphra's face, but she was not even paying attention.

"Did I upset you? I was merely teasing you," he said.

"No, Your Highness. I was just distracted for a second. I am sorry," she said.

"What is it? Maybe I can help," he said.

"It is nothing important, Your Highness," she replied.

"I still want to know. I insist," he said.

"I was thinking of continuing to practice painting at home and not coming to the court anymore. I believe I have learned enough from the master," she said.

"Is something bothering you here? Are you not comfortable?" he asked.

"No, Your Highness, but I think I can concentrate more if I do not come to the court," she replied.

"Are these meetings between us the problem? Because if they are, we can stop. You can just come to see the master," he said.

"It is not the problem, Your Highness. You are very kind and considerate, and I am forever thankful to you, but things have become so different lately, and I just want to live the same life I had before. I want to ride in the forest and paint by the lake as I used to," she said.

"It is all my fault. I thought I was helping. Forgive me," he said.

"It is me who should apologize, Your Highness. I know you have a kind heart, but I need to be alone now and away from the court," she said.

Larko agreed to what Aphra had asked, but he was disappointed. The painting class was the only excuse for him to see her at the court, and she did not want to come anymore. She was either upset with something or tired of seeing him. Things had become different for Larko from the day he had met Aphra. She was usually calm, yet full of energy, and her eyes were typically dazzling with happiness and excitement, like anything magnificent was possible with her. Larko missed her, but he did not want to ruin her peace. He followed her everywhere for days without her noticing. He could watch her sing and play without even blinking. She was beautiful, like a painting. Court and the matters of the kingdom did not matter much to him then. All he cared about was looking after Aphra. He did not want to leave her alone in the forest.

Days and weeks passed with Larko's absence from the court, and everyone knew it had something to do with the girl he had met in the forest before. He was rarely at the court, and he missed most of the critical meetings, and when he was present, he was completely distracted. So, finally, some of the lords decided to talk with the king.

"We have heard rumors about a girl who used to come to the court to learn painting at Prince Larko's command. I am sure you are aware of it, Your Majesty," Lord Casper said.

"Yes, I am aware. She is very talented, as Larko has told me," King Alger replied.

"She is very talented not only in painting but also in stealing the prince's heart, Your Majesty," Lord Julian said.

"What do you mean, Lord Julian?" King Alger asked with anger.

"Please forgive me, Your Majesty, but unfortunately, Prince Larko and this girl have been very close lately," Lord Julian replied.

"And how does that concern you, Lord Julian?" King Alger asked.

"I am sure Lord Julian is just worried about our young prince, Your Majesty. If you have noticed, the prince is rarely at the court lately, and when he attends the meetings, he is completely distracted. We have news His Highness rides in the forest every day, hoping to see that girl. Our prince is still very young, and he might have wrong ideas about love. We must warn him, Your Majesty," Lord Casper said.

"That is right, Your Majesty. Prince Larko might think he loves this girl, but this is just a temporary phase in his life. His Highness is supposed to marry Queen Lamia, and if this union does not happen, we will lose our most powerful ally," Lord Julian said.

"Even if Prince Larko does not want to marry Queen Lamia, there are still so many noble girls in the kingdom he can choose from, Your Majesty," Lord Casper said.

King Alger shouted, "Nonsense! Will you two stop? Larko knows more about life and love than any of you idiots at the court. All you do is eat, sleep, and spread rumors. If he wants to spend his time with that girl, I am certain he has a good reason for it. I trust his judgment." Then he looked at Lord Casper and said, "Even if Larko does not marry Queen Lamia, he will never marry that ugly daughter of yours. I know how badly your wife wants it, but it will never happen."

"That was not what I meant, Your Majesty," Lord Casper said.

"I have heard enough. Leave me alone now!" King Alger said.

The king was a stubborn man, but he loved his son more than anything. He never let anyone at the court doubt Larko's judgments or undermine his decisions. He was angry with himself for not realizing what was happening with Larko and hearing it from the lords. He was well aware of Sinkaba's wealth and power, but Larko was more important to him.

Sinkaba was a smaller kingdom than Kalastra, and it was right in the middle of the desert. It was a rich land with several turquoise mines. People had good lives there, and merchants always traveled from Kalastra to Sinkaba, and vice versa. Queen Lamia was a brilliant woman with great military strategies. She was exquisitely charming. She was a beauty beyond description, and her charm and wisdom had turned her into an idol for the people of Sinkaba. Several kings and princes wished for her hand in marriage, but she had her eyes on Prince Larko Dejovian of Kalastra. King Malik had arranged her marriage with Prince Larko years before his death, and everyone seemed happy with the arrangement except Larko. The king decided to talk with Larko, but he knew his son was as stubborn as him, and if he had already decided to marry Aphra, he would not change his mind.

"How is everything with you, Son? I feel like I have neglected you recently," King Alger said.

"I am great, Father. Everything is fine," Larko replied with a smile.

"I am glad to see you happy, Larko, but the lords have told me you spend most of your time alone in the forest recently. Is everything all right?" he asked.

"Everything is fine, Father. I just wanted to be alone to think," he replied.

"Is something bothering you?" Alger asked.

"Yes, and I should have told you sooner. I cannot marry Queen Lamia," Larko said firmly.

"Does this have anything to do with the girl who used to come here to learn painting? What was her name?" Alger asked.

"Aphra. Her name is Aphra, but she has nothing to do with the decision I made about Queen Lamia. I know for sure that I do not want to marry her, and I told you this years ago when you and King Malik arranged our marriage without asking our opinions," Larko replied.

Alger sighed, his shoulders sinking. "I was hoping the rumors weren't true."

"I do not want to argue with you, Father, but I will not change my mind," he said.

"Do you know how important it is for our kingdom that you marry Queen Lamia? Your marriage with her will secure the future of our kingdom. Sinkaba is powerful, not to mention wealthy, with so many turquoise mines, which will be all yours and Kalastra's after our nations are united. But if you call off this wedding, you will start a war, Larko! Queen Lamia will take this as an insult, and we will lose our best ally," Alger said.

"I cannot marry for politics, Father. I do not love her. I understand they are powerful and wealthy, but they are not more powerful than us. We have the bravest and the most skillful knights in the world, and we have the best military," he said.

"Larko, love has no meaning when you become the king of this vast land. When you have a kingdom to protect, sometimes you need to sacrifice the things and people you love," he said.

"This is your ideology, Father, not mine. I have chosen to believe in love. I cannot be like you and my mother. You never loved each other," he said.

"Yes, we never loved each other, but we were both happy with what we gained. I built this kingdom with your grandfather's help, and your mother became the queen of this land," Alger said.

"Father, we shall end this conversation right here! I will not change my mind. I will not marry Queen Lamia, and I am sure she will understand. She is a wise and considerate woman. Besides, we are the most powerful kingdom in the world. We do not need Sinkaba's support. I love you, and I respect you, but I cannot do as you say. I believe I can build an even better kingdom if I love the woman I live with," he said.

"I will not disagree with you, Son, but remember this: Women become extremely dangerous when their feelings are hurt. If you do not marry her, be prepared to pay the price for it. The whole kingdom might pay. I may not live much longer, Larko, and I want to warn you. You know I have a bad heart, and I will die soon, but that does not mean I am not worried about you, my son," he said.

"Please do not say that, Father. Nothing is certain yet," he said.

"I am ready, Son. I have been ready for a while. I am sure you will be a better king than me," Alger said.

The lords' meeting with the king had no outcome for them, and they were not happy with the answer they had received from King Alger. If there was one thing everyone at the court was certain about regarding King Alger, it was his love for his son. Larko was the king's only child, and he loved him dearly. Calling off the wedding with Queen Lamia was not in anyone's interest, and not the lords' either, and after talking with King Alger, they were certain he was not going to do anything to help them out, so they decided to take things into their own hands and solve the problem differently. They were ready to do whatever was needed, and they started by threatening Aphra's family to get them to leave Kalastra.

It was a quiet night, and Aphra and her parents were having supper when they suddenly heard a few men galloping toward their house.

"Who are they, Father? Are they the rioters?" Aphra asked.

"I doubt that. They have never been to the city before. These men should be from the court, I think," Sebastian, Aphra's father, said.

"But why are they here? We have paid our taxes on time. What do they want from us?" Titiana, Aphra's mother, said.

"Stay calm and let me do the talking!" Sebastian said, then

opened the door and left the house. Aphra was worried. Three men had surrounded her father, and she could hardly see their faces.

"Who are you, and what do you want from us at this time of the night?" Sebastian asked.

"We have a message for you from the court. You and your family need to leave Kalastra before sunrise and never come back," the man said.

"Why? I have done nothing wrong. Who is this order from?" Sebastian asked.

"You have made many people angry at the court, and if you are wise, you will not argue and leave immediately to save your lives," the man said.

"I have always been a good citizen, and I have never been late to pay my taxes. How can a simple merchant like me make anyone at the court angry?" Sebastian asked.

"How dare you question us! We delivered you the royal message, and if you disobey, you shall bear the consequences. You should be happy we let you and your family live," the man said.

"My whole life is here. I cannot just leave Kalastra," Sebastian said.

"Then you should have told your daughter to stay away from the prince," the man said, and all three of them left.

Aphra could not believe what she had just heard. She had not seen the prince for weeks, and yet the court was worried about her acquaintance with Prince Larko. She loved him secretly in her heart, and she did not even dare to imagine that the prince would have the same feelings for her. Whatever it was, she felt guilty for causing problems for her family.

"I am sorry, Father. This is all my fault," Aphra said, wiping off her tears.

"There is nothing to be sorry about. We are a family, and we will get through this together," Sebastian said.

"I have not done anything wrong, Mother. The prince just saw me a few times after my painting class, but I stopped going to the court weeks ago because I could not stand the looks of the lords and the ladies there," she said, looking at her mother.

"You do not need to explain anything, Aphra. We believe you, and we know how things work at the court, but right now, we need to find a solution to this problem. We cannot leave Kalastra. It is our home," Titiana said.

"No matter what, we will not leave Kalastra. If the message was from the king, they would have read it for us, but they did not show us any royal message," Sebastian said.

"Even if the king is unaware of what is going on, it does not mean that they cannot harm us," Titiana said.

"We need to be more careful, but we will not do what they want. Our ancestors have lived in this land for centuries, and you will raise your children here, Aphra, so do not be afraid. Life will be the same as before tomorrow morning," Sebastian said.

Aphra could not sleep that night. She felt horrible, and she was worried for her parents. She was certain her father would not change his mind, and he was right in not wanting to leave Kalastra, but she could not stop thinking about what would happen in the future.

"Why are you still awake, Aphra?" Titiana asked.

"How can I sleep, Mother? I am ashamed of myself. I should have never gone to the court," Aphra said.

"There is no shame in love, and do not deny it, my dear. You are my daughter, and I know you. I have noticed how different you have been lately. It is all over your face, and it is the most beautiful and the purest feeling anyone can experience in life," Titiana said.

"Are you not going to tell me that I am stupid?" Aphra said.

"No. Your father and I have never banned you from wanting anything in your life. We have always supported you, and we will do it as long as we live," Titiana said.

"But I will not forgive myself if anything happens to you and Father because of me," Aphra said.

"Do not think about such things. Your father is a wise man, and he knows what he is doing. We will not leave our homeland for no reason, and the mother of the forest will protect us. Now close your eyes and try to sleep," Titiana said.

The next morning, when Aphra opened her eyes, everything seemed normal. Her mother was baking bread, and her father was collecting firewood. The day passed without an incident, and she was happy and thankful. The lords, on the other hand, were angry, and they were not going to give up easily.

"Threatening him did not work. We need to show him that we are serious," Lord Julian said.

"You are right. We should take action, and we shall not waste any time. What do you have in mind?" Lord Casper said.

"This man is a merchant, and his barn is full of wheat right now. We need to set fire to his stash before he gets a chance to trade them. My spies told me he will probably leave Kalastra to trade his wheat in two days," Lord Julian said.

"Even if he is tough, losing his assets will bring him to his knees," Lord Casper said.

That night, three men from the court set fire to Sebastian's barn. The barn was full of wheat, and they burned down everything. The whole village was there with Sebastian and his family, but no one could do anything. The harm was already done, and the whole barn and everything inside it had turned into ashes.

"We need to talk with the king. We cannot let them do whatever they want," Aphra said.

"You cannot see the king. This is all coming from the court, and they will not let you even pass through the gates," Sebastian said.

"But surely there must be something we can do," Aphra said.

"There is. We will build another barn, and we will continue with our life here," Sebastian said.

"What if they set fire to the new barn?" Aphra asked.

"Then we will build another one, but we will not leave," Sebastian said.

Unlike what Aphra thought, she did not need to go to the court and talk with the king to let them know what was going on, because Larko checked on her secretly every day, and he had learned about the fire. He knew it was not an accident, and Lord Julian and Lord Casper were definitely behind it, but he could not accuse them without any proof. He needed to talk with his father and ask for his help.

"Are you aware of what the lords are doing behind our backs, Father?" Larko asked.

"What is it, Son?" King Alger asked.

"Someone has set fire to Aphra's father's barn last night, and I am certain Lord Julian and Lord Casper are behind it," Larko said.

"So, it is about that girl again. I was hoping you wanted to talk about the estate's matters with me," King Alger said.

"I care about Kalastra, Father, but we are responsible for keeping our people safe too. The lords cannot do whatever they want behind our backs. They need to be punished," he said.

"Do you have any proof that they were behind the incident?" King Alger asked.

"No, Father. I do not, but we both know that they did it," Larko said.

"I cannot punish two of my lords with no reason because you fell in love with a merchant's girl," King Alger said.

"Fine! I said it before, but I suppose you did not take me seriously. I will cancel my wedding with Queen Lamia, and I will publicly announce it. No more hiding, Father!" Larko said.

"You are making a huge mistake. Love has blinded your eyes, but I can see everything, Son. You do not want Queen Lamia as your enemy," King Alger said.

King Alger was furious with the lords for what they had done, and not simply because what they did was wrong but because they had encouraged Larko to be more protective of Aphra and to cancel the wedding with Queen Lamia even sooner. On the other hand,

Lord Julian and Lord Casper were plotting their next move to force Sebastian to leave Kalastra. It seemed like money was not an issue for Sebastian, and to scare him off, they decided to harm one of his loved ones, but they were scared of Larko, so they could not even think of hurting Aphra. They waited for ten days, when everything calmed down; then one afternoon, when Titiana was all alone at home, two men, who had completely covered their faces, barged into the house and kidnapped her. Later that day, when Aphra came home, everything was strange to her. The pot was on the fire, and the vegetables were scattered all over the table. Her mother never left without letting them know, so she was certain something was wrong. Her father was not in the village that day. He had gone to the market in the city to buy supplies for the barn, and she had to find him and let him know.

"What is wrong, Aphra? Why have you been running?" Sebastian asked, stepping forward as his daughter came stumbling toward him, breathless and wide-eyed.

"Mother," she murmured, catching her breath. "Mother is not at home, and everything looks weird. I think someone might have taken her."

"These people will not leave us alone," Sebastian said with anger. "Go home and lock the door. Do not worry. I will bring your mother home."

He then hopped on his horse and started galloping. He was worried and angry. He was certain the king and the prince were not behind all the harassment, but he did not know who it was either. He checked out every possible location that Titiana might be at, but hours of searching were useless, and she was nowhere to be found. It was getting dark, and he could not convince himself to go back home empty-handed, but if there was a slight chance that she was home or stranded somewhere close, he had to try it. Sebastian's house was located on a hill, and there were few pine trees not so far from the house. Getting almost close to the house, he heard a muffled scream. He stopped the horse to listen carefully and heard the scream coming from a distance.

It must be Titiana, he thought. He followed the sound, and as he got closer, he could hear her more clearly. He finally found her. They had tied her to a tree, there was a cloth in her mouth, and they had blindfolded her. Sebastian ran toward her and took the cloth out of her mouth.

"I am sorry, darling. I am so sorry. What have they done to you?" Sebastian said, untying her and taking the cloth out of her mouth.

Titiana started crying and jumped into his arms. He let her cry for as long as she needed. He was angry with himself for being so stubborn and endangering his family.

"We will leave, Titiana. You, Aphra, and I will leave Kalastra, and we will never come back. This is all my fault. I did not take them seriously, and I see where we are right now," he said.

"No, Sebastian. We will not leave. They cannot have what they want. Do not be scared for me, and do not be scared for Aphra, for if they dared to hurt her, they would not have come for me," she said.

"But we cannot just sit back and do nothing. They have to pay for what they did to you," he said.

"We do not even know which one of the lords this is coming from, and it does not matter, because they are powerful and we are not," she said.

"I will do anything for you and Aphra. I will go to the court tomorrow morning. There is justice in this land. The king is fair, and he will listen to me," he said.

"No, Sebastian. Do not do it. I am certain the king is aware of everything, and even if he is not, do you think he will punish his lords for commoners like us?" she asked.

Sebastian was helpless, and he did not know what to do. He took Titiana's hands and looked at them; there were scratches all over her hands and feet. They had made her walk barefoot in the forest and imprisoned her in a deserted cabin in the middle of nowhere. After hours of mentally abusing and threatening her, they'd finally tied her to a tree somewhere close to her house.

Nothing was the same after that incident. Aphra felt even worse after knowing what had happened to her mother, and she wanted to talk to Prince Larko so many times, but she could not find the courage in herself to face him. She kept thinking that maybe she had imagined everything and her feelings for the prince were not mutual, but she was wrong.

Larko could not forget about Aphra. He was sure about his decision. He loved her, and nothing was going to stop him from marrying her. She was a kind soul, full of life and energy. Her courage had given him hope for the future, but he knew he had to deal with Queen Lamia first. Larko had to explain everything to her, so he grabbed his pen and wrote a letter to Queen Lamia.

Dear Queen Lamia of Sinkaba,

I am writing to you not as a prince but as a man who has found love, true love, a transformative love. Our fathers arranged our marriage years ago without seeking our opinions. We met each other only once when we were both very young. I know about your flawless beauty, wisdom, and sophistication, and I am confident any man who marries you will be tremendously lucky, but that man will not be me. I have fallen in love with a girl who is neither a queen nor a princess. However, she is so precious to me. I am certain a queen of your values does not want to marry without love and just for politics. So please forgive me for calling off our wedding, and I hope Kalastra and Sinkaba remain allies, and that this incident changes nothing in our friendship.

Your forever ally,
Prince Larko Dejovian of Kalastra

When he finished the letter, he sealed it with a royal stamp and gave it to one of his most trusted men to deliver to Queen Lamia, hoping everything could be resolved with discussion and without war. Even if Aphra did not love him and he had just imagined everything, he could still not marry Queen Lamia, so he had to be honest with her and tell her everything. Writing the letter to Queen Lamia was not as hard as talking to Aphra about his feelings. He had been following her for weeks, and he watched her closely, and with each passing day, his feelings were growing more and more. It was finally time for him to talk to her. The next day, he went to the forest again and waited for Aphra to show up. He knew she sat by the same tree near the lake the whole day and worked on her painting until she got tired. After a short wait, she finally showed up. Larko tried to get closer to her that day while hiding behind the trees, but despite his efforts to stay as quiet as possible, Aphra heard rustling in the bushes.

Aphra shouted, "Who is there?" Larko did not know what to do. He was embarrassed to show himself. Finally, after a few seconds, she asked again, "Who are you? Why are you following me?"

He finally came out of the trees and said, "It is me, Aphra."

Aphra was shocked to see Larko but happy at the same time. She missed him and did not expect to see him again.

"Sorry, Your Highness. I did not realize it was you," she said.

"I was riding when I saw you. I just wanted to make sure you were safe," he said.

"Thank you, Your Highness. You are very kind to me," she replied.

He glanced at the canvas propped against a tree nearby. "What are you painting?"

"A baby deer alone in the forest," she replied.

"I thought you only painted things that did not move," he said with a smile.

"I was an amateur back then, but now I can imagine what I am painting in my mind," she replied with a smile.

"I think you forgot what you promised me," he said.

"I have not, Your Highness. I will paint a portrait of you anytime you command," she said.

Larko took a few steps toward her, close enough to touch her hands, then asked, "Does my presence bother you?"

Aphra stared at him for a few seconds. She had not dared before to look straight into his eyes, but that day she forgot that he was the prince. Her heart was beating so fast that she thought Larko could hear it, but she pulled herself together and said, "No, Your Highness."

"Did you find the peace you wanted?" he asked.

"I thought I would, but something has happened to me, and I cannot undo it," she said.

"Why do you want to undo it? Let it thrive," he said.

Aphra took a step backward and asked, "Why are you here, Your Highness?"

"To see you. I lied to you. I did not see you by accident today. I think you must have figured it out. I was waiting for you to come. I have been watching you paint and sing for weeks. I know when you leave your home, what songs you sing every day, what you have painted so far, and what flowers you pick on your way home. I have been watching you, but I still miss you."

"Why are you telling me these things, Your Highness? It will take me an eternity to forget what you just told me," she said.

"Do not forget it then! You cannot look me in the eye and tell me you did not miss me."

"I have to go, Your Highness," she said and turned back.

"I love you," he burst out as she moved to leave.

Aphra could not move. She felt lightheaded, and it seemed like everything around her was spinning. Her heart was exploding, and her tears were pouring into her chest like a river. She turned back gently, and as she wiped away her tears, she said, "Princes do not fall in love with ordinary girls like me in real life."

"Maybe, but you are a fairy tale to me. You take my breath away.

You are unlike any girl I have known, Aphra," he said.

"How can you love two people at the same time? One is lust, for sure," she said.

"I only love you, Aphra," he replied.

"How about Queen Lamia?" she asked, her voice cracking. "Everyone in Kalastra knows you will marry the queen of Sinkaba."

"I have no feelings for her. My father and King Malik arranged our marriage years ago when we were both very young, but what I feel for you is genuine. Let me enter your world, Aphra! Do not push me away!" he said with a firm look in his eyes.

"I want to, Your Highness. I want it with all my heart, but I am scared. What if you get tired of me one day?" she asked.

He took her hand in his, gently but firmly. "You are like a thousand-page book to me, ancient and rooted. I will read a page of you every day, and once I reach the end, I will read you from the beginning, but I will never get tired of reading you. I promise you."

"No one at the court will be happy with your decision, Your Highness. They have already made it clear to me and my family," she said.

"I am sorry for everything you and your parents went through because of me, but I will make everything right. I promise you, Aphra," he said.

"I love you, Your Highness, even if the price is to die," she said with a trembling voice.

"Live for me, Aphra! Live so I can live too. I loved you yesterday, I love you today, and I will love you even if I no longer breathe and my body rots and my soul enters the land of the dead. So let this tree witness what I told you today," he said as he opened his arms to her.

Aphra took his hand and said, "I believe you, Your Highness. Let everyone say I have gone crazy for falling in love with a prince. Nothing matters anymore."

Larko embraced her and held her tight to his chest. She was trembling, and he could count the number of breaths she was taking. Her hair smelled like a fresh daffodil, and her hands were soft like clean linen. She laid her head on his shoulder, and a love story began that day.

CHAPTER TEN

L AMIA WAS A beautiful woman, and anyone who had seen her would testify to her indescribable beauty. She was created perfectly, and she was a masterpiece carved by the hands of her creator. She was the absolute meaning of perfection and attraction. When she touched her long, dark, wavy hair, it crashed on her slender waist like waves on the beach. When she talked, everyone was bewitched by the curves of her lips and agreed to whatever she asked for, and when she looked at others with her piercing black eyes, no one could resist not telling the truth.

Her palace was as alluring as her face, and it was a glorious scene when she sat on her throne wearing her jeweled crown, showing off her exquisite beauty. Queen Lamia was the most powerful woman in the world, and she had everything in her grasp. She had rejected all the princes who had asked for her hand in marriage and was patiently waiting for Prince Larko. So many things had changed for Lamia since she had last visited Kalastra and seen Larko, except her feelings for him. She was no longer the weak and scared girl who used to hide in her chamber and wanted to run away from Sinkaba; instead, she had turned into a strong woman who was proud of ruling over Sinkaba and cared about her people. She was an exemplary woman, and she was loved and respected by everyone in the kingdom, famous not only for her charm but also for her talent in riding and archery. Queen Lamia thought she could have anything she wished for in life, and there was nothing she could not gain with her beauty and power, until she received a letter from Prince Larko.

"A messenger from Kalastra is here to see you, Your Majesty. He says he has an important letter from Prince Larko Dejovian of Kalastra for you," Jabeer, the queen's most trusted adviser, said.

There was not a single day in the past few years when Lamia had not thought about Larko, waiting to receive a letter from him, but every time she wanted to send a message to him, her pride stopped her.

"Finally! He has finally written to me. Tell him to enter," Queen Lamia said with excitement.

The messenger entered the crown room and bowed for Queen Lamia.

"Queen Lamia of Sinkaba! I have a message from His Highness, Prince Larko Dejovian of Kalastra. His Highness said the letter is of utmost importance, and he will be expecting a reply," the messenger said as he handed the letter to Jabeer.

"Very well! You must be exhausted after riding here from Kalastra. I will make sure you are well rested, and I will give you a letter in response to your prince's letter in the morning. You can leave now!" Queen Lamia said.

Jabeer handed the letter to Queen Lamia, and she opened it eagerly, but after she read it, the smile on her face disappeared, and she started shivering with anger. It was not what she expected, and her imaginary heaven turned to hell in just a few seconds.

"How dare he? How can he allow himself to insult me and my kingdom? I cannot believe this," Lamia screamed with rage as she tore the letter into pieces.

"What was in the letter, Your Majesty?" Jabeer asked as he picked up the pieces of the letter from the floor.

"He is calling off our wedding because he has fallen in love with a commoner. He is rejecting me for a girl who has no status. She is not even a princess; she is a simple girl, and now he wants to cancel all the arrangements we had for years," she said, shivering with fury.

"This is an insult, Your Majesty. Your marriage with Prince Larko was arranged years ago by your fathers. He cannot just cancel everything. We should send a message to King Alger immediately," he said.

"To ask what, Jabeer? To beg him to talk with his son so he marries me? Never!" she said.

"Then we should kill the messenger and attack Kalastra at once," he said.

"They are way more powerful than us. We will have no chance of defeating them. War is not the solution," she said, then paused for a few seconds. "Leave me alone, Jabeer! I need to think. Do not do anything without my knowledge!"

Jabeer bowed low. "As you command, Your Majesty."

Lamia was hurt. She had spent the last few years of her life thinking about Larko, and he wanted her to forget him suddenly, like there was nothing between them. The memory of seeing him for the first time was still alive in her mind, and she cherished every second she had spent with him in Kalastra, but it was all nothing to him. How could he fall in love with someone else while she was thinking of him every single day? Trusting a man was never easy for Lamia, especially after what her father had done to her mother, but something about Larko invited her to trust and fall in love with him. She felt Larko had shattered her pride. She was a queen whom every prince and king in the world wanted to have, yet Larko had rejected her for an ordinary girl. It was true that he had never shown her any affection, but he had not disagreed with the marriage either. It was all a nightmare to her, but she would not let any man break her, not even Larko. She was a strong woman, and all she needed was one night to think and cry, and what a dark and gloomy night it was for her. She was alone in her chamber, looking at the only drawing she had from Larko, the one she had stolen from him when she had secretly entered his chamber. All she needed that day was something that belonged to Larko so she could look at it and reminisce about the amazing days she had in Kalastra with him, so when she saw a drawing of him in one of the drawers, she took it without hesitation. That night, alone in her chamber, she looked at his drawing and kissed it again and again. The drawing was old, and she was sure he had changed a lot over the years. He was probably more masculine and more handsome, but that drawing was all she had from him, so she had kept it for years. She opened the window so the cool breeze touched her face, and then she suddenly burst into tears.

"Is everything fine, Your Majesty?" Aesha asked as she entered the chamber.

Lamia didn't look up. Her back was turned, shoulders tense. "Yes, everything is fine, Aesha. You can go back to sleep."

"You are crying, Your Majesty. You are not fine. I have never seen you this sad before," Aesha said as she approached her.

"I was never this sad, even when I lost my mother. I do not think I can ever be the same person I was before," Lamia said.

"Is it because of Prince Larko, Your Majesty?" Aesha asked.

"Yes, it is. He broke my heart into pieces. Why did he do this to me? How could he prefer an ordinary girl to me?" Lamia asked.

"That girl is nowhere even close to you. She must have bewitched the prince, Your Majesty. There is no other explanation," Aesha replied.

"I do not believe in witchcraft, Aesha. It was all my fault. I knew from the beginning that he was not in love with me, but I fooled myself. I waited years for him, but he never came to visit me or wrote a letter, and I let myself believe that he was fine with all the arrangements our fathers had made. Now he expects me to reply, and I do not know what to write back. I do not even know why I am crying for him. I do not love him," Lamia said.

"I think you do, Your Majesty. You love Prince Larko. You never told me how you felt about him, but it was all over your face. You are deeply in love with him," Aesha said.

There was no doubt Larko was sweet and gentle, and Lamia was much in need of love, something she had neither received from her father nor remembered from her mother; she was only a kid when she lost her. But, despite her beauty and power, Lamia was a fragile woman. She had built a dream world for herself with Larko, and he had ruined everything with just a letter. She felt betrayed and insulted, but she decided not to show her anger. Instead, she wrote back a heartwarming letter to Larko and assured him that everything was fine, and he did not need to worry about anything. Lamia was a wise woman. She decided to hide her anger so she could exact her revenge upon Larko at the perfect time. Her love for Larko had turned into hatred in the blink of an eye. Before handing the letter to the messenger, Jabeer tried to convince her to reply firmly and threaten to attack Kalastra, but she was not going to change her mind.

"I still believe we should attack Kalastra, Your Majesty. We should give them a lesson never to forget," Jabeer said.

"They have a huge well-trained army compared to us. We stand no chance against them. The military attack is the last option, Jabeer. We should wait for now and let him think we are on good terms with them. I am a patient woman. I will take my revenge when the time is right."

As days and weeks passed, Lamia's anger grew more and more, and she was not herself anymore. Everyone in the palace was worried about her, especially her servant. She ate less, she was reluctant to do anything at all, she locked herself up in her chamber, and the only thing she did was think about all the details of her plan and the best way to make Larko suffer. She had no rush in taking her revenge.

"It has been two days that you have not eaten anything, Your Majesty," Aesha said quietly, placing a tray of untouched food on the side table.

"I'm not hungry," Lamia replied, her voice flat as she stared out the window.

"You should eat a little, even if you are not hungry, Your Majesty. You should stay strong for the sake of your people. They all look up to you," Aesha said.

"I know that, but I cannot help it," Lamia said.

"I wish you had attacked Kalastra and were done with it by now instead of hurting yourself," Aesha said.

Lamia let out a cold laugh, bitter and sharp. "It is not that simple. I will never attack Kalastra. They will slaughter us in just a few hours. I would rather die here with sorrow than lose my only chance of exacting my revenge upon Larko and that wicked girl."

Aesha took a cautious step closer. "What are you planning to do, Your Majesty?"

"I do not know yet, but I will make them pay. I do not care if he kills me at the end, but I want to see the pain on his face," Lamia replied.

"What if he realizes you lied and somehow knows you want to take revenge, Your Majesty?" Aesha asked.

"It is impossible. He is a smart man, but it seems like love has blinded him; otherwise, he would not send me such a letter. All he needed from me was approval to marry someone else, and I gave it to him. He did not even bother to break my heart in person or write back and thank me for understanding him. Tell me, Aesha! Does he deserve any mercy?" Lamia asked.

"No, Your Majesty. He does not. He deserves the worst, and I will help you in any way I can," Aesha replied.

A slow smile curled at Lamia's lips, cold and deliberate. "I will wait for them to get married and to feel happy and safe, and once they think they have it all, I will take everything from them."

"I am fine with everything you want to do with them, but do not torture yourself, Your Majesty. Your life is precious. Your people are worried about you. Being a queen is not easy, and you cannot hide in your chamber because you are heartbroken. You need to show yourself to your people. Let them know you are still in charge, and everything is under your control," Aesha said.

"You are right. I will visit the villages today. Tell them to prepare my horse," Lamia said.

Later in the afternoon, she got on her horse and left the palace. Aesha, Jabeer, and a few soldiers usually accompanied her. People were all eager to see her, and they praised her wisdom and affection. They were all cheering for her as she made her way into the city. She was always generous with her people and had lowered their taxes after her father's death. She had built several buildings in the city when she became the queen of Sinkaba, and she had expanded her realm even more than her father had done. When she got to the city square, she stopped, and people gathered around her. She knew her people were worried and wondered what she would do after Prince Larko canceled the wedding, so she had to smile and give them hope even when she had none.

"My great people of Sinkaba! I stand here in front of you today, as I know you have all heard about what happened with Prince Larko Dejovian of Kalastra. We decided to part ways, as our marriage was only arranged by our fathers years ago when we were both very young, but this changes nothing between us, and Kalastra is still our ally. Do not fear, as there will be no war. I will choose a proper and suitable husband in time, and I will give Sinkaba and all you people an heir to the kingdom. Be happy and celebrate, as good days are coming to our land," she said to her people.

Then the crowd started cheering for her and repeatedly said, "Long live the queen."

CHAPTER ELEVEN

PEOPLE IN KALASTRA were happy knowing their prince had decided to marry a simple girl from the village, but they were worried at the same time because they knew he'd had to call off the wedding with Queen Lamia, who was the most powerful ruler in the South. When the messenger returned from Sinkaba and handed Queen Lamia's letter to Larko, he read it immediately and shared it with his father.

"The messenger I sent to Sinkaba just arrived, and as I told you, there is no problem, Father. Queen Lamia is a wise woman. Calling off the wedding has not changed anything in our diplomatic relationships. We are still good allies, and I do not understand why you are so worried," Larko said.

"I cannot explain it, Son. It is just a feeling I have. I do not trust her, and we should be cautious, especially on the wedding day. We should have guards everywhere," King Alger said.

"As you command, Father. I promise you to be careful. You look very tired today. Why do you not rest in your chamber? I will take care of everything," he said.

Alger studied his son for a long moment, then let out a tired breath. "I am old and sick, my son. It does not matter if I rest or not. My time will be up soon."

"You are fine, Father. Worrying and too much thinking has just made you a little weak, but it will all pass," he said.

Larko was wrong. The king's condition got worse, and he got weaker and weaker every day. Even the court physician could not help him anymore. He was in bed most days, and Larko was in charge of almost everything. The physician had told him that the king's situation would not improve, and they had to be ready to say goodbye to him at any minute, but Larko was just not ready yet. For the first time in years, he was starting to feel whole again after meeting Aphra, but he knew the mother of the forest was going to take his father from him when he most needed him. He wanted to postpone his wedding to take care of his father, but the king insisted on seeing his son's wedding before his death.

One year had passed from the day Larko and Aphra had met for the first time. One year ago, Aphra was an ordinary girl, like other girls in Kalastra, but soon she would marry the prince. She was supposed to be the happiest girl in Kalastra, and she loved Larko more than anyone and anything in the world, but she could not hide her fear. Like King Alger, she had not believed Queen Lamia's good intentions. After all, she was a woman, and she knew how a woman would react when a man hurt her feelings, but she could not persuade Larko to believe her. She met Larko, fell in love with him, and would marry him soon. It was all so magical that she thought something terrible was going to ruin it. Aphra tried to talk Larko out of the marriage and asked him to wait until they knew what Queen Lamia was planning to do, but Larko did not listen.

Larko and Aphra usually rode together and went as far as they could, deep into the forest, and the day he received Queen Lamia's letter, he was supposed to meet her in the forest in the darkness of the night for the first time. It was a beautiful and soothing night in Kalastra, and the sound of the crickets and the hoot of the owls were all welcoming Larko into their territory. He no longer wanted to be Prince Larko that night. He just wanted to be Larko, a young man who was in love and anticipating seeing his lover.

"I am sorry to keep you waiting, my love," Aphra said.

"What can be better in this world than waiting for you, Aphra?" Larko said, holding her hands.

"I love being in the forest. It does not scare me. It is like home to me, and I wanted to experience this with you one last time before I start living at the court," she said.

"Marrying me does not mean you cannot have the life you had before. You can still do whatever makes you happy. We will ride together in the forest, you will paint here, and we will spend as much time as you need in the wilderness," he said.

"Do you still think we should marry now? Maybe we should wait for a while," she said.

"No more waiting, Aphra! We should even hurry. I do not want to spend one more day without you," he said.

"I am scared, Larko. Something does not feel right. Queen Lamia did not show any sign of disappointment in her letter. Do you not think this is strange?" she asked.

"I do not understand why you and Father are so worried. Queen Lamia knows her army is not even comparable to Kalastra's army. She is a smart woman, and she does not want to start a war that she knows she will lose. It is that simple," he replied.

"I wish I could think like you," she said.

"Relax! I promise you everything will be fine. Just think about our wedding, and I will take care of everything else for you," Larko said; then he kissed her on the forehead. Aphra tried to steal her eyes from him, hiding the uncertainty and the fear she still felt, but Larko raised her head, looked into her eyes, and said, "Do you know you have the most beautiful, innocent eyes in the world?"

"Do you think I am innocent?" she asked, her voice nearly a whisper.

"Of course I do. What makes you think you are not?" he asked.

"I feel guilty for ruining Queen Lamia's dream of marrying you. I am sure she hates me," she said.

"I never loved her, Aphra. It was a political arrangement between our fathers. No one even asked us how we felt. I was young back then. I did not even know what love meant until I met you. I am sure Queen Lamia will find the love of her life too. We could never be happy together," he said.

"I hope so, Larko," she said.

"It is enough worrying," Larko said, his tone turning playful. "Tonight, I want to sleep next to you, here, under the sky."

Aphra laughed and said, "You want to sleep under the sky? I am sure you are teasing me. You have never slept anywhere except on your comfortable bed, Your Highness."

"I know, but as I always say, there is a first time for everything, right? I have brought lots of blankets. So, shall we?" Larko said while smiling.

Aphra folded her arms, amused. "I have to warn you, it is not easy sleeping on the ground."

"I have the stars in the sky to light up our night, and I have you by my side to light up my heart. It is a beautiful night, and I am going to sleep next to a beautiful woman. What else can I want in life?" he asked.

"If marrying me means losing everything you have, your title, and your wealth, will you still do it?" she asked.

"I will do it without hesitation. I will choose you over anything and anyone. I will even drop my right to the throne if I have to, but I will not lose you, Aphra," he replied.

Aphra did not ask anything else; she just placed her head on his chest and closed her eyes. She had never slept that peacefully in her life before. The moon was complete, and the sound of the lake by their side was mesmerizing. It was a breathtaking night, and they both felt they needed to be alone with each other, away from everyone's eyes, before starting their new life at the court. Aphra hoped to persuade Larko that night to postpone the marriage, but he was too proud and young to listen to anybody, so she finally gave up. She no longer wanted to fight with the things that insisted on happening in her life.

No one could understand how crazily Larko was in love with Aphra, not even her. He was so in love with her that he was even ready to go to war with Sinkaba if he had to. He had changed everything at the court to Aphra's satisfaction. Larko had commanded the gardeners to plant one thousand daffodil flowers in the garden because they were Aphra's favorite.

Finally, the wedding day arrived, the day everyone had waited for, and it was exactly one month after receiving Queen Lamia's letter. It was a glorious day for Larko and Aphra and the whole kingdom. It was not an ordinary wedding; it was a royal wedding, a magical and indescribable experience. Aphra looked stunning in her wedding dress, made from the finest silk and lace in Kalastra. It was a long white embroidered dress, and it fit her beautiful body, showing off all her curves. Her veil was the longest anyone had seen, and ten of her servants had to carry it, and her flower bouquet was from the daffodil flowers planted in the garden. Her soft hair was flowing down on her slender shoulders, and the jasmine flowers in her hair had magnified her innocent beauty. Aphra's heart was beating fast as her servant was helping her get dressed, and she occasionally blushed as she thought about Larko's sudden intrusion into her chamber the night before.

"Open the door, Aphra! I need to see you," Larko said.

Aphra opened the door and said, "It is past midnight, Larko. What are you doing here at this time?"

"I could not sleep. I wanted to make sure you had not run away," Larko said as he pushed himself into her chamber.

"Why would I run away, dear? I am counting the hours to be your wife," she said with a smile.

"Then be my wife now! I cannot wait any longer," he said.

"You cannot be serious. We have waited so long for the magical moment to arrive. Why should we ruin it now?" she asked.

"Because I say so, and I am the prince, if that means anything to you," he said.

"I think you should leave now. Someone might see you here," she said as she pushed him out the door.

He moved toward the door, reluctant. "Wait! I still have something to tell you."

"I think you have said enough, Your Highness," she replied coolly, opening the door. "I will see you in the morning when you are sober."

"I am not that drunk. All I want is these last few hours to pass so I can have you in my arms," he said.

"Have you been thinking about Queen Lamia like me?" she asked.

"I do not think that she can or will do anything to harm us. I am just bothered that you are not enjoying yourself. Let it go! I assure you that we will both see the dawn, and I will see you in your white wedding dress, and I will wait for you at the end of the aisle, and you will be my queen, and there is no power in this world to stop that. I love you, Aphra, and our love for each other is greater than anything Lamia plans for us," he said, holding her hands.

"Thank you for telling me these things. I needed to hear them from you," she said and kissed him on the cheek.

"Goodnight, my bride," Larko said, stepping back with a quiet smile. "I will see you in the morning."

It was all too good to be true, but all the waiting and worrying was going to end soon. Aphra was about to start a new chapter in her life, and she could finally hold Larko's hands forever. She wore her white shoes and grabbed her daffodil flower bouquet, but she was so excited that she could barely walk.

"Are you excited, my lady?" Iris asked.

"Very much, Iris. I feel like my heart is about to explode," she replied.

"It is all normal, my lady, but focus only on Prince Larko, and everybody else fades out," she said.

"I was worried last night, and Larko tried to calm me down, but I cannot stop thinking about Queen Lamia. I feel like she is going to appear any minute," Aphra said.

"The guards are everywhere, my lady. You do not need to worry about anything. You are just overthinking," she said.

Aphra took a deep breath and said, "You are right. I should let go of her. It is my wedding day."

"That is better, my lady. We can go whenever you are ready," she said.

Finally, the huge doors of the ballroom opened, and Aphra appeared in her dazzling white dress, and behind her, Iris and the rest of the servants were carrying her veil. The crowd in the ballroom was more than she imagined, and she barely knew anyone. They were all staring at her with their curious eyes, still in disbelief that a simple girl was going to marry the prince of Kalastra. As she walked down the aisle, she could see the jealous looks of other girls, not believing how she had stolen Larko's heart; however, all the knights looked at her with admiration. She was trying her best to walk straight with the flower bouquet in her hand, and as she randomly glanced at some of the lords, she could see their cold and indifferent looks, but what warmed her heart was seeing Larko at the end of the aisle. He looked at her with his big hazel eyes like he was seeing her for the first time. Larko took her hands, and the joy and excitement she felt at that moment were so immense and powerful that she was sure they were going to stay with her for an eternity.

Larko and Aphra married that day in Kalastra, and 300 years later, a girl from Aseeta saw everything in her dream that had happened in their lives until they got married. Esther woke up in tears. She had seen them in her dream, and she had felt whatever

Aphra had felt: her excitement, her fear, her joy, and the love she had for Larko, like somehow, she knew her from a different world.

CHAPTER TWELVE

EVERYTHING WAS DREAMY for Aphra and Larko. They had finally married, and life could not get any better. The king was happy for his son but worried at the same time. He could see how Larko had changed for the better after falling in love with Aphra, and he was proud of him, but he could not convince himself yet that Queen Lamia was fine with everything. Larko, on the other hand, was starting to think about Aphra and his father's opinion about Queen Lamia because everything was too perfect to be true. He could feel something was off, but he did not want to scare Aphra. So, to prepare for any possible attack from Sinkaba, he fortified the castle in the South and increased the number of soldiers on the southern borders. He even traveled to Sinkaba anonymously, with a few of his knights, to make sure Queen Lamia was not plotting against Kalastra. After marrying Aphra, he was responsible for keeping her and his people safe, and he felt the burden every day. Larko was the best warrior in Kalastra, and everyone looked up to him, but to make Kalastra even more powerful, he needed more warriors who could fight like him. After consulting with his father, he announced to the public that, in the annual tournament, instead of ten knights, twenty knights would be chosen, and to make everyone more interested in joining, he increased the reward for the chosen knights. Being a knight of Kalastra was a prestigious title, and every young man in Kalastra wished to be a knight and fight alongside Larko.

A few weeks after the wedding, Aphra was completely used to life at the court, and she tried her best to be worthy of her title. She still assisted her uncle with the sick people in the city, and marrying the prince had not stopped her from caring about her people, yet she felt more responsible. She loved politics and insisted on attending all the meetings regarding the matters of the estate, and Larko applauded her wisdom and courage. She had even asked Larko to teach her how to fight. She believed every woman needed to know how to use a sword and not rely on men to protect them, and the forest was the best place to practice.

"Are you ready for your sword fighting class, my wife?" Larko asked, his voice full of mischief.

"Only if you are my teacher," Aphra replied with a smile.

"I will not be an easy teacher," he said with a smile too.

"Fine, I will accept the challenge, Your Highness," she said with a teasing curtsy.

"You need to start with a small sword, something that you are comfortable holding and is not too heavy for you," he said, then handed her the sword.

Aphra grabbed the sword, but she had no idea how to hold it in her hand.

"I look completely funny, I know," she said.

"No, dear, you are doing fine. Just look at how I hold the sword!" he said, holding his sword in his hand.

Larko was patient with Aphra, and he was certain she was a fast learner, and Aphra tried to imitate him and followed all his instructions.

"Now hold your sword up and attack me!" he said.

"I do not know how to attack. What if I hurt you?" she said.

Larko burst into laughter and said, "Are you serious, dear? You think you can hurt me?"

"Do not underestimate me! Maybe I can," she said and attacked with her sword.

"I see you are offended, but never attack out of anger. Always concentrate and plan your move," he said, defusing her attack and pointing his sword at her throat. Aphra's sword had dropped to the ground, and she was looking into Larko's eyes.

"We cannot get anywhere today if you keep looking at me with those beautiful eyes of yours," he said.

"Did you not just tell me to concentrate when fighting?" she said with a smirk.

"I did, but I've never had an opponent as charming as you," he said, lowering his sword and placing his hand on her lower back. Then he pulled her to his chest and kissed her gently on her lips. Although the first session of practicing in the forest had not gone as Aphra and Larko had planned, it was memorable and joyous. Aphra was playful like a child when she was not in the court, and Larko was a completely different man. He was not just a prince but a man deeply in love. He kissed her over and over, made love to her, and the only thing they did not do was practice sword fighting.

Breathless and resting against him, Aphra whispered, "This cannot happen again, or I cannot learn anything from you."

Larko smiled against her forehead. "It was our first class, so we could technically cheat. Do not worry! I will make you a great fighter in just a few months. I can see the passion in your eyes. There is nothing that you cannot do, Aphra."

"That is because I have a great supporter like you. I love you, Larko, and I love you more with each passing day," she said.

They practiced again after that day, and as Larko had said, Aphra excelled in sword fighting. In just a few months, she had become a great fighter. She was fast, she was smart, and she was courageous. Aphra was loved and respected by everyone at the court, and even the lords who were against the prince's marriage to her were starting to understand why Larko had chosen her.

Larko and Aphra's happiness was contagious, and the whole kingdom was joyful, but in just a few months, everything changed. King Alger died almost one year after their marriage, and with his death, Larko became the king of Kalastra. He was devastated, and although he knew his father's death could happen any day, he was not ready for it, and he could not believe that his father was gone forever and that he was responsible for the whole kingdom. King Alger's death was a shock to everyone. Nobody knew the king was sick, except Larko and the court physician. King Alger wanted to keep it a secret to have an advantage over Lord Henry and the insurgents loyal to him. If they knew the king would die soon, they would prepare an army and attack Kalastra at once. A few weeks after the king's death, Larko's coronation happened. He became the legitimate king of Kalastra, as did Aphra as the queen of Kalastra, and just as everyone had predicted, it did not take long for Lord Henry to attack Kalastra, and so Larko had to spend most of his time traveling to different parts of the kingdom, suppressing the rioters. In Larko's absence, Aphra was responsible for the kingdom, and she was well fit for the position, as if she was born to be a queen. She was smart, caring, wise, and Larko's best consultant, not to mention she was a physician, a painter, and an excellent rider.

Rioters attacked from every corner of the country, and Larko was constantly away. He was going to leave again that morning, and Aphra could not confide her feelings.

"When will you return, my love? I am already worried about you," Aphra said.

"Sooner than you think. Do not worry! I have my finest men with me," Larko said.

"Every time you leave, I feel like you take a piece of my heart with you. I will count the days and nights until you come back," she said.

"And you have my whole heart in your hands. There is nothing in this world that I want more than being next to you, but you know I have to go," he said.

"Take this bracelet!" she said, reaching into her satchel. She pulled out a small woven bracelet—blue-and-gold threads twisted with tiny carved beads. "I made it for you. It will protect you. Wear it and bring it back to me in one piece, just like yourself."

Larko smiled and took the bracelet from her. He loved her more than anyone and anything in the world, but he was never good at expressing his feelings. He sometimes thought that Aphra did not know how much he loved her and the things he would sacrifice to keep her safe. It was not easy for him to leave her either, but he had to go. He had no choice; he was the king of Kalastra and responsible for protecting his people and land.

Larko had a unique personality. He was hard on his decisions, and once he made up his mind, no one could persuade him to change it, not even Aphra. She could see how Larko had changed over one year. He was more mature and determined, and although he was still young, his hair had grown gray. However, in Aphra's eyes, everything about Larko was charming. His hazel eyes were stunning, and she could stare at them for hours. Larko was the most persuasive person Aphra knew, and she always ended up doing what he wanted without even noticing when and how he had made her change her mind. However, nothing mattered to her that day. Larko was going to leave Kalastra, and she could not bear being away from him. It was not the first time he would leave the court, but she felt the same unexplainable feeling in her heart every time he left. He had to be away from the court for weeks, and every day was torture to her. Nothing was beautiful when Larko was not with her—the court, the garden, the forest, everything was the same. Days were dull and monotonous, and there was nothing to cheer her up, not even the sound of canaries.

For a second, the thought of Jasper passed through her mind again. She still felt guilty for breaking his heart, but she did not want to think about him that day. All she cared about was Larko and when he could be back at the court again. How could she tolerate the lonely days and nights without him? Larko put on his armor, grabbed his sword, kissed Aphra on the forehead, and left, and just like that, her days of loneliness started. Larko was calm when saying goodbye, and Aphra always envied the control he had over his emotions. She wished she could be more like him, indifferent sometimes; at least she would not have to suffer.

Aphra walked up the stairs reluctantly and went straight to her chamber. If only she could fast-forward the time until Larko was back at the court again. She looked at her chamber, and it was nothing except stone and bricks, cold and spiritless. Everything had changed after Larko left. It was freezing that morning, and a cold wind was blowing through the window. As she covered her neck with her fur shawl, she reached out to the curtains and drew them. The room felt cozier with the curtains drawn. She sat on the bed, took her shoes off, and stared at the first painting she did for Larko. He was modest and charming, and she'd been so lucky to steal his heart. She could vividly remember the first day she laid eyes on him. He was the prince of Kalastra and every girl's desire. It was more like a dream that a prince fell in love with a simple girl, but sometimes dreams came true.

Even the memory of that day riding with Larko made her smile. She had not known him then, yet he had made her feel safe and protected. Her life would be so different if she had not met Larko in the forest that day, but she knew it was in her destiny to meet him and fall in love with him. As she wanted to lay down on the bed and continue her daydreaming, someone knocked on the door and said, "Your lunch is ready, Your Majesty."

"I am not hungry. You can take it back," she said.

Her heart was heavy, and the only thing that calmed her down was thinking about Larko, but then she remembered that Larko always wanted her to stay strong and fulfill her duty as the queen of Kalastra when he was away, so she called her back and said, "I changed my mind. I will have my lunch in the garden today."

The garden was Aphra's favorite place at the court. It was impeccably beautiful, a piece of paradise, and the gardeners had planted all her favorite flowers in the garden as Larko had commanded. The garden's serenity gave her new energy: the rose bushes, the jasmines, the lilies, and the daffodils, which were her favorite flowers. The garden had a spectacular view of the city. Nothing had changed with the city of Kalastra, and it was still the same as before; only, she had changed. She'd fallen in love with Larko, and everything changed for her after that. It was a cold day, and a thin fog hovering over the city made it a little hard to see what was exactly going on, but she could tell the city was alive and busy, like always. Aphra took a deep breath and filled her lungs with fresh air.

"It is a little chilly today, Your Majesty. Do you need a cover-up?" Iris asked.

"No, I am fine. I love this time of the year when it gets cold and foggy. When is your favorite time of the year, Iris?" she asked.

"I am not sure, Your Majesty, maybe summer," she replied.

"It was summer when I saw Larko for the first time," Aphra said.

"I am sure the king will return safe and sound, Your Majesty," she said.

"I hope so, Iris. I've just had a bad feeling since this morning, and I do not know what it is," she said.

"Maybe Lady Ingrid can help," Iris said.

"I doubt it, but send for her anyway," Aphra said.

Aphra was always worried when Larko left, and she tried her best to ignore the negative thoughts in her mind; however, it was different that time. Lady Ingrid was Aphra's most trusted adviser at the court, and she always tried to help her out.

"What is troubling you, Your Majesty?" Lady Ingrid asked.

"I do not know what it is, Ingrid, but I can feel something horrible is going to happen. Larko is away, and I cannot stop thinking about him. I know I tell you the same thing each time he leaves, but it is different this time," she said.

"Did you have a bad dream, Your Majesty?" she asked.

"No, I did not, but I have this fear that I will not see Larko again," Aphra replied.

"It is all normal, Your Majesty. You are worried about the king," she said.

"It is not just worrying. I feel like it is the end of everything, as if our time together has come to an end. I feel death, Ingrid," she said.

"Are you still thinking about Sinkaba and Queen Lamia, Your Majesty?" she asked.

"I would be lying if I said no; I am scared of her," Aphra replied.

"One year has passed since your marriage, Your Majesty, and she has not done anything. I think the king is right. You must let go of your fear. She cannot harm you or the king anymore," she said.

"Then what is this feeling I have? I have no control over it," Aphra said.

"You are overthinking, Your Majesty. You have to face your fear and see with your own eyes that it does not exist. Maybe you should invite Queen Lamia to Kalastra and put this animosity behind you," she said.

"I do not think that is a good idea. It may make everything even worse if she sees us together," Aphra said.

"As you wish, Your Majesty, but try to eliminate the negative thoughts and focus on the country's affairs. If you occupy your mind, you will have less time to think and worry," she said.

"I will try my best. Thank you, Ingrid. Talking to you always makes me feel better."

Later that day, Aphra decided to continue working on her painting. It was the only thing that kept her sane and made her worry less, but it was impossible not to think about Larko when she painted.

CHAPTER THIRTEEN

IN SINKABA, QUEEN Lamia was thinking about exacting her revenge upon Larko and Aphra. She was ready to do anything to destroy them, but she needed a powerful ally. She needed someone at the court of Kalastra whom she could trust, someone close to the king and queen, and after months of searching, she finally found that person, someone whom both Larko and Aphra trusted, someone with power, and someone who hated them both as much as she did.

"Any news, Jabeer? Have you found anyone who can be valuable to us?" Queen Lamia asked.

"Yes, Your Majesty. I think I have," Jabeer replied.

"Who is this person?" she asked.

"His name is Jasper, Your Majesty. He is one of the king's best and most trusted knights," he replied.

"Why do you think he is willing to betray his king?" she asked.

"He was Aphra's best friend since childhood, and he was secretly in love with her. He expressed his love to her, but Aphra turned him down and said she had no feelings for him. He is emotionally hurt, Your Majesty, and I think he is the perfect bait," he said.

"So, he is hurt like me. How is it that life is so unfair to some people?" she asked.

"Larko could never make you happy, Your Majesty. You fell in love with him when you were weak and scared of your father, and he was just a refuge. You are in love with the memories you made with him years ago, but I am certain if you see him now, you would not want him to be part of your life anymore," he said.

"I am not in love with him anymore, but he shattered my pride, and he has to pay for it," she replied with hatred in her voice.

"Jasper will help us make it happen. He is exactly the one we need," he said.

"We need to make sure he is not in love with Aphra anymore, or he will ruin everything," she said.

"Do not worry, Your Majesty. He is not in love with her any longer. I am completely certain," he said.

"That is perfect. I would like to see him myself. Send him a message through one of our spies in Kalastra, and tell him I would like to meet him at Mount Zaka. It is better not to attract any attention at this time," she said.

"As you wish, Your Majesty. I will send the messenger at once," he said.

Once Queen Lamia realized Jasper had been in love with Aphra before and how she had rejected him and married Larko a year later, she knew he was the perfect partner in crime for her. She was sure his love for Aphra had turned into hatred by then, and she could use him a lot in taking her revenge. Jasper had never forgiven Aphra, and when Queen Lamia approached him, he was hurt and confused. He was full of hatred, and he did not know how to cope with rejection.

Larko knew that Aphra and Jasper were best friends, but Aphra had never told him about Jasper's feelings for her. She was afraid of what he might do if he realized his best knight had loved her once. Aphra did not know how to react if she saw Jasper at the court either. Their last encounter in the Crystal Cave was not so pleasant, and she hated that she had lost her best friend that day. She wished Jasper had never talked about his feelings for her, but he seemed completely different when she saw him at the court two years later. They talked like two old friends, and there was no sign of jealousy and hatred in him, or at least that was what Aphra felt, but in reality, it was all a game well played by Jasper, to make Aphra trust him again, and that was what Queen Lamia needed. Jasper and Queen Lamia had let their suppressed love turn into hatred, and they were both ready to do anything to take their revenge.

At some point, Jasper had even thought about killing Larko, but he changed his mind later. Being rejected by Aphra was hard enough for him, and when he heard about the prince's engagement with her, he assumed Aphra had known him for a long time, which was why she did not want Jasper. He would have been the happiest man on earth if Aphra had told him that she loved him too, but his fears were all real. As much as he loved Aphra and wanted her to be his wife, he could never imagine his life with her, like she was too perfect to marry him. He had only two wishes in life—becoming a knight and marrying Aphra—and he only got one. He did not even dare to dream about her. He just praised her. He was close to her and saw her almost every day, yet he felt she was so far away. He was always afraid of losing her, and it had finally happened; the universe took her from him. When he entered the court as a knight, he was full of rage and sorrow. Gradually, his sadness was gone, and all that was left was rage. He tried so hard to forget about Aphra, but destiny wanted to play games with him. At the court, he heard rumors he could not believe. Everyone talked about a girl from the village who spent time with the prince in the garden. They said her name was Aphra. *Aphra! She cannot be my Aphra,* Jasper thought when he first heard the rumor, but he was curious like everybody else.

Everyone at the court knew Prince Larko was supposed to marry Queen Lamia, and this new girl was interesting to everyone, even Jasper, until he saw her at the court one day. *It cannot be true.*

What is Aphra doing here? She cannot be the prince's mistress, Jasper thought. He knew Aphra well, and he was sure she would never agree to be anyone's mistress, not even the prince's. *If she is not the prince's mistress, what is she doing at the court? Why do they always walk together in the garden?* Jasper kept thinking, and the thoughts were killing him. People said the prince was going to marry her, but how was that even possible? What about Queen Lamia? Did they see each other before he was a knight? Did she turn him down because she wanted to marry the prince? The thoughts did not leave him alone, and he was losing his mind.

When a messenger from Sinkaba told Jasper that Queen Lamia wanted to see him somewhere in private, he did not even hesitate and left Kalastra right away to meet her at Mount Zaka. Jasper was always arrogant, but he was not evil; however, he'd changed into a different person after being heartbroken by Aphra. He got vicious, or maybe his evil side just found a reason to emerge. Whatever it was, the old Jasper was gone, and he was ready to do anything to hurt Aphra and Larko.

Everyone in Kalastra had heard about Queen Lamia's exquisite beauty, but only a few people had seen her. When Jasper arrived at Mount Zaka, he did not know what to expect. He had no idea why Queen Lamia wanted to see him, and he did not care either. He knew whatever the reason was, it could not be peaceful; otherwise, there was no point in meeting secretly. He waited for hours until she finally showed up, and what he saw was way better than what he had heard about her. He had never seen any woman that attractive in his life. She was different from Aphra. Her beauty was wild and scary, like she could kiss you and watch you choke to death at the same time. She was a masterpiece and every man's desire. He kept staring at her until the voice of Jabeer brought him back to reality.

"This is Queen Lamia of Sinkaba. Get off your horse and bow for Her Majesty!" Jabeer said.

"Of course! Please forgive me, Your Majesty. Your beauty has completely distracted me," Jasper said as he got off his horse.

Queen Lamia's lips curled into a faint smile. "I see you know how to talk to women. I like you already."

"It is my pleasure if a beautiful queen like you praises me. To what do I owe the pleasure of meeting you, Your Majesty?" he asked.

"It seems like we have common interests, or I shall say common enemies," she said.

"I am not sure who you are talking about, Your Majesty," he said.

"I think you are. Do not disappoint me, Jasper! You are a clever man. I know you hate Larko and Aphra as much as I do," she said.

"What else do you know about me, Your Majesty?" he asked curiously.

"I know that you were in love with Aphra, but she turned you down and married Larko instead. I know that you are one of the best knights in Kalastra, and I know that you have been friends with Aphra since childhood. Is that enough?" she said with a smug look on her face.

"You are quite right. I hate Larko," he said.

"How about Aphra?" she asked.

"There is nothing left in my heart for her, not anymore," he replied.

"Are you willing to betray the kingdom you serve to take your revenge?" she asked.

"I serve no one, not even you," he replied.

"Fair! I do not want you to serve me. I want us to work together and take our revenge. We deserve it," she said.

"I will do whatever you ask as long as they pay for what they did to me," he said.

"Are you sure you have no feelings for Aphra anymore? If you are hesitant, tell me now!" she said.

"I am not hesitant, Your Majesty. Nothing would give me more pleasure than seeing both Larko and Aphra suffer," he said.

"I thought you knights had a certain code of ethics that you had to abide by, but apparently, you do not care," she said.

"What I care about right now is spilling Larko's blood, cutting off his head, and offering it to Aphra, and I am ready to do anything you ask, Your Majesty," he said.

"Impressive, but I am not planning on killing Larko. I want him to be alive and suffer," she said.

"What do you want me to do then?" he asked.

"For the start, I need you to act normal with Aphra. Do not avoid her! Try to talk to her whenever you can, like how you did before. She should believe you have no feelings for her anymore and that you have forgiven her," she said.

"Is that all? What is your plan?" he asked.

"That is all I want you to do for now. Once you have her trust again, I will tell you what to do next. Be careful and let no one know we met!" she said.

"Why do you not tell me what you are planning to do? Do you not trust me, Your Majesty?" he asked.

"I trust no one except myself. Remember that I can take my revenge even without you, and my spies are everywhere at the court, so if you change your mind and tell anyone about me, you will not see the next dawn," she said.

"I will not change my mind, but let today be the first and last time you threaten me, Your Majesty," he said.

"Fine! I will not threaten you again," she said with a smirk. "I will send a messenger when the time is right. If you do just as I tell you, you will be well rewarded."

"All I want is to take my revenge," he said.

"Very well! Until next time, Jasper," she said as she kicked at her horse to move.

When Jasper returned to the court, he did exactly as Queen Lamia had asked him. He waited for an opportunity to see Aphra, and it happened on a beautiful afternoon when she was walking in the garden alone. She was wearing a delicate lavender dress that was tight on her waist and long enough to drag on the ground. Her hair was up high, and a strand of it was loose in the air, moving around with each gentle breeze. She touched the flowers as she walked, and when she reached the daffodils, she stopped, bent down, and smelled them all. He knew the daffodil was her favorite flower. He knew everything about her. He could not believe how he had survived without her; it had been two whole years without seeing her face and hearing her voice. It was more like a nightmare, but it had happened. It seemed easy for Aphra not to see him anymore, but he was going through hell trying to forget her. He tried so hard to forgive Aphra, but he could never succeed. He had avoided her when she came to the court after marrying Larko because he was afraid of losing his control if he saw her. He hated her for what she had done to him, and the hate was the only thing that had kept him sane. He could not afford to feel sad, because it was a sign of weakness, and he needed his strength then more than any other time.

Aphra was there with her pretty face, silky hair, and childish enthusiasm for small things. She was still the same Aphra he knew, and for a second, he wanted to forget everything and let all his anger and hatred go, but he stopped himself. She was Queen Aphra, and she was not his childhood friend anymore. She was married to the king, to Larko. If only he could abduct her and run away with her to a land where no one could find them. If only she loved him as much as she loved Larko. He would do anything for her, but she was never going to leave Larko. She had made her choice. She did not love him. He could still remember the tone of her voice and how disappointed she was in him when he told her he was in love with her in the Crystal Cave. Nothing could heal his broken heart, nothing except revenge.

"It is a beautiful day, Your Majesty, is it not?" Jasper asked, his voice calm as he stepped into the garden.

"Jasper! I did not expect to see you here. It has been a long time,"

Aphra said as she turned back.

"It has been two years, Your Majesty," he said.

"How are you? How is your life as a knight?" she asked.

"Just like what I expected, exciting and full of adventures," he replied.

"I am happy for you. I know being a knight meant the world to you," she said.

"It still does. I was just passing by, and I saw you in the garden. I wanted to congratulate you on your wedding. I should have done it sooner than this," he said.

"Thank you, Jasper, but you do not need to be so formal with me. I am still the same person you knew. I have not changed," she said.

"You have married the king, and you are the queen of Kalastra. It is quite a change, I think," he said with a smirk.

"We could never talk after that day in the Crystal Cave. I wanted to come to the court and talk to you so many times, but I could not. I thought you hated me," she said.

"Anyone who hates a kind and loving creature like you will be doomed forever, Your Majesty," he said.

"Are we still friends then?" she asked.

"We are, and it is my honor to serve you and His Majesty," he said.

"I am thankful, and I am glad you are here. I want you to know that," she said, looking at him.

"I will remember it, Your Majesty. You can always count on me because there is nothing I will not do in this world for you," he said, kneeling for her.

Aphra reached out, her tone gentle. "Please rise, Jasper! Know that there is no one I trust more than you at this court."

"I am happy to hear that, Your Majesty," he said.

"I know that some of the lords hate me here at the court," she said.

"Time will fix everything, Your Majesty. They do not know you, and they are afraid of the things that might happen in the future," he said.

"You mean Queen Lamia?" she asked.

"Yes, but there is no need to worry. If she was planning to do anything, she would have attacked Kalastra on the wedding day. No one will disturb your peace, Your Majesty," he said.

"I hope so, Jasper. It is good to have you at the court. I feel much safer knowing that you protect us," she said.

"It is my honor, Your Majesty. I should leave now, but I am always at your service," he said, bowing for her.

"Thank you, Jasper," she replied, her voice touched with genuine warmth.

Aphra was relieved after finally talking to Jasper. She felt so guilty after what had happened in the Crystal Cave, but when she'd seen him in the garden, he seemed calm and composed, and there was something different about him. It appeared he was not in love with her anymore, and she was happy that he was no longer suffering and had moved on.

CHAPTER FOURTEEN

WHEN THE NEWS of King Alger's death had spread, many small regions in the kingdom started rioting, assuming King Larko was young and inexperienced, hoping to conquer Kalastra. Larko had to leave the court constantly, and Queen Lamia was aware of that. She knew it was the perfect time to carry out her plan. She had one whole year to think about all the details, and she was not going to miss her chance. She needed Larko away from the court, and Lord Henry's riots favored her because that meant Aphra was alone at the court with only a few knights protecting her. She had even sent a spy to Kalastra's court to monitor Jasper to ensure he was not in love with Aphra anymore and remained intent on his vengeance.

"Tell me, Jabeer! What did our spy say about Jasper?" Lamia asked.

"Do not worry, Your Majesty. He is loyal to you. He is doing as we want. It seems Queen Aphra trusts him completely," he replied.

"That is great. We must make sure Larko does not come back to the court anytime soon. We need to help Lord Henry keep him busy for now," she said.

"I do not trust Lord Henry, Your Majesty. He is not an honorable man," he said.

"I agree. That old fox should die, but I only need him to keep Larko busy. As soon as we execute our plan, we will kill him too. Where is Larko now?" she asked.

"Near the Northwest border of Kalastra," he replied.

"Good! We need him as far away from Kalastra as possible," she said.

Queen Lamia was pleased. It was only a matter of time until she could finally take her revenge. Conquering Kalastra was never her intention, but she knew she could easily do that after breaking Larko. On the other side, in Kalastra, Aphra was very worried about Larko. She knew he had his best warriors with him, but she was still not at ease. Anything could happen at any minute, and even the court was not safe. There could be traitors everywhere, but she knew she could trust Jasper. Larko had asked him and a few other knights to stay at the court and look after the queen and the city.

There was a temple at the court where Aphra usually went to pray for Larko. Like other Kalastrians, she believed in the mother of the forest, and she asked her every day to keep Larko safe. She was worried about him all the time, and all she could do was pray and ask for his safe return. There was not a single night that she had slept well without Larko, and the only times she felt calm and at peace were when she painted or walked in the garden. Painting was her first connection to Larko, and she lost track of time when she started painting. One night when she was painting in her workshop, Jasper came in to talk to her.

"I did not know you could paint, Your Majesty!" Jasper said with surprise.

"It has been a while. I am not an expert, but I enjoy it," Aphra replied.

"You are very talented. There is nothing you cannot do: healing, singing, playing the lute, riding a horse, and now painting," he said with a small chuckle.

"I owe this to Larko," she said.

"How come?" he asked.

"He was the one who encouraged me to paint and learn it professionally," she replied, her gaze fixed on the strokes of her brush.

"What are you painting, Your Majesty?" he asked.

"A unicorn," she replied, then paused for a few seconds. "Do you think unicorns exist?"

"Anything is possible in this world, Your Majesty," he replied.

"Sometimes, I want fairy tales to be real. I want to find a unicorn, get on it with Larko, and leave this place forever. I know something horrible is going to happen, but no one believes me, and I am tired of trying to persuade others," she said.

"You are safe here, Your Majesty. I will not let anything happen to you," he said.

"It is Larko I worry about, not myself," she replied.

"If it makes you feel at ease, I can leave now, and I will be by the Northwest border by tomorrow night," he said.

"Your presence there does not change anything. I want Larko back at the court," she said.

"But he is the king, Your Majesty. This is not the first time, and it will not be the last time he leaves for battle. You have to get used to it," he said.

"This is what everyone keeps telling me, but I know it is different this time. I know it," she said.

"I promise you everything will be over soon. He defeated Lord Henry at the Northwest border, and he will come back to you in no time," he said.

"Does he have to go back again?" she asked.

"Maybe, but next time I will be with him. I should fight alongside my king instead of staying behind at the court," he replied.

"Do not say that, Jasper! Your presence here means everything," she said.

"I hope to be worthy of what you think of me, Your Majesty, and if anyone, either Lord Henry's men or Queen Lamia's men, tries to harm you, they will have to kill me first, so do not worry," he said.

"I pray nothing like that happens. All I want is peace in the kingdom, and I am not worried about myself, but I do not want my people to suffer in any way because I fell in love with their king," she said, then put down her brush. "I shall retire to bed now, although I know I cannot sleep even for a bit."

"You are a strong woman, Your Majesty. Do not lose your hope. I am certain when the king comes back, you will not even remember these days," he said.

It was the second time Jasper had found Aphra alone, and with each conversation, he felt he was getting closer to her and had gained her trust back. He was certain Queen Lamia's plan was going to work, and all he needed to know was what exactly she had in mind, so he decided not to wait for her message. He would go to Sinkaba to visit her, but he could not just leave Kalastra without reason; he needed an excuse.

In the morning, he talked with Aphra again. He needed to convince her that he had to leave the court.

"I have not such good news, Your Majesty," Jasper said.

"What is it, Jasper? Is it about Larko?" Aphra said.

"No, Your Majesty. When I went to my chamber last night, someone slipped a letter under the door, and he disappeared before I could catch him," he said.

"What was in the letter?" she asked.

"I do not want to scare you, but there is a chance Queen Lamia might want to attack Kalastra from the South as well. I need to ride south and make sure our southern borders are safe," he said.

"An alliance between Queen Lamia and Lord Henry makes complete sense, but she is smarter than attacking Kalastra and making us her enemy. I assume she would just provide supplies and men to Lord Henry," she said.

"You might be right, but we cannot take any chances. We need to make sure," he said.

"Then take a few men with you. Do not leave alone," she said.

"There is no need, Your Majesty. We need all the men we have at the court here. I will be fine riding alone, and I will be back with good news," he said.

He left the same day and rode nonstop for a few days until he finally arrived at Sinkaba. Everything was amusing to Jasper in Sinkaba, and it was nothing like what he had heard. People looked different, and the houses made of straw and mud were not the same as the houses in Kalastra. Men wore long, loose garments up to their feet, with keffiyehs on their heads, and women had long tunics with loose pants underneath them. Sinkaba was vast and entertaining, and one could easily lose their way in the bazaar. It was very crowded and much bigger and busier than the market in Kalastra, and merchants were all selling their products at each corner. As he was walking in the bazaar, he stopped at a jewelry stall and looked at the colorful earrings and bracelets on display, and among them all, one caught his eyes; it was a round green earring in the shape of a snake, and he instantly thought of Aphra. He'd always wanted to buy her nice clothes and jewelry and wanted to take her wherever she desired, but she never loved him, and he never had the money to do so until he became a knight. Aphra was in Kalastra, and she was worried about someone else, not him. He was sad and desperate, and pretending to be friends with her to gain her trust back had made him even more vengeful.

The man who owned the jewelry stall was talking to him, but he was so lost in his thoughts that he had not heard him.

"Sir, do you want to buy these earrings?" the man said again, this time a little louder so Jasper could hear him.

"No. I do not have anyone to buy these for," he said with a sad voice.

Jasper was ready to sacrifice everything for Aphra, but nothing mattered anymore. He did not want to waste his time thinking about her even one more second. He got on his horse and rode straight to the palace. All he wanted to do was impress Queen Lamia and prove to her that he was a fine knight, had excellent qualities, and was far better than her soldiers in Sinkaba. He wanted her to share her plan with him. When Jasper got to the palace, he could not believe his eyes. The palace was shining from afar, a piece of jewelry right in the heart of the desert, and it was huge and so much bigger than the Kalastra castle. When Jabeer realized Jasper had come to Sinkaba, he was certain Queen Lamia would be furious.

"Something unexpected has happened, Your Majesty," Jabeer said.

"What is it? Is it about Kalastra?" Queen Lamia asked.

"Jasper is here to see you, Your Majesty," he said.

"Jasper? What is that idiot doing here?" she said with an angry voice.

"I do not know, Your Majesty. He says he wants to see you," Jabeer said, keeping his head bowed.

"I should not have trusted him. It was a big mistake. He is going to ruin everything."

"Should I tell him to leave?" he asked.

"No, let him in, but we need to make sure no one has followed him," she said.

"Sure, Your Majesty," he said.

The beauty of the palace astonished Jasper. It was huge and glorious, and the Kalastra court was not even comparable to the Sinkaba palace. All the columns were delicately carved and decorated with turquoise stones, and the water fountains and gardens had multiplied the enchantment of the palace.

"Her Majesty will not be pleased to see you here," Jabeer said as he directed him to the main hall.

"Why not? After all, we are working together," Jasper replied, looking around and checking everything on his way.

"Queen Lamia does not like to be surprised. She told you to wait for her message," Jabeer said.

"I remember, but I could not wait any longer, and so here I am," Jasper said.

"Fine! Bear the consequences then," Jabeer said, opening the giant doors of the main hall for him.

When the doors opened, the view of the hall room was magnificent. The columns and the walls were decorated with gold and jewelry, and the floor was made of marble. It was a huge room, and Queen Lamia was sitting on her throne and wearing her jeweled crown.

"What a magnificent and glorious palace you have, Your Majesty! It is as beautiful as you, I shall say," Jasper said, bowing to Queen Lamia.

"Why are you here, Jasper? I thought I made it clear that you had to wait for me in Kalastra," Queen Lamia said.

"Maybe I missed you, Your Majesty," he replied with a sly grin.

"Enough! I commanded you to stay in Kalastra and watch out for Aphra. If I wanted to see you in Sinkaba, I would not have come to Mount Zaka," she said.

"You are not my queen, and you cannot command me to do anything. I did what you asked because I wanted to. Do I need to remind you again that I am doing this for myself and not for you?" he said.

Before he could finish his sentence, all the royal guards in the room drew out their swords and pointed them at him, but Queen Lamia commanded them all to stay back and sheathe their weapons; then she said, "You are either an idiot or very brave. I guess you have a death wish talking to me like this."

"I am not scared of you and your men, Your Majesty, and I assure you that my presence here does not ruin our plan," he said.

"Very well! You better be right, Jasper," she said.

"Can we talk alone now?" he asked.

"We can," she said, then commanded everyone in the room to leave, and when they were alone, Jasper came closer and said, "Larko is an idiot for leaving you. You are outrageously beautiful."

"Be careful, Jasper! You are not in a position to flirt with me," she said with a smirk.

"You cannot resist me, Your Majesty. I can see it in your eyes," he said.

"Is that why you came here? To know how I feel about you?" she asked.

"No," he replied.

"Then tell me why you came," she said.

"Aphra trusts me now. She thinks I have forgiven her and I am loyal to her and the king. Larko is still fighting at the borders, and it is the perfect time to do whatever you have in mind. We should not waste any time. I want to know what your plan is," he said.

"Why do you want to know my plan so badly?" she asked.

"Why do you not share it with me? Do you not trust me yet?" he asked.

"You would be dead if I did not trust you, but I need you to be careful. No one should suspect you," she said.

"I am certain everyone trusts me at the court. Do you think I do not consider everything when I make a move?" he asked.

"Fine! You can stay for the night, but you will have to leave in the morning," she said.

"I did not come all this way for nothing, Your Majesty. You will have to tell me what your plan is, or I will not leave," he said.

"If there is one thing I like about you, it's your audacity. Go and rest for now! We will talk later tonight at supper," she said with an amused smile.

"Thank you, Your Majesty," Jasper said, dipping his head in a half-bow.

They gave Jasper a nice chamber and prepared him a hot bath. He had ridden for days without rest, and he was exhausted. He had come to Sinkaba to find out Queen Lamia's plan, and he was not going to leave without knowing it. Queen Lamia was a woman who was capable of doing anything to get what she wanted. She scared him more than anyone, and he knew that to survive her rage, he needed to get close to her. Unlike Queen Lamia, he did not want Aphra to suffer, as there was still a little affection left in his heart for her, and he could not hurt her, even if he did not love her anymore. All he wanted was to kill Larko, and he was determined to find out what Queen Lamia's plan was, using any method. So, at supper, he asked the question again, hoping to get an answer.

"You look much better after a hot bath and a good rest," Queen Lamia said.

"Yes, Your Majesty. Thank you for your hospitality," Jasper said.

"How do you like Sinkaba?" she asked.

"It is beautiful and unique, Your Majesty. I wish I could explore it more," he said.

"Maybe later. I am sure there will be lots of time for exploring in the future," she said.

"As you say, Your Majesty, but you have not given me an answer yet. What is your plan for Larko and Aphra?" he asked.

"You only need to know the parts that concern you. Our spies told me that Larko has defeated the rioters at the Northwest border and will be back in Kalastra soon. You need to be back before him!" she said.

"But you told me before that you needed Larko away from the court to carry out your plan," he said.

"That is right. We have made sure he leaves soon after he is back in Kalastra. Let him see his dear Aphra one last time. Let them spend some time together and make memories. Once they are separate, the agony of remembering those memories will kill them both," she said with hatred.

"What is going to happen to Aphra when Larko leaves again?" he asked, trying to hide his worry.

"We will separate them forever, and he will never see her again," she said with a devilish smile.

"Why did you need me to get close to Aphra? Why did you want her to trust me?"

"You will know soon. Do not be impetuous, and do not ask further questions. I can change my mind about you at any minute and have you killed or thrown in the dungeon."

"We both want the same thing, Your Majesty. I will not betray you. You have my word."

"That is good. I need loyal men like you for the future I am building," she said.

After supper, Jasper went straight to his chamber. He was disappointed because he had not found out about Queen Lamia's plan yet. Lying in bed, he thought about what she meant by separating them forever. *Does she want to kill them both or just one of them?* he thought, and he did not know why he still cared about Aphra. He was worried about her. "She deserves to die for what she has done to me, but how can I kill her or let anyone harm her?" he said. He was confident that whatever Queen Lamia's plan was, it was nasty. She hated Aphra. He could see it in her eyes. It was past midnight, and he could not sleep. Suddenly, he heard a knock on the door.

"Open the door, please! I am Aesha, Queen Lamia's servant," she said.

Jasper opened the door and asked, "What are you doing here?"

"Her Majesty wants to see you in her chamber. Hurry up! Do not keep her waiting."

Jasper did not expect Queen Lamia to call for him. He thought she was too proud to ask for anything. It was late, and Aesha was leading the way to her chamber. Nights at Sinkaba were magical. The sky was cloudless, and the stars were shinier than in Kalastra. When they got to Queen Lamia's chamber, there were no guards by the door. Aesha knocked and said, "He is here, Your Majesty."

"He can enter," Queen Lamia said.

Jasper entered the queen's chamber. It was magnificent, a truly royal chamber. It was huge, with four pillars, which were all beautifully carved. A dim light was on, and a nice desert breeze was blowing through the balcony. Jasper took a step forward and saw a shadow in the darkness. Gradually, a feminine figure appeared in front of him. It was Queen Lamia, with her hair loose on her shoulders, in a see-through silk nightgown. Jasper could not move for a second. He had imagined Aphra in a nightgown, walking toward him so many times, a dream that never came true, but instead of Aphra, Lamia was in front of him. She was the most beautiful woman he had seen, and he was speechless. *How could someone be that perfect?* he thought.

"Do you want to keep staring at me?" she asked.

"I am sorry, Your Majesty. I am a little shocked," he said.

"No need to call me Your Majesty for tonight," she said, then came closer to him, touching her hair playfully. Her body was glowing under the moonlight.

"You are beautiful," he said.

"Do I take your breath away?" she asked.

"You do. I have never seen a woman as beautiful as you," he said, his voice rough with desire.

"Who is more beautiful? Me or Aphra?" she asked, watching his face closely for any hint of hesitation.

"I cannot compare you to each other. You are distinct in many ways. All I know is that you are the most attractive, desirable, and beautiful woman ever created so far," he said.

"Then you need to prove to me you are worthy of my attention," she said as she placed her hand on his chest.

"I will do anything you want. I am yours. My loyalty is only to you," he said.

"I trust you, and I know we will conquer so many great lands together," she said.

"We will, but first, I will conquer you tonight," he said as he pulled her to his chest and sealed her lips with a kiss.

She was magnificent, but she was not Aphra. Being with her excited him, and it was like he was on a ship in a stormy sea, and the turbulence of the waves could throw him off the ship at any second. Jasper left at dawn. He had to get to Kalastra before Larko. He had finally realized what Queen Lamia's plan was, and he knew that the next time Larko left Kalastra, everything would change.

CHAPTER FIFTEEN

"WE HAVE THIRTY men wounded, Your Majesty, but the good news is that the enemy is retreating," Hadrian, one of Larko's faithful knights, said.

"Make sure to treat all the wounded soldiers properly. We cannot afford to lose anyone. They will attack at dawn again," Larko said.

"I am sure they will, but I feel like they are distracting us, Your Majesty," he said.

"What do you mean, Hadrian?" he asked.

"I think Lord Henry is preparing a larger attack from somewhere else. It is very unlikely for him to retreat. They want us to keep all our forces in one place," Hadrian said.

"You might be right. This could be a trap. We should not keep all our men here," Larko said.

"Where do you think the next attack will be, Your Majesty?" he asked.

"We have defeated them in the north and northwest. The next strategic point is southeast. They probably want to take possession of Castle Beldo," Larko said.

"That is too important for us, Your Majesty. We cannot afford to lose it," he said.

"You are right. We must hurry. Do you think you will be fine with only fifty men here?" Larko asked.

"It is even more than enough, Your Majesty. Do not worry about us here," he said.

"Excellent! We shall ride for Kalastra after a short break. I will take the wounded with me as well. We need supplies and more men ready to fight," Larko said.

"Do not worry, Your Majesty. We will defeat Lord Henry. He can never conquer Kalastra," he said.

"I have no doubt, Hadrian. I am not worried when I know I have knights like you by my side," he said.

It had been precisely forty-five days since Larko had left Kalastra to fight with the rioters at the borders. It had been forty-five days that he had not seen Aphra's face and had not heard her voice. He sometimes dreamed about Aphra, coming to his tent in her milky silk robe and her hair open in the air, then sleeping next to him and touching his hair with her dainty fingers, but he did not need to imagine her in his dreams anymore. He was going to Kalastra the next day for his wounded men, gathering more soldiers, and seeing Aphra for one night before leaving again.

Jasper, on the other hand, arrived at Kalastra right before Larko. He knew Larko was coming, and it was probably the last time he could see Aphra. Queen Lamia had told him what he was supposed to do, and all he needed was Larko to leave again.

Larko and his army arrived at the gates of Kalastra at sunset. The sunset at Kalastra was unimaginably beautiful. The sky was just a palette of colors: light blue, wine red, and gray. It was sunset when Larko kissed Aphra for the first time, and now that he was at the gates of the citadel, he could not contain his excitement to see her.

When Larko arrived, Aphra was in the crown room talking with Jasper and some of the knights. She needed to know all the details of

Jasper's trip to the southern borders. Jasper lied and told her and the knights in the room that everything looked normal, but to be safe, he suggested sending more soldiers to the border with Sinkaba. As he was talking, Aphra heard the watchman shout, "The king and his men are here! The king is coming!"

Aphra felt lightheaded for a second. She had heard it right. Larko had come back, and her prayers were finally answered. She left the room and ran down the stairs to the courtyard. There he was— Larko, in his armor, getting off his horse. His dark brown hair was all messy, and his face was tired but still strong and determined.

"Larko, you are here," she murmured as she walked toward him. He was just a few steps away from her, but she could not feel her legs anymore. Suddenly, all her strength was gone, and she fell to the ground.

"Aphra!" Larko shouted as he ran toward her. He held her in his arms and took her to her chamber.

"Open your eyes, my dear. I am here," Larko said, kissing Aphra's hands.

Aphra slowly opened her eyes, and it was just like the first time she had seen him in the forest.

"Are you real, my love?" she asked, trying to stop her tears.

"I am. You have no idea how much I missed you," he said.

Aphra held Larko's face with her hands and said, "I missed you even more. I thought I would never see you again. I was so scared."

"I know, darling. I promise to make it up to you. We have our whole life ahead of us. You just have to trust me," he said.

"I trust you with all my heart. Please tell me you are not leaving again," she asked anxiously.

"Just one more time. I promise you it is going to be the last time for a while, at least."

"No, Larko! I beg you. I cannot stand being away from you anymore. It is like stabbing my own heart every time I say goodbye to you. I cannot do it again," she said, sobbing.

"Do not cry, Aphra! I cannot see your tears. Is this how you want us to spend our night together?" he asked, trying to look into her eyes while she was hiding them from him.

Aphra looked down and gently said, "No."

"Look at me!" he said commandingly. "Your face is all I have in my dreams when I am away from you. Do not deprive me of that. We only have one night," he said.

Aphra raised her head and said, "I love you so much. I love you more than my heart can take." She threw herself into his arms.

"I am here, Aphra, and everything will be fine. Trust me!" he said while stroking her hair, trying to calm her down.

After a few seconds, Aphra raised her head and said, "You smell, Larko!" and burst into laughter.

"I know. I smell disgusting," he said and started laughing. "I have been riding nonstop."

"I will tell your servant to prepare the bath for you," she said as she got off the bed.

"Will you join me?" he said, catching her hand in the air with a fading smile on his face.

She smiled back and said, "Well, I am not sure yet, Your Majesty."

She had only one night to see Larko, and then he was going to leave again. She had no choice except to surrender to his will, and there was no point in crying or begging him not to leave her alone. She knew the consequences of her choice. It was the price she had to pay for marrying a king, but she would have married him even if he was a knight or a merchant. Larko was going to leave at dawn, and she still had so many things to tell him. All she wanted to do was watch him for hours and hold him tight, but time was passing quickly that night, as if it was her enemy. She wore her robe and looked at Larko playing with the papers on his desk.

"Is everything all right?" she asked.

"Yes, darling. You do not need to worry about anything. I need to prepare a few things before bedtime, and then I will be done," he said, giving her a reassuring smile.

"How long will you be away this time?" she asked.

"Not long. I promise." He touched her face; then there was a knock on the door. "This must be Jasper. I need to talk to him before I leave tomorrow," he told Aphra; then he said, "You can come in!"

Jasper entered the room, bowed for Larko and Aphra, and said, "Welcome back, Your Majesty. I am very relieved to see you safe and sound here in Kalastra."

"Thank you, Jasper. How was everything here? Did anything unusual happen?" he asked.

"No, Your Majesty. Everything was calm," he said.

"Aphra told me about your short trip to the southern borders. Is Queen Lamia preparing an attack?" Larko asked.

"No, Your Majesty. It was a false alarm. Everything is under control in the South."

"That is good. I will ride again tomorrow at dawn. This time, it should not take me so long, but I will leave feeling assured that you will protect the queen and the court," Larko said.

"Please let me accompany you, Your Majesty. I feel useless here," he said.

"How can you say that? I am trusting you with the most precious thing I have in my life. I cannot leave Aphra unprotected, and I trust you more than anybody else. You two are childhood friends, and I know you will keep her safe," he said.

After a few seconds, Aphra said, "I am certain I will be safe here with Jasper," looking at him.

After an awkward silence, Jasper said, "Of course, Your Majesty. I will protect you with my life."

"Thank you, Jasper. You can leave now," Larko said.

I have no feelings for you anymore, and I will take away your precious Larko from you. If you do not want to be mine, you cannot be his either, Jasper thought as he stood behind the chamber's door. He could not stay at the court that night; it would either be him or

Larko. *I swear this is the last night you spend with him, Aphra*, he thought; then, he got on his horse and rode straight to the Crystal Cave. When they'd found the cave, they were both very young, and Aphra did not even know that Jasper loved her, or maybe she knew and pretended not to realize it, but it did not matter anymore. All Jasper wanted was to be alone with Aphra's memory that night.

There was a magical peace in the cave, like time did not pass there. Jasper could see Aphra everywhere; she was his in the cave. It was the only place that belonged to them. The cave was his and Aphra's. He lay down on the cold stones and closed his eyes. Nobody could take her from him in his imagination, and all he wanted to do was remember the time he had spent with her, her smile, her face, when they went horse riding together, when she played the lute, and when he sang along.

It was a dark, cold night, and there was no noise to be heard in the forest, not even the hoots of owls, as if the forest was dead. Jasper was slowly falling asleep when he suddenly felt the presence of someone in the cave. When he opened his eyes, he saw an old man staring at him.

"Who are you?" Jasper asked, reaching for his dagger.

"There will be no need for your dagger. I am not here to harm you," the old man replied.

"What do you want from me?" Jasper asked.

"Do not do what she asks. If you do it, there will be no turning back. Nothing will be the same after that. Aphra will never forgive you," the old man said.

"Who are you? How do you know these things? Has Queen Lamia sent you here to test me?" Jasper asked.

"No one has sent me, my child. I am here to warn you. If you help her, what you do will haunt you for eternity," the old man said.

"I am not scared of the future. It cannot be worse than what I am going through right now," Jasper said.

"You are just angry, but you will heal in time. You are not like

Lamia. Do not give in! Fight it! Fight the desire to avenge! If you love Aphra, let her be happy," the old man urged.

"What about my happiness?" Jasper asked.

"Does it make you happy to see her suffer?" the old man asked, peering into Jasper's eyes.

"No, but I want Larko to suffer," Jasper said.

"I did what I had to do. You will regret this, Jasper. Farewell." He turned his back.

"Wait! You cannot just show up and threaten me. Tell me your name!" Jasper asked, panting with fear.

The old man shouted, "Zelmata," and left the cave.

Jasper could not sleep that night. He did not know who Zelmata was or how he knew everything about him and Queen Lamia's plan, but he could not erase his voice from inside his head. What if he was going to be haunted? What if Queen Lamia did not keep her word and killed Aphra instead of giving her to him? When he was in Sinkaba, he had finally persuaded Queen Lamia to tell him everything about her plan, and she had told him that she was only going to avenge Larko for what he had done to her and did not care about Aphra. She promised him that after killing Larko, she would let Aphra leave and that she would never know he had assisted her, but what if the old man was right? It was almost dawn, and Jasper had to ride back to the court before Larko left again. When he got there, it was still dark, and everyone was asleep. He went straight to the armory and sat there in silence.

"I guess it was not just me who could not sleep last night," Larko said.

"Sorry, Your Majesty. I did not realize you were here," Jasper replied.

"The past few months have been hard for Aphra and me, but we have always found our way together," Larko said.

"I am sure this time will be the same, Your Majesty," he said.

"I cannot be certain this time. I have a bad feeling, something I have never experienced in my life before, not even when my father died. I do not know what it is, but there is no escape from it," Larko said with deep sorrow in his eyes.

"Let me come with you, Your Majesty. Let me fight alongside you," he said.

"I am not worried about myself. I could not tell Aphra, but I am terrified for her. I have no explanation for this feeling, and I know she should be safe here, but I do not know why I am so nervous, and that is why I need you to stay here and keep her safe. You are the only person I trust with her life," Larko said.

"As you wish, Your Majesty. I will protect the queen with my life," he said.

"Very well! I shall get ready and leave. I do not want to wake her up. It is better if she does not realize when I leave or her tears will not let me go," Larko said with a sad voice.

It was in the early morning of a cold winter day that Larko left. He was not the same Larko everyone knew, like something had changed inside him over one night. He could feel something terrible was about to happen, but he did not know how to stop it. He was too proud to change his mind and stay. It would be the last battle with Lord Henry, and all he wanted was to come back home gloriously. Aphra saw him from the window getting on his horse, but she did not have the strength to say goodbye to him. He looked magnificent in his armor, like always. He was confident, and all his knights had surrounded him. Most of the knights were going to accompany him to the battlefield, except for a few who had to stay in Kalastra.

"Please look up, Larko! Look at me one last time, my love!" Aphra whispered to herself as she looked at Larko behind the window.

Larko finally looked up, but he could not bear to look at her begging eyes. He had to leave instantly, or it would be impossible to leave at all, so he left.

"He left," Aphra murmured with tears in her eyes. "He left," she said again, collapsing on the floor.

"Your Majesty!" Iris screamed as she ran to her.

Aphra was so weak that she stayed in bed for hours after Larko left. The court physician said she had to rest and stay in bed to regain her strength, and there was nothing wrong with her health. She stayed in bed all day, and it was almost nighttime when she opened her eyes. The chamber was almost dark, with one candle burning on the table, and Iris was sleeping on the chair beside her bed. Despite the dizziness she felt, she decided to get out of bed and walk.

"Please forgive me, Your Majesty. I do not know when I fell asleep," Iris said as she tried to sit up.

"Do not worry. I just woke up. I need some fresh air," Aphra said.

"You should not get out of bed, Your Majesty. The physician said you needed to rest," she said.

"I am better. I cannot stand this bed anymore. I want to walk. Help me get dressed, please," Aphra said.

"As you wish, Your Majesty," she said.

Iris then brought Aphra's favorite blue dress, and as she was helping her get dressed, she said, "Do not worry, Your Majesty. I am sure the king will return without even one scratch."

"I hope so, but today when I looked at him, I felt like it was the last time I would see him. Have you ever had an unexplainable feeling before?" Aphra asked.

"I suppose, Your Majesty. I sometimes have bad feelings too, but nothing bad happens in the end. You are worried because you know this is the last battle His Majesty has with Lord Henry, and you are just impatient," she said.

"You might be right. I cannot think anymore," Aphra said.

"It is dark, Your Majesty. Where do you want to walk?" she asked.

"I just want to walk in the garden. I need to think and pray," Aphra replied.

Aphra put on her shawl and went straight to the garden. It was freezing cold, but she did not feel the cold much. The fire inside her was burning her up. She wanted to be optimistic, but the negative thoughts did not leave her alone. She could feel Larko's presence everywhere at the court and in the garden, more than anywhere else. They used to walk in the garden every day when things were normal, when King Alger was still alive. They had planted most of the flowers together. Each flower reminded her of a memory she had with him, and if flowers could talk, they would testify to their pure and passionate love, the love between two strangers from two different worlds, the love between a prince and a simple girl. Iris followed her with the lantern, walking two steps behind her. She was always loyal to Aphra, and she adored her queen. All the servants at the court loved and respected Aphra for her kindness and wisdom, especially because she never treated anyone as an inferior, and she had stolen everyone's heart, not just Larko's.

"You have been walking for an hour, Your Majesty. It is too cold, and you might get sick," Iris said.

"What do you think he is doing now? Do you think he is somewhere safe and warm?" Aphra asked with a desperate voice, like she was living in another world.

"Please do not do this to yourself, Your Majesty. I am sure the king is safe, and he will come back to you victoriously like always," she said.

"I need to tell you a secret. The physician knows, but I asked him not to tell anyone," Aphra said.

"What is it, Your Majesty?" she asked.

"You need to take an oath that you will not tell anyone," Aphra said.

"I take an oath that I will not share your secret with anyone, Your Majesty. You can trust me," she said.

"I am pregnant with Larko's child," Aphra said.

"This is great news, Your Majesty. Does the king know this?" she asked with excitement.

"No. I wanted to tell him last night, but he was so distant from me that I did not even know how to start, and I regret it now. Maybe if I had told him I was pregnant, he would not have left. I should've stopped him from leaving any way I could," Aphra said with tears in her eyes.

"Please do not blame yourself, Your Majesty. Nothing will happen to the king. You are so worried about His Majesty that you have completely forgotten about yourself. You need to be strong for the sake of your child," she said.

"Will you pray with me tonight?" Aphra asked.

"Of course, Your Majesty, but please eat something first, even just a bit. You need to keep your strength. I beg you," she said.

"I will. Thank you, Iris. I do not know what I would do without you," Aphra said, managing a faint smile through her tears.

"It is my honor to serve you, Your Majesty. You are the queen this kingdom has always desired to have. You are brave and wise. People love you and the king," she said.

"Thank you. You have always been very loyal. We should better go inside now," Aphra said.

Aphra knew Iris from years ago when she used to go with her uncle to check on sick people in the city. Iris's mother was sick, and her situation was so severe that the physician could not help her anymore. Her father was a cruel man who never cared about his family, and when his wife died, he wanted to sell Iris to make money out of her. Iris was a young girl at that time, and Aphra could not let anything happen to her. She tried to reason with her father, but he did not listen, and he was going to sell his daughter to an old fisherman for only ten coins. Aphra was heartbroken, and she had to do something, so she asked her uncle to save that girl and take her to the court as a maid. That was all Aphra could do for Iris at that time, and when she moved to the court after marrying Larko, all Iris wanted was to serve her, and Aphra chose her as her maid.

It was a long night for Aphra, but it passed somehow. It was not the first night without Larko, but it was the hardest one for her since she could not silence the voices inside her head. Praying did not help either. It only calmed her down for a few hours, and then she was alone again with her fears. The fear of losing Larko had devastated her, and the only thing that kept her going was knowing that she was carrying his child and going to become a mother soon.

CHAPTER SIXTEEN

FOUR DAYS HAD passed since Larko had left the court, and Aphra was more impatient than ever. She sat by the window all day waiting to see Larko come back, and nothing made her happy anymore except seeing him. Jasper watched her every day as she went for her walk in the garden, and he knew the time for revenge was getting closer. He was heartbroken to see how she tortured herself when she was not next to Larko. Jasper could be the happiest man in the world if Aphra had shown him even one-hundredth of that attention, but he had realized it was impossible to win her heart as long as Larko was alive.

Later that day, a letter was slipped under Jasper's door, asking him to see someone in the city's outskirts outside the gates. Jasper left immediately, as he was certain the message was from Queen Lamia.

"Why did you ask me to come here?" Jasper asked.

"It is time," the man replied.

"What should I do?" Jasper asked anxiously.

"You should convince Aphra to leave the court tonight. Tell her Larko is wounded, and he is waiting to see her; then take her to the cave you used to go to together. Be careful! She should not suspect anything," the man said.

"What is going to happen after that? Queen Lamia promised she would let me leave with Aphra," Jasper said.

"Do not worry! Nothing will happen to you and Aphra. Her only desire is to kill Larko, and to do that, she needs bait. Aphra is just the bait. After he is dead, you two are free to leave," the man said.

"But Aphra will never forgive me if she knows I am involved in all this," Jasper said.

"She will not know. We will abduct you on the way, and she will think we are Lord Henry's men. We just need to use her and threaten Larko to come to us. We will keep you in two different cages, and after everything is over, you can leave with her. She will even think you are her savior," the man said with a smirk.

"But if I tell her Larko is waiting for her in the cave and she realizes it was not true, she will know I was lying from the beginning," Jasper said.

"Tell her you received a message from one of the knights who was with Larko, and you are not sure if it is a trap or if he is really wounded. Let her decide whether to leave or not, but we both know she will leave if there is even a one percent chance of seeing Larko," the man said.

"Okay then. I will bring her to the cave tonight," Jasper said.

"Jasper! Do not make any mistake, or Queen Lamia will never forgive you. Remember that!" the man said.

When Jasper left, he was confused. He could feel something was not right, but he could not think straight. He did not trust Queen Lamia, and he knew once Aphra left the court, anything could happen to her, so he had to choose between his desire to avenge them or his love for Aphra. *What if she does not keep her word and kills Aphra?* he thought. But on the other hand, the thought of seeing Larko dead was so sweet that he could not resist it. Nothing could make him feel better than to see Larko die and Aphra grieve for him. Maybe after his death, Jasper could have a chance with her, and he did not want to throw away his only chance of revenge. It was now or never.

Jasper returned to the court and waited for Aphra to be alone in her chamber. It was dark, and Iris was preparing Aphra's bed. Right after Iris left her chamber, Jasper entered without knocking.

Aphra was surprised to see Jasper. She raised her voice. "What are you doing in my chamber, Jasper? You cannot be here."

"Please forgive me, Your Majesty, but it is a matter of life and death. I had to see you alone," he said.

"What is going on? Is it about Larko?" she said, trying to control her fear.

"Yes, Your Majesty. The king is wounded badly, and he has been taken to a safe place by some of the knights. I just received a message from one of them now. The king does not feel well, and he is waiting to see you," he said.

Aphra almost passed out. She barely grabbed the bed rod so as not to collapse on the floor.

"Are you fine, Your Majesty?" Jasper asked, reaching a hand toward her.

"I am fine," she said with her hand forward, trying to stop him from coming close. She then sat on the bed and said, "Larko cannot be wounded. My love cannot die. He promised to come back to me." She waited for a minute. "Why is he not coming to the court? The court physician can help him get better here."

"I am afraid to say that we might have traitors among us, Your Majesty. We cannot risk His Majesty's life, but I am sure his wound is not lethal. Do not worry, Your Majesty," he said.

"How do you know that, Jasper? We do not know anything. I must see him. Take me to him right now! I beg you, Jasper," she said while crying.

"I am not sure this is a good idea, Your Majesty. What if this is all a trap? What if His Majesty is not wounded at all?" he said.

"What if it is true and we do not do anything? Larko needs our help. I've had this bad feeling since he left, and I knew something horrible was going to happen," she said.

"We should not act hastily. You are the queen of Kalastra, Your Majesty. Your people need you. What if something happens to you? You should not leave the court," he said.

"Do you expect me to sit here and do nothing while Larko is in danger?" she demanded, glaring at him through her tears.

"No, Your Majesty. That is not what I meant. It is better that I go to His Majesty alone and that you stay at the court," he said.

"Impossible! We will leave immediately. I will not leave him alone," she said.

"Then no one should know that we are leaving, not even your most trusted person. It is vital for the king's safety," he said.

"I will not tell anyone," she said.

"I will go to the infirmary now to grab medicine and all the supplies we need. Meet me in the stable in thirty minutes," he said.

Aphra could think of no one and nothing except Larko, imagining him wounded and alone somewhere, waiting to see her heart shatter into pieces. She could not wait to see him and hold his hands. *All those bad feelings were real*, she thought. She got dressed as quickly as she could and went straight to the stable. There, Jasper was waiting for her.

"Are you ready, Your Majesty?" he asked.

"Yes, I am ready. We must go. We should not waste any time," she replied.

"Did anyone see you coming here?" he asked.

"No. I was cautious. Nobody saw me," she said.

"Okay then. We shall go," he said.

Aphra and Jasper got on their horses and started galloping. They had just left the city gates when a crazy rain started to pour. It was a thunderstorm, heavy and forceful, as if nature was showing its anger for what was about to happen.

"We should take shelter until the rain stops," Jasper said.

"No. We cannot stop. We must get to Larko," Aphra replied.

She was wet and cold, but the thunderstorm did not scare her. All she cared about was getting to Larko. She kept thinking about whether her fears were all real from the beginning or if she had made them real by believing something terrible was going to happen. Nothing that night was the same as before, as if the darkness of the night, the magnitude of the thunderstorm, and even the unusual noises the animals were making were all signs warning her to go back, yet she heard everything and felt nothing. Not long after they entered the forest, twenty men showed up with black masks and blocked their way.

Jasper shouted, "We have been ambushed, Your Majesty. These must be Lord Henry's men. Stay close to me." He took out his sword.

"I will either die tonight or reunite with my love. There is no third option," she said while taking out her dagger and galloping toward the men.

He shouted, "No, Aphra, wait!"

They both started fighting with the men, but it did not last long. They were only two, fighting off twenty men, and they had no chance of winning over them. Even if they had, Jasper had no intention of killing them since they were all Queen Lamia's men, not Lord Henry's.

"You are all cowards. How dare you attack your queen! King Larko will kill you all and your commander. You have no chance of surviving," Aphra said, shouting as one of the men was tying her hands and feet up.

"We are not Lord Henry's men, bitch! We are from Sinkaba. Queen Lamia cannot wait to see you," one of the men replied, laughing hard.

"Queen Lamia!" she whispered.

"Do not be afraid, Aphra! I will not let them harm you. I will keep you safe. I promise," Jasper said.

"I always knew she was lying. I knew she would finally take her revenge. She might be helping Lord Henry. Maybe she was the one who attacked Larko," she said.

"Calm down, Aphra! I will find a way for us to flee. Nothing will happen to you and His Majesty," he said.

"Put them in two separate cages! We should leave at once. I hate this crazy weather here," one of the men said.

"Where are you taking us?" Aphra asked with anger.

The man leaned down, grinning like a jackal.

"Have you not realized yet? You are going to Sinkaba. You two are Queen Lamia's belongings now."

"King Larko will not let you get away with this. He will attack Sinkaba and that dear queen of yours. You will all die soon," she said.

"Nobody can save you from Queen Lamia, not even your king. Forget about him. Forget about everything in Kalastra. You will never come back." The man looked into Aphra's eyes and said it with a voice filled with hatred.

"How can you hate me so much? I have done you no harm," she said.

"You lived the life that belonged to my queen, you lowlife merchant girl," he said and spat on the ground.

Jasper shouted, "Watch your mouth, bastard, or I will kill you and your queen."

The man then punched him in the face and said, "I am not allowed to touch her, but I will kill you if you tempt me, so shut your mouth!" he shouted at Jasper. "Enough wasting time! We are leaving now," he told his men.

They put Aphra and Jasper in two different cages and rode for the whole night. Aphra had never been so far from Kalastra before. Something inside her heart told her it was the last time she would see Kalastra. The last time she would breathe its air, see its lakes and mountains, and the last time she would see the land she had spent her whole childhood in, the land in which she had fallen in love with Larko, but none of that mattered compared to Larko's sufferings.

Aphra thought Larko was wounded and alone in the forest, waiting for her to come, and the only thing she could do at the time was pray, so the mother of the forest would keep him safe.

Two days later, they arrived at Mount Zaka, which separated Kalastra from Sinkaba. It was a huge mountain and very tough to pass. Nature completely changed on the other side of the mountain, and there were no pine and oak trees, no brisk breeze.

"We will camp here for the night. It will be a difficult day tomorrow," the man said. Then he grabbed a piece of bread and threw it inside Aphra's cage. "Eat it! My queen needs you alive."

"I do not want anything from you and your queen," Aphra said, throwing the bread out.

"Eat it, or I will shove it into your mouth," he said, throwing it back inside the cage.

A few feet away, Jasper gripped the iron bars of his own cage. His voice cracked with worry.

"You need to eat something, Your Majesty. You must maintain your energy. You cannot continue like this. I am worried about you."

"I cannot think of myself right now. I am not even hungry. I am only thinking of Larko. What do you think he is doing now?" she asked with tears in her eyes.

"I do not know, Your Majesty, but I am certain he is better. Our mighty knights will not leave their king alone. You do not need to worry," he said.

"How can I not worry? Now I am certain we have traitors at the court. Someone must have followed me when I left my chamber," she said.

"We will find that traitor once we get back to the court," he said.

"Do you still think we can go back?" she asked.

"Of course we can, Your Majesty. Everyone must have realized our absence by now. I am certain they are looking for us. Do not lose your hope!" he said.

It was nighttime, and it was so dark that nothing was visible.

There was a chill breeze in the air, and there was no sound except Queen Lamia's men's voices in the distance. Aphra closed her eyes and tried to block their voices in her head. She wanted to remember a few nights ago, when everything was perfect. Larko was by her side, and she could touch his face. He was so close to her that she could even hear his heartbeat. She should have never let him go. She wanted to cry and beg him to stay and ask him to send his men instead, but she knew he would not listen. He would have never left his men alone in the battle. She wished she could turn back time to the happy days she had with Larko, to the day she met him for the first time in the forest, to the day he held her hands and looked into her eyes, to the day he kissed her lips and told her he was in love with her. *I will come back to you, love; I promise. We have not even started our journey yet*, she thought. She remembered the day she married Larko, and she would marry him a thousand times over and over, even if she knew she had to pay a big price for her love. All she wanted since the day she met Larko was to be with him for eternity, but now she was hundreds of miles away from him.

She could barely sleep that night, and soon it was dawn. They had to pass through the mountain, and Mount Zaka was an extremely challenging mountain. They could not be in the cage anymore, and Lamia's men had forced them both to walk on the stones barefoot. She could hardly walk, let alone climb the rocks. She had not eaten anything for two days, and she finally lost consciousness halfway through the day. She was so exhausted that she just collapsed on the stones.

"What happened, Your Majesty? Open your eyes, please! Aphra, open your eyes!" Jasper said when Aphra fell to the ground.

"Useless woman! She cannot even walk," one of the men said.

Jasper shouted, "Shut your filthy mouth, bastard! How dare you talk about my queen like this?"

The man punched him in the face and said, "I will talk however I want. Do not make me tell her everything. Do you think she will even look at you when she realizes you were behind all this?" he said.

"This was not our agreement. Queen Lamia promised me," he said.

"Queen Lamia promised you nothing. If you make me angry one more time, I will make sure she knows everything about you before cutting her throat. Now carry her! We need to move," he said.

Jasper was devastated. It was too late to regret what he had done. He must have known from the beginning that Queen Lamia was not trustworthy and hated Aphra and wanted to kill her. He felt stupid for believing her and giving her the only woman he truly loved in his life. He still loved Aphra, even if she was not his. He carried her for hours, climbing the mountain, and when she opened her eyes, it was almost time to make camp for the night. Jasper put her on the ground gently and said, "My queen, open your eyes, please."

After a few seconds, Aphra opened her eyes slowly. "What happened? Where are we?"

"We are still in the mountain, Your Majesty. You were unconscious for a few hours, so I carried you," he said.

"Thank you. My head hurts so bad," she said while trying to sit up.

"Be careful, Your Majesty! You are very weak. You need to eat something. You cannot help Larko by torturing yourself. Please eat this piece of bread. It is not much, but you will gain your strength back," he said, giving the bread to her.

"How much farther is it to Sinkaba?" she said while biting on the bread.

"Probably another day on the mountain, and after that, a few more days, I think," he said.

"What do you think she is going to do with us?" Aphra asked.

"I will not let her do any harm to you, even if I have to sacrifice myself for you," he said.

"Jasper, you have always protected me no matter what, but I do not want you to sacrifice yourself for me. She only hates me. I knew this from day one. I knew she would want to take her revenge someday. I never believed her friendship act," she said.

"Then why did you marry him, Aphra? Why did you marry Larko when you knew your life would be in danger?" he asked.

"I love Larko, and I could not imagine my life without him. I would still do the same if I could go back in time. I would choose him every single time. He is my lover. He completes me. He is the air I breathe and the heat that warms me up. I belonged to him even before I met him. I am not scared of anything, Jasper. I will happily die knowing that I lived when I was alive," she said.

"Did you ever have any feelings for me?" he asked desperately.

"I did, but it was not love, and as we grew older, I realized something was missing. We were just used to spending time together. It was a familiar feeling for both of us because we knew each other since childhood, but our shared feeling was not love. I am sorry, Jasper, and I wish things were different. I wish one girl someday steals your heart and loves you the way you deserve because you are a good man," she said.

"That day will never come, Aphra. If you die, I will die too," he said.

"No, you will not die. Queen Lamia's problem is only with me, not you. Promise me that you will save yourself, and you will go back to Kalastra," she said.

"Oh, Aphra, you do not know what evil I have done. I deserve to die," he said.

"What could you have possibly done? I know you, Jasper. You have a kind heart."

Then there was a deadly silence in the mountain. Jasper had never wanted to listen to Aphra before. He had valued his pride more than her feelings, and he was always angry with Aphra for rejecting him, and he let his anger consume him. Now it was too late to make up for his mistakes. Even if he could find a way to keep her alive, sooner or later, she would realize he had betrayed her, and he would lose her forever. He did not dare to look into her eyes and tell her he was the reason for all the pain and suffering she was going through. How could he tell her what he had done? How could he confess his sins and be forgiven? What he had done was unforgivable. He felt ashamed, and he hated himself. By this point, he was certain Queen Lamia wanted to kill Aphra, and he could not think of any way to save her.

CHAPTER SEVENTEEN

EVERYTHING SEEMED TO be in Larko's favor on the battlefield. Lord Henry had lost many of his men, and soon he had to retreat. He had waited years for King Alger's death to attack Kalastra, and when Queen Lamia approached him and offered to assist, he accepted instantly. However, even with the help of Queen Lamia, they were still outnumbered, and Larko and his knights massacred them. Lord Henry was a threat to the kingdom from the beginning, and unlike King Alger, Larko had no intention of letting him live and riot again. After two days of continuous triumph over Lord Henry, Larko was confident he would not attack again, but he was still alive, and he wanted him dead. On the third day of the battle, when Larko was talking with his knights, a messenger from Kalastra entered his tent hastily and said, "I have come from the capital, Your Majesty. I have bad news."

"What is it? Spit it out!" Larko said.

"The queen, Your Majesty," the man panted, his voice trembling.

Larko shouted, "The queen? What has happened to the queen?"

"Her Majesty has gone missing for two days. Her maid saw her last when she prepared her for bed, and when she went to her chamber in the morning, she was not there, and her bed was untouched," he said.

Larko shouted, "This cannot be possible. How can the queen have gone missing with all the guards at the court? Who has dared to steal her from inside the castle?"

"It must be Lord Henry's men, Your Majesty. They must have taken the queen as a hostage," one of the knights said.

"He has kept us busy here to attack the capital," another knight said.

"Lord Henry is helpless now, and he is capable of doing anything. We must save Her Majesty," someone else said.

"Enough! Nothing matters now except the queen's life. We leave at once," Larko said with a voice trembling with anger. "Sir Naya, you stay here with the army! Lord Resko and a few other knights will come with me," he said.

"There is one more thing, Your Majesty," the messenger said.

Larko snapped his head toward him, his eyes wild.

"What is it?"

"Sir Jasper cannot be found at the court either," the messenger said, barely meeting Larko's eyes.

"I had commanded him to protect the queen. If they are both missing, Jasper is with Aphra, which is a good sign. We have to go back immediately before they get too far," he said.

"Yes, Your Majesty. Do not worry. We will find the queen safe and sound," one of the knights said.

Larko and his knights left immediately. They rode the whole night without stopping and arrived at Kalastra in the morning. It was in the forest just before getting to the citadel that one of the knights shouted suddenly. "I think I found something. This fabric must belong to Her Majesty's attire." Larko looked at the fabric, and he was sure it belonged to Aphra's shawl. There was also a broken branch just a little farther from where the fabric was, but one thing did not make sense to him. The fabric and the broken branch were both in the direction of the South, and if Lord Henry's men had stolen Aphra, why would they take her to the South?

"Are you also thinking about the same thing I am thinking, Your Majesty?" one of the knights asked.

"Yes, I am, but I cannot believe it. Can this be Queen Lamia's doing?" Larko said.

"We all knew she hated you and Her Majesty. She must have found an opportunity to take her revenge," the knight said.

Larko's shoulders sagged as the horse's hooves pounded the earth beneath him. He let out a ragged breath.

"How could I be so naive? How could I not see anything when I went to Sinkaba? My father and Aphra were always right. This is all my fault. This is all on me." His voice was raw, torn between fury and regret.

"Please be calm, Your Majesty. We will find the queen. We will not let Queen Lamia do any harm to Her Majesty. Do not lose your hope, please," he said.

Nothing he or anyone else said could calm Larko down. He was helpless and hopeless, and now his love was in the hands of his sworn enemy, and he had no idea whether she was still alive or not. The only thing he could do was ride to Sinkaba without wasting time, but the people who had taken her were two days ahead of him.

Larko's soul died the moment he realized Queen Lamia had taken Aphra. His body was riding the horse toward Sinkaba, but his soul was gone. His heart was heavy like a piece of stone, and his hands were ice-cold, like there was no blood in his veins. He had started a trial in his mind with himself, and he had condemned and sentenced himself to die in agony. Deep down in his heart, he always knew his father and Aphra were right, but he had decided to ignore his gut feeling because he did not want to live his whole life in the constant fear of a woman, and now Aphra was paying the price. Life without her had no meaning for him. It was empty, like a gaping hole. He remembered the last night he had spent with her and how worried she was. She had begged him not to leave her alone, but all he wanted was to triumph in his last battle and come back home victoriously, and he wanted his people to remember him as a powerful king in the future. The last time he saw her, she was standing by the window, staring at him, but he had ignored her pleading look. He wished he had kissed her more that night and held her tighter, but he could not turn back time; all he could do was ride with all the life that was still left in his body. He could not stop thinking about Aphra, not even for a second, and his knights were getting worried about him since he did not talk, eat, or drink anything. He was just riding with all the power he had.

CHAPTER EIGHTEEN

IT WAS HOT. The harsh rays of the sun were lashing down on her frail body and draining out the last sips of life left in her. There was no cloud in the sky, and all she could see was the endless blue with the blazing sun in the center. There was sand everywhere, and the hot desert breeze blew sand into her eyes. The sun had burned her skin, and her lips were dry and cracked. There were dunes everywhere, and there was no tree or even rock to provide shade. Aphra was in Sinkaba, somewhere she had never been before.

Queen Lamia's men had covered their bodies and faces so the sun did not burn them, but they had made Aphra and Jasper walk barefoot, with nothing to protect themselves. She had lost her hope of survival, and she thought Larko was dead too. She did not even try to fight for her life anymore. It was pointless when her reason to live was gone, and even if Larko was alive, she would never beg Queen Lamia for her life. She could go to hell, for all Aphra cared, but every time she wanted to convince herself that she was done with life, she remembered that she was pregnant, and she felt guilty for not thinking about her baby. *Why am I pregnant if my baby is supposed to die?* She had asked herself that question so many times in the past few days, but she had not found an answer. After a long walk in the desert, the men finally stopped. It was still the middle of the day, so Aphra was sure they did not want to camp for the night. Something was about to happen. After all, they had reached their destination.

"She needs water. She is not feeling well," Jasper said to the men.

"Do not beg for me, Jasper!" Aphra said, barely able to talk.

"She does not want our water, and she will not need it anyway," the man said.

"What do you mean? What is going to happen?" Jasper asked with a terrified look in his eyes.

"Queen Lamia will be here soon. She will decide if she can have water or not," the man replied.

"I will talk with Queen Lamia. She will listen to me. She likes me. I know that. I will beg her to let Aphra go. That is the only way," Jasper said to himself, like a maniac, but Aphra knew the end was close. Queen Lamia was finally coming to take her revenge, and she regretted nothing. She would marry Larko again, even if she knew she would die shortly after. She felt no pain any longer. She was neither dead nor alive, somewhere between worlds. There was a deadly silence in the desert. No one talked, the air was still, the breeze had stopped, and no creature moved, not even the lizards. After a short wait, four horses appeared on the horizon. Jasper could hardly see, but he was sure one of them was Queen Lamia. The riders got closer; they were all wearing black veils and had covered their heads. Suddenly, all the men knelt for one rider.

"Welcome, Your Majesty!" one of the men said.

Queen Lamia got off her horse, took off her veil, and said, "You did great. I will reward you well for your service."

"Thank you, Your Majesty," the man said.

Queen Lamia then looked at Jasper and said with a smirk, "Look who we have here! The brave knight of Kalastra!"

Jasper stumbled toward her, his voice breaking.

"We need to talk," he said.

"The time for talking is over. It is time for action, thanks to you," she said.

"You promised me. You said all you wanted was Larko. Let Aphra leave, and I promise I will bring his head to you," he said.

"You are an idiot, Jasper. No wonder Aphra did not choose you," she said, looking into his eyes.

He shouted, "I will kill you, bitch. I will slit your throat and feed you to the dogs."

"Take him away! Take his eyes out and leave him in the desert. He deserves to die with agony," she commanded her men.

"Wait! You can tear me into pieces if you want. Take my eyes out, do whatever you want with me, but please let Aphra go. I beg you. It was all Larko. She did not even know about you two," he said, trying to save Aphra's life with his last words.

"You are pathetic, you know that?" she said.

"Not as much as you. You are a mad queen who wants to kill her rival because she is too weak to compete with her," he said.

She yelled at her men, "Take him away and make sure he suffers!"

Queen Lamia was furious. She had waited too long, and she was not letting anyone or anything take her chance away from her.

She yelled again, "Bring that bitch to me!"

Two men grabbed Aphra by her wrists and dragged her on the sand; then they threw her in front of Queen Lamia's feet.

"Do you know who I am?" Queen Lamia asked as she raised Aphra's head with her hand, looking right into her eyes.

"The crazy queen of the South!" Aphra snapped back, her voice low and defiant.

"Maybe I am crazy, as everyone says, but everything was fine before you showed up. Larko and I were going to marry. We would rule over Kalastra and Sinkaba together. He was mine, but you took him from me. You ruined everything; you took my love and lived the life I was supposed to have. You do not even deserve to be a servant at his court, let alone be the queen of Kalastra. Now, it is time for atonement. You will pay for what you did, and you will wish you had never married Larko," Lamia said.

"Do what you want to me. I do not regret what I did. He never loved you, and you know it. It was just a political marriage arranged by your fathers. You can continue deceiving yourself and blaming me, but do not tell me you loved him. You are just thirsty for power," Aphra said.

"I have enough power, and I will have what I want with or without Larko. Love was the only thing I was looking for, and you took it from me. Now, it is time to pay for what you did, and you will beg for your life after you know how I am going to make you suffer," Lamia said.

"I will never beg no matter what you do to me," Aphra said.

Queen Lamia smiled and said, "Well, at least you are not pathetic like Jasper, who begged me for his life."

"Jasper is a knight of Kalastra. He does not beg for his life. He dies with dignity," Aphra replied.

"As much as I would like to continue this game, I think you should know the truth before you die. Jasper is not the person you think he is. He betrayed you and Larko. He was the one who helped me bring you here, but of course, he did not know I was going to kill you. I told him I would let you go so you two could run away together, if only he brought you to me," Lamia said.

"I do not believe you. Jasper would never do such a thing. He is loyal to his king and me," Aphra replied.

"Loyalty has no meaning compared to love. He never stopped loving you. All he wanted was to kill Larko, and that was what I told him I would do. The poor man thought he could have you after Larko's death," Lamia said.

"So, he lied about Larko too. He is not wounded in the battle then," Aphra said with a faint smile.

"I can see you are not as stupid as I thought," Lamia said.

"Larko will kill you. You cannot get away with this," Aphra said.

"I cannot wait to host him in my palace," she said with a smirk, then looked at her men. "You two, start digging!"

The men started digging a grave, and as it got deeper, Queen Lamia became more anxious. She hated Aphra as much as she was afraid of Larko, and she was sure he had realized Aphra's absence at the court by then and was on his way to Sinkaba.

"Enough! Bring her here!" Lamia said to her men.

"Are you thirsty?" she asked Aphra.

"I want nothing from you," Aphra replied.

"It does not matter if you are thirsty or not. It will be all over soon. Do you not fear what I am going to do to you?" Lamia asked.

"I do not. I have thought about my death so many times, and I always knew it would be by you somehow," Aphra replied.

"You are smart, but I am sure what you did not know was how I would kill you," Lamia said; then she looked at her men. "Throw her in the hole!"

The men did not move for a few seconds; then one of them asked, "Shall we kill her first, Your Majesty?"

"Did you not hear me? Throw her in the hole and bury her alive! She does not deserve to die easy," she said.

"But the sand is scorching, Your Majesty," one of the men said.

"How dare you disobey my orders and question me? Do as I say, or you will suffer the same fate!" she yelled at them.

They threw Aphra in the hole and started pouring the sand down on her. Aphra had not yet believed what was about to happen to her. The sand was hot, and her skin was burning, but she was not going to say anything. She did not even cry. She killed the fear inside her. One of the men finally said, "Please stop looking at us. Just close your eyes!"

"Do you think it will make it easier for you if I close my eyes? What you are doing here will haunt you forever," she said.

Lamia leaned over the edge, shadows dancing on her face. "What is it, Aphra? Do you want to beg me for forgiveness?"

Aphra lifted her chin, her voice a death knell.

"I have done nothing wrong to need to ask for forgiveness, but today, here, I curse you to live the rest of your miserable life in agony and your soul to be haunted for eternity and to never have peace in the world of the dead when you die."

"Faster! Bury her in there! Let her suffocate!" Lamia yelled at her men.

The men poured the sand faster, and Aphra closed her eyes not because she was scared but to imagine Larko's face for one last time in her mind. She did not feel the heat of the sands anymore; she did not even hear Lamia's voice. There was no one there except Larko and her. They were in the forest in Kalastra, and a cool breeze was blowing. She was lying down under a tree, and Larko was holding her head, looking at her with his hazel eyes. She opened her eyes, smiled at him, and said, "Were you watching me the whole time?"

Larko grabbed her hand and said, "What can be more joyful than watching you sleep?"

"I love you, Larko. I never thought I could love someone so deeply. I want you to know that I need you like the air I breathe. You are my past and my future. You are everything that there is in this world for me. You are the reason I exist, and I was born to find you and to fall in love with you. Do not leave me alone, for I am broken without you," she said.

"I will never leave you, Aphra. You are the missing part that completes my soul. I loved you even before I met you; I love you now, and I will always love you in this world and the other world." He kissed her on the cheek.

Aphra put his hand on her belly and said, "We are going to have a child, Larko. A part of you is growing inside me."

Larko's eyes were wet with tears of happiness. He looked into Aphra's eyes. "You have given the world to me, Aphra. This child is a miracle, and I will give him the best life he deserves."

"How do you know we will have a prince?" she asked.

"I saw him in my dream," he replied.

Suddenly, there was complete darkness, the darkest black possible, but she was not scared. Her soul had left her body, and the light replaced the darkness.

"She must be dead by now, Your Majesty," one of the men said. Queen Lamia was silent. She was staring at the sand. Aphra had shown no sign of fear, and she had not even begged for her life. She had said nothing when they poured sand on her head, as if she was not even there.

"Can you hear me, Your Majesty? She must be dead now," the man said again.

"Fine! We will go back to Sinkaba," Lamia said.

"What will happen now? Will King Larko attack us?" one of the men asked.

"King Larko will not let us get away with this," another man said.

"She cursed us. I cannot forget her eyes staring at me," someone else said.

"Silence! No one should fear her curse. It means nothing. She is dead, and she cannot hurt anyone," Lamia yelled at them.

"How about King Larko, Your Majesty?" one of the men asked.

"Larko is weak. We will trounce him," she replied.

"We shall go back to the palace and fortify the city walls, Your Majesty. He must be on his way as we speak," one of the men said.

Queen Lamia and her men rode back to Sinkaba. She knew Larko was coming after her, and even though she was shaking with fear, she regretted nothing. She doubled the number of soldiers at each corner of the palace. Lamia was terrified for the first time in her life. She feared Larko's rage and Aphra's curse, but she had no intention of showing any sign of weakness to her people.

CHAPTER NINETEEN

LARKO WAS RIDING as fast as he could, but he was still behind. He had not eaten for days, and his knights could not catch up to his pace. He was finally in Sinkaba, near the city gates, and he thought Aphra was probably in the dungeon. He did not even want to think about the possibility of her being dead.

"We should wait until it is dark, Your Majesty. Just a few more hours, and then we can set the queen free," Lord Resko said.

Larko rested one hand on the pommel of his sword, his eyes fixed on the distant lights of the city beyond the dunes.

"How are we going to do it? There are only eight of us, and I am certain they are fully guarding the palace. We should come up with a plan," he replied, his tone edged with tension.

"We are not even sure Her Majesty is in the dungeon. They might keep her somewhere else. After all, they know you will come after the queen, Your Majesty. They are waiting for us," one of the knights said.

"We have not come all this way to wait behind the gates, Your Majesty. We must rescue the queen and kill as many of them as we can," someone else said.

"We are only here to set the queen free, without attracting any attention. We are outnumbered, and we need to be smart. I know you all want to help, but I cannot risk your lives knowing that they are waiting for us. I believe it is best if I enter the palace alone in the middle of the night," Larko said.

"I understand that we are not on a suicidal mission, but we will not leave you alone either, Your Majesty," Lord Resko said.

"I believe in all of you, but we do not know what is awaiting us in the palace, so you must wait for me outside the city gates in case anything happens to me in there," Larko replied.

"I agree with you, Your Majesty, but please let me come with you, just the two of us," Lord Resko said.

"Okay fine, just you, Lord Resko, but the rest of you stay here and wait for my signal!" Larko said.

After an hour, it was completely dark, and they had arrived at the city gates, but surprisingly, there were no guards at the gates, and it was dead quiet everywhere.

"It is too quiet, Your Majesty. This cannot be a good sign," one of the knights said.

"He is right, Your Majesty. There are no guards at the gate. This is a trap," Lord Resko said.

Larko clenched his jaw, fury simmering beneath the surface. "What do you suggest, Lord Resko? To go back? To leave Aphra here in Queen Lamia's hands?" Larko asked, his voice like the edge of a blade.

"No, Your Majesty, but I think we should come back with our army," Lord Resko replied.

"There is no time. They might kill her any minute. I will go in there either with or without you," Larko said.

"If you are persistent about going into the palace tonight, I will accompany you, as I am worried about your life, not mine, Your Majesty," Lord Resko said.

"Thank you, Lord Resko. You have always been loyal to the

queen and me," he said with a smile, then looked at his knights. "If anything goes wrong and we do not come back within an hour, leave and bring help! This is an order. Do you understand?"

"Yes, Your Majesty," they said.

Larko then looked at Lord Resko and said, "We need to find the dungeon. They are probably keeping her there."

"You are right, Your Majesty," he said.

Larko and Lord Resko entered the city easily while the rest of the knights waited outside the city gates. There was no one in the alleys, not even a beggar. When they arrived at the palace, there were only two guards at the tower who were drunk and did not realize anything. Larko was sure something was wrong, but he could not go back. He had to find Aphra; there was no other choice. They found the dungeon easily, but what was important was how to pass by the guards without making any noise. As they got closer to the guards, they realized they were both asleep.

"How come all the guards are asleep everywhere, Your Majesty? It cannot be this easy," Lord Resko said.

Larko grabbed the keys off one of the guard's pockets as slowly as he could and whispered, "We have come this far. Easy or hard, we cannot go back now." Then they started looking at every cell, but Aphra was not in the dungeon.

"Her Majesty is not in the dungeon. Queen Lamia is probably keeping her somewhere else in the palace with high security. This is the only explanation I can find, Your Majesty," Lord Resko said.

"We should separate now. I will find Queen Lamia's chamber, and you look everywhere else. I will kill her if I have to, but she will tell me where Aphra is," Larko said.

"It is too dangerous, Your Majesty. There must be many soldiers guarding her chamber now," he said.

"I am going in, Lord Resko, so leave if I am not back in thirty minutes," he said.

Larko had no intention of going back alone. He reached out for his sword and pressed it hard to his body, making sure it was still there with him. He grabbed one of the torches in the hallway and made his way to where he thought Queen Lamia's chamber would be. Two soldiers were guarding her chamber, but this time they were awake. He reached out for his bow and shot an arrow at one of the guards, and as soon as he wanted to shoot another arrow, the other guard fell to the ground, and they were both dead. Larko looked back and saw Lord Resko behind him.

"I think I told you not to follow me," Larko said with an angry voice.

"Hang me later if you want, Your Majesty, but we should not waste any time now," he said.

"Fine, follow me!" Larko said.

Larko opened the door as quietly as he could, yet the sound of the door squeaking echoed in the hallway. He took his sword out and entered the room. Queen Lamia's chamber was massive, with several open balconies that allowed lots of air in the room. There was only one torch in the chamber that had slightly lit up the room, but it was still hard to see. Larko and Lord Resko approached the bed, and Larko could finally see Queen Lamia sleeping in her bed. He put his sword on her throat and said, "Open your eyes! I know you are not sleeping."

A few seconds later, Lamia opened her eyes, with a devilish smile on her face, and said, "Welcome, Larko! I was expecting you sooner."

"Where is Aphra?" he asked with fire in his eyes.

"Why are you so angry, Larko? You were always nice and gentle before. What has she done to you?" she asked.

"Do not tempt me to slit your throat here, for I will gladly do it," he said.

"Who is he? Is he one of your loyal knights, like Jasper?" she asked while looking at Lord Resko.

"What did you do to them?" Larko asked.

"I did not do anything. This was all your doing when you decided to choose her instead of me," she replied.

"Do not pretend like you loved me. You and your father were just thirsty for power."

"I do not deny that I wanted to become the queen of Kalastra, but I wanted you more. We were supposed to get married," she said.

"It was just a political arrangement made by our fathers. I was very young back then. I did not even know what love was, and I never promised you anything," he said.

Her eyes narrowed, yet they glistened with something darker than sadness.

"But I knew what love was, and I fell in love with you."

"You still do not know what love is," he said.

"Say what you want, Larko, but I loved you. I could not see myself marrying anyone else except you. I never told you, but I counted down the days until I would meet you in Kalastra; instead, I received a letter from you saying you were sorry and you had fallen in love with someone else. You did not even bother to come here and tell me everything in person. You married your precious Aphra, and you were so stupid to think that I had forgiven you," she said.

"Do whatever you want me with me, but let Aphra, Jasper, and Lord Resko leave."

"You are too late, Larko, just like always," she said.

His voice cracked like dry wood.

"Where is Aphra?"

"In hell, I hope," she replied. Larko raised his sword to kill Lamia, but the whole chamber lit up before he could do anything. There were men with swords everywhere in the room; one was pointing his sword at Larko, and another was pointing his sword at Lord Resko.

"Did you think it would be that easy to enter Sinkaba and get into my palace and my chamber if I did not want you to?" she asked.

"What did you do to her?" Larko asked again with a shaky voice.

"I buried her alive in the desert," she said with a maniacal smile.

"You cannot be that cruel. You are lying. You have imprisoned her somewhere in the palace, I know it," he said with a desperate voice.

"I confess that she was smarter than you and Jasper. She said she knew from the beginning that I would kill her someday, and she was right," she said with a smirk.

Larko shouted, "I will kill you, bitch!" but Queen Lamia's men attacked him, took his sword away, and made him kneel. He was shivering with rage, and nothing mattered anymore. Lamia then got out of her bed and took a few steps toward him, and with a victorious face, she asked, "Are you not curious to know what I did to your knight Jasper?"

Larko was staring at Queen Lamia. He could hear what she was saying, but he was unable to process and take it in. The hope of seeing Aphra alive, holding her tight in his arms, was the only thing that had kept him going in the past few days, but everything was over for him; she was dead.

"Okay fine! I will tell you what I did to him. I told my men to take out his eyes and leave him in the desert by himself. I suppose he should be dead by now, or maybe he is not, but do not worry. I punished him for betraying you," she said.

"Lord Jasper is a man of honor. He is a knight, and a knight of Kalastra never betrays his king," Lord Resko said.

"Dear Lord Resko, not all knights are loyal like you. Some fall in love with the queen and betray their king," she said.

Larko then raised his head and looked at Lamia. "I do not believe your lies," he said.

"I suppose your dear wife never told you that Jasper was always in love with her, and she had rejected his pure passionate love before meeting you," she said.

"They were just childhood friends," he said.

"Oh, my poor Larko. How do you think I lured Aphra out of Kalastra? Obviously, with the help of your loyal knight Jasper," she said.

He shouted, "You are lying!"

"Jasper always loved Aphra, but I suppose she did not love him back. He confessed his love to her on the day he became a knight, and Aphra told him she had no feelings for him; then she met you after a while, you two married, and you thought you could live happily ever after. How pathetic of you both!" she said.

"Aphra would have told me if there was such a thing. I do not believe you," he said.

"I found out about his passionate burning desire to have Aphra, and then I told him he could have her if he brought her to me, and of course, he accepted. I just told him a tiny little lie, of course. I said I would kill you and let Aphra leave with him, but instead, I killed her. He was very shocked," she said.

"Shut your filthy mouth! How can you be so disgusting?" he said.

"How can you be so stupid, Larko? You should thank me for showing you Jasper's true face," she said.

"Where did you bury her?" he asked while looking into her eyes.

"Why do you want to know? Do you want to dig her up and kiss her goodbye?"

"Just tell me where you buried her!" he asked again.

"Somewhere in the desert. She is all sand now, I suppose," she said.

Larko had never felt so desperate in his life. Lamia's words were like a sharp dagger tearing his heart apart, and it felt like the world had ended for him. Aphra was his whole life, and he could not believe that she was dead. He could not even imagine how he lived before her and how to live after her death. Aphra had changed him in so many ways. She was a light in the darkness of his life, and now that light was off. He did not move; he did not shout; he did not even blink; he just stared at the floor. His body was cold as ice.

"Take Lord Resko to the dungeon!" she said.

"How about him?" Jabeer asked.

"King Larko and I are still talking. You can all leave, except you, Jabeer!" she said.

Queen Lamia's men took Lord Resko to the dungeon, but Larko still did not move. It was just Larko, Lamia, and Jabeer in the room, and nobody talked. Finally, Lamia grabbed a chair and sat in front of Larko, looked at his head that was still down, and said, "You are pitiful."

"Kill me, or I will kill you, I swear," he said.

"He is right, Your Majesty. We should kill him here," Jabeer said.

"Death would be too easy for you, Larko. I want you to live and suffer every day of your miserable life. I want you to pay for what you did to me," she said.

"You are crazy. You think playing the victim will justify your doing, but you are wrong. I am not the one who pays in the end, Lamia; it is you, and it will be big. I assure you," he said.

"It is big talk for a king who will have no kingdom soon. Lord Henry is attacking Kalastra as we speak. There will be nothing left of your empire. You will be forgotten, she will be forgotten, whatever you and your father built will be forgotten, your people will be my slaves, and I will make sure nothing remains of Kalastra," she said.

"It is not in your power to erase my kingdom. My knights will never let you and Lord Henry take over Kalastra. You and that coward have no chance," he said.

"We probably did not have any chance before, but things are different now. They know we have captured you, and their queen is dead. They are hopeless, Larko," she said.

"What is your plan for me? Do you want to keep me here all night?" he asked.

"There was a time I wanted you in my chamber before, but that time is history," she said with a smirk; then she looked at Jabeer and said, "Take him to the darkroom in the tower and make sure they guard it heavily!"

"As you wish, Your Majesty," Jabeer said.

Jabeer took Larko to the room on the highest level of the palace, and as they went up the stairs, the lights gradually died until there were no more torches in the hallway of the highest level. It was pitch-dark, and the room was at the end with a huge wooden door hinged with iron nails. Larko was walking slowly, dragging his feet along, and the four men who were supposed to guard his room pushed him forward occasionally. When they finally arrived, Jabeer opened the door and said, "Welcome to your hell, Your Majesty."

Larko paused for a few seconds and said, "I will make sure you beg my knights for your life before they slit your throat."

Jabeer looked at him and said, "You do not scare me."

"Then why are your hands shaking?" Larko asked.

Jabeer shouted at his men, "Throw him inside!"

Jabeer was not a brave man. He was simply an opportunist who had gained King Malik's trust and had become his adviser after the king killed his first adviser, whom he believed was helping his wife in treason. He was sneaky and intelligent and always found a way to survive the worst situations by first looking out for himself. After the king's death, he became Queen Lamia's adviser too, and she always listened to him, but what happened with Larko and Aphra was different, and everything was out of his control from the beginning. He preferred to kill Larko that night on the spot instead of imprisoning him, but he did not have the power to disobey Queen Lamia, and he could not convince her either. He feared Larko, and he was certain imprisoning him was a big mistake.

The guards threw Larko into the room. It was pitch-black. Larko sat on a corner and rested his head against the cold stone wall. He hated himself for what he had done to Aphra. If only he had listened to her and his father, things could be very different. They had both warned him about Lamia, but he had underestimated her power and was too proud to believe she could do any harm to him, and now Aphra was gone. He could not even cry; his eyes were dry. He just stared at a point in the darkness of the room and hit his head against the wall occasionally. All he wanted was to kill Lamia and anyone who had helped her in any way to kill Aphra. Then he remembered

Jasper, a man he had trusted with his life, kingdom, and love. If all the things Lamia had told him about Jasper were true, he would kill him with his own hands. How did he never realize Jasper was in love with Aphra? How could he be so blind? After hours of sitting in the darkness, which felt like an eternity to him, he felt a presence in the silence and loneliness of the room, and after that, he heard Aphra's voice. He knew he was losing his mind.

"Do not blame yourself, Larko! It was not your fault," the voice said.

"Everything is my fault. I did not listen to you, and I could not even save you. I was late. You should hate me, Aphra. I hate myself for what I did to you," he said.

"I can never hate you, Larko. My love for you is eternal, and nothing will ever change that. Believe me that everything happens for a reason. You were not late, my dear. It was my destiny to leave you," she said.

"I cannot even imagine the pain you went through when that monster buried you alive," he said, and a few drops of tears fell on his lap.

She came closer, knelt, looked deep into his eyes, and said, "You are my king, Larko. Wipe your tears off your face and be strong, like always. Do not let her break you. We will meet again," she said.

"Am I dead, or are you here in this room?" he asked.

"You are not dead. You needed me, so I came," she said, then vanished into thin air, and there was just the darkroom again.

"Do not leave me, Aphra! I still need you. I need you to stay," he said; then he whispered, "I will not tell anyone you were here, just you and me. She cannot harm you anymore. I am going to kill her, Aphra. Do not worry. I will kill her for you."

There was nothing more important in Larko's life than avenging Aphra's death. All he wanted was to kill Lamia, but he was still uncertain about Jasper. He could not believe his best knight and the man he had trusted with his life had betrayed him. *If Jasper betrayed me, what are the chances there were other knights who betrayed me? What if they all helped Lamia and Lord Henry?* he thought.

Time did not pass in that darkroom. No light entered the room, and there was no window to catch some fresh air. The room was specifically designed to make the prisoners crazy, and it was working on Larko. He was imprisoned for three days, and all he did was stare at one point in the darkness and talk to himself. Queen Lamia wanted to keep him in the room until he completely lost his mind, but Jabeer disagreed.

"It is a mistake to keep him alive, Your Majesty. We must kill him instantly. He will become even more dangerous if he loses his mind," Jabeer said.

"How can a lunatic be dangerous, Jabeer? He has no power and no kingdom to rule. He will be no danger to us," Queen Lamia replied.

"That is why he is dangerous, Your Majesty. Every day he spends in that darkroom alone gives him a chance to plot against us," he said.

"I do not want to kill him, Jabeer. He must be alive and suffer. Hearing him shout in pain and misery is the only thing that makes me happy now, and I do not want to hear anything else from you," she said.

"As you wish, Your Majesty," he said, but he knew he had to take things into his own hands. It seemed to him Queen Lamia could not think straight anymore. She had taken her revenge, but she was still not happy, and nothing could quench her thirst for revenge. He was certain Larko would kill him if he had the chance, so he had to kill him first. He could not wait for Queen Lamia to change her mind, so he called one of his most trusted men and told him to take Larko to the desert and kill him there.

"Is this Her Majesty's command?" the man asked.

"Her Majesty cannot make a rational decision now. She wants to keep him alive so he suffers for the rest of his life, but we both know if he lives, he will finally find a way to flee, and he will kill us all. You were one of the men who buried his wife alive; do you think he will let you live?" Jabeer asked.

"He will never have a chance if we keep him chained," the man replied.

"How long can we keep him in the darkroom? Not all his knights are like Jasper. They will finally come here for their king, and he will run away, and when he is free, he will come back for all of us. It is up to us now to make a decision, so do the right thing and kill the bastard!" Jabeer said.

"When Queen Lamia realizes we disobeyed her, she will kill us all," the man said.

"Leave that to me. I will talk to her later. She always listens to me, but we have to act fast now," Jabeer said.

"Fine, I will do it," the man said.

"Make sure he is dead and bring me his head!" Jabeer said.

After three days of solitude, someone finally opened the door and entered the room. Larko was sitting in a corner with his head down and his arms at his sides. He seemed to be murmuring something, but it was hard to understand him.

"Move! It is time to end your miserable, pitiful life," the man said.

Larko raised his head; the light of the torch in the man's hand had lit up his face a little. He looked at him, determined, right in the eye, and said, "I will not die until I kill you all: you, the dogs around you, Jabeer, and your bitch queen."

The man did not move for a few seconds; then he pulled himself together and shouted at the two men by his side, "Enough! Take him! Do not listen to him; he has lost his mind."

They put a black pouch over his head and took him out of the palace. They rode for about thirty minutes; then, they stopped somewhere in the desert.

"I think we should stop here and get it over with," one of the men said.

Larko could not see anything, but he knew they were about to kill him. He heard them getting off their horses and taking their swords out, but then he suddenly heard them falling on the sand, and there was just absolute silence after that. His hands were tied, and he could not see or do anything. After a few seconds, he heard horses galloping fast toward him, and then there was a familiar voice.

"Are you fine, Your Majesty?" one of his knights asked.

"Is it you, Elliot?" Larko asked.

"Yes, Your Majesty," he said as he took the pouch off Larko's head and cut the rope around his hands. Next to Larko, there were three dead bodies, all shot with arrows. Elliot and the rest of the knights who were with him and Lord Resko had not left Sinkaba, and they all knelt before Larko when they saw him.

"Please rise! You saved my life," Larko said to his knights.

"It is our duty and honor to serve you, Your Majesty. When we did not receive any signal from you and Lord Resko, we knew something was wrong. We were waiting for you outside the city gates for three days. We had finally decided to split, so some of us stayed here in case anything happened while two rode back to Kalastra to bring help, but as we prepared to separate, we saw them taking you outside the palace today, so we followed you," Elliot said.

"Thank you for saving my life. I did not want to die before killing Lamia," Larko said.

"Did you find Her Majesty? Where is Lord Resko?" Elliot asked.

Larko covered his face with his hands and turned his back on his knights; then he shouted as hard as he could in the desert. He wanted to let all his rage and resentment out. He wanted to shout for hours; he wanted to weep; he wanted to dig up every inch of that desert until he could find Aphra's body, but he could not. He was a king, and he could not seem weak to his people.

"What is it, Your Majesty? What happened in there?" one of the knights asked.

Larko took a deep breath and said, "The queen is dead. Lamia killed her before we got here. She buried her alive in the desert."

He then looked at his knights; they were devastated, broken into pieces, and unable to speak.

"How is that even possible, Your Majesty? How could she dare to touch our queen? Was she not scared of Kalastra and our mighty army?" Elliot asked while still in shock.

"Please let us mourn with you, Your Majesty. You are not alone. We will avenge Her Majesty's death," another knight said.

"I will kill her myself, and I will make sure she suffers," Larko said.

"What happened to you and Lord Resko in the palace, Your Majesty?" Elliot asked.

"They knew we were coming. They were waiting for us. They took Lord Resko to the dungeon, and I do not know if he is still alive or not," Larko said.

"How about Jasper, Your Majesty? He was with the queen," Elliot asked.

"Bring that bastard to me if you ever see him alive. He must be somewhere in the desert if he is not dead already," Larko said with anger; then he grabbed Elliot's sword off his belt. "I only live from now on to kill Lamia and anyone who helped her kill Aphra. I do not want you to come with me. Go back to Kalastra without me! I have to do this alone," he said.

"We cannot leave you, Your Majesty," Elliot said.

Larko shouted, "Did you not hear me? As your king, I commanded you to go back to Kalastra, if that means anything to you, or maybe you are all traitors like Jasper."

"What has Jasper done, Your Majesty? He has always been loyal to you and the kingdom," Elliot said.

Larko put the sword under Elliot's neck and said, "Did you know what his plan was? You two were friends," he asked.

"I do not know what you are talking about, Your Majesty. Kill me if you want, but I have never betrayed you, and I never will," he replied.

"What has Jasper done, Your Majesty?" one of the knights asked.

Larko lowered his sword and said, "That bastard was in love with Aphra all along. He was helping Lamia plot against us. He thought Lamia would kill me, and he could have Aphra after that," he said.

"Unbelievable! He was always so loyal," Elliot said.

"Has he run away, Your Majesty? I will bring his head to you if you command me," one of the knights said.

"Lamia took out his eyes and left him alone in the desert. He might be dead, but if you ever find him alive, just bring him to me. Anyone who has helped Lamia in any way must die by my hands," Larko said.

"Let us serve you, Your Majesty. You might not believe in your knights anymore, but we are all loyal to you until our last breath, and we will gladly give our lives for you. I am certain it is the same for Lord Resko. We are not like Jasper, and we will never betray you," Elliot said.

"I have to do this alone, Elliot. This is my revenge. Besides, there is probably nothing left of my kingdom anymore. Lord Henry attacked Kalastra with the help of Lamia the day we left for Sinkaba, so I am no longer your king, and you do not need to be loyal to me anymore," he said with a sad voice.

"Do not lose your hope, Your Majesty. I cannot even imagine how you feel after the death of Queen Aphra, but you have not lost everything. We have the greatest kingdom and the best knights in the world. Kalastra cannot be defeated easily. Lord Henry has no chance of conquering Kalastra even with the help of Queen Lamia. Let us come with you and take our revenge, and then we will all go back to Kalastra together," he said.

"Elliot is right, Your Majesty. We will never leave you. We would rather end our lives here than go back without you," Leo, one of the knights, said.

"You have all underestimated her. She is crazy, and she will do anything to conquer Kalastra. She was plotting this for a year," Larko said.

"If she conquers Kalastra and there is no country to go back to, I would rather die by your side and avenge Her Majesty's death as the last thing I do in this world," Elliot said.

"She cannot win this time. There is nothing in this world I want more than ending her life with pain," Larko said with rage.

"We want the same thing, Your Majesty. We will come up with a better plan this time, and we will kill whoever had a role in Her Majesty's death," Leo said.

"We need to leave this place, Your Majesty. When they realize their men are not back yet, they will know something is wrong and soon will come for you," Elliot said.

"We need to find shelter and food. His Majesty looks pale. He has probably not eaten for days," Leo said.

The six remaining knights were ready to do anything to protect their king and avenge their queen's death. They had taken an oath to always be loyal to King Larko and Kalastra under any circumstance. With no food and drink, trapped in a barren land that smelled like death, they were determined to bring those responsible for their queen's death to justice. All they needed to do was rest and then create a perfect plan to kill Queen Lamia and destroy her kingdom.

CHAPTER TWENTY

ESTHER GLANCED AT her map; she was very close to where once was a great kingdom. Kalastra was a dreamland for everyone, and people used to migrate from different parts of the world to live there. The nature was breathtaking, the people were kind and friendly, and the king and knights of Kalastra cared about the well-being of the citizens. However, Hila and the chief of the village had both warned her that nothing was left of that glorious kingdom and culture anymore; people were aggressive, and they were living in constant fear of looters and rebellions. So, as much as Esther was excited to see Kalastra, she was afraid of what she might encounter as well.

She had passed the desert behind her, and she was sure the route ahead was all beauty; it was so scenic that it made her ride slower. She wanted to absorb the charm of that evergreen land into her veins and inhale its fresh air into her lungs. After riding for half a day in the meadow, she saw a forest in the distance. It was vast and green, majestic and mysterious. She had no control over herself anymore, and she was drawn to the forest. Something was inviting about it, which urged her to proceed. It was the first time she was setting foot in that forest, yet it felt so familiar to her, like she'd known that place all her life, and somehow it felt more home to her than Aseeta.

Esther could not find any rational explanation for why she felt that way, so she decided not to fight it anymore and to embrace anything ahead of her because everything was magical there. She entered the forest riding very slowly, then stopped and got off her horse. She wanted to feel everything in the forest: the air, the soil, the sunshine, and the trees. She liked to touch anything alive and vibrating, and the forest was very much talking to her; she just had to listen. She looked up and saw the sunlight breaking through the branches of oak trees, lighting up the path ahead of her. The warmth of the sun felt wonderful. She looked down and saw the twigs and leaves beneath her feet. She liked the sound of cracking them; it was like wood burning in a fire. She bent down and picked up an acorn, then smelled it with all the power that she had in her body. She could smell the whole forest in that acorn; it was fresh and cleansing. She placed her hand on the rough bark of a tree and hugged it with her eyes closed. The tree was ancient yet alive. She could see happy moments and laughter through the eyes of the tree; she could see lovers kissing under its shade and children playing around it. The forest was enchanting. It had given her the ability to see through things, and all the feelings she was experiencing were intensified. It was so quiet that she could fall asleep there, and the only sounds she could hear were from animals: birds flapping their wings and rabbits moving through the bushes. If she could, she would stay there forever, but she had to continue. A voice inside her kept saying it was just the beginning and things were about to get even greater. After walking a short distance, she came across a lake in the middle of the forest. It was not a big lake, but the water was refreshing and much needed. She thought it would be the perfect spot to stay for the night. She had not eaten all day, and she was starving, so she decided to look for some food.

Esther started looking around for berries, acorns, and hazelnuts. The forest was lush, and there was plenty of food to eat. Having a rabbit or a squirrel could be more satisfying, but she had never hunted in her life before, and she did not know how to catch one of those. It soon got dark, and she made a fire for the night. Nights were getting colder as she moved farther north. She pressed the blanket tight to her chest to keep herself warm, but it was still cold, even with the fire burning. She was staring at the flames, hoping to see Aphra again. She had so many questions to ask her, and she knew she was somehow related to her. The rhythmic movement of the flames from side to side was pleasing to watch, and the heat of the fire had warmed up her face. She took off her boots and laid her feet in front of the fire to warm them up. Sleeping in the forest was very different from sleeping in the desert. It was impossible to hide in the desert, with no rock or tree, since it was just sand and the sky and shining stars, but in the forest, there could be a wolf lurking around, waiting to eat her alive, or maybe someone was hiding behind the bushes until she fell asleep to cut her throat. Yet, she was not scared, or perhaps she must have been a little cautious, if she was wise enough, because her first morning waking up in the forest was not what she had imagined the night before. She was having sweet dreams until a sharp and cold object touched her neck; then she heard someone say, "Time to wake up, beauty!"

When Esther opened her eyes, a young man was standing on top of her, pressing his sword at her throat. She wanted to scream, but she was so terrified that she could not even move.

"Who are you, and what are you doing in my territory?" he asked, pressing the sword closer.

"Good morning, sir! I had just camped for the night here. I did not know it was your territory," she replied.

The man laughed and said, "Nobody has ever called me sir before. What is your name, stranger?"

"Esther, sir!" she replied.

"You do not need to call me 'sir' anymore. Tell me where you are coming from, and do not think about lying to me," he said.

"I am coming from the South," she replied.

"Where in the South, exactly?" he asked.

"Do you want to keep pointing that sword at me?" she asked.

"I ask the questions here, and you just reply, understood?" he said, then pushed the sword a little forward.

"Okay, I am sorry. I am coming from Aseeta," she said.

"Where the hell is Aseeta?" he asked.

"It is in the South," she replied.

"Are you mocking me, girl?" he asked with an angry voice.

"Oh no, I am not. Aseeta is the name of my village. It is very south, to be accurate."

He moved the sword away and said, "Come on, move! Show me where it is on the map."

Esther reached out for her map and laid it on the ground, then pointed at a place on the map, and said, "There! That is where I am from. Aseeta."

The man looked at her and said, "Girl, do you have a death wish? Why do you lie to me? Do you know how far that area you showed me is from here?" he asked.

"Well, I know. I have been traveling for a while," she said.

"How old are you?" he asked.

"Nineteen," she replied.

"And you have been traveling from Aseeta to here on your own?" he asked.

"Why is it so hard to believe? I am nineteen, and I have been traveling alone from Aseeta to here," she said, then paused for a few seconds. "Oh, I know why. You have never left your safe zone. You have always been living in your territory."

"You think you are smart, huh? No one in their right mind leaves this paradise behind to see just the sand in the desert. People here do not like strangers who come from the other side of Mount Zaka.

Do you understand?" he said.

Esther brushed dirt off her knees, eyes glinting with mischief. "People here are not so friendly, and I can see that."

"We have been like this for centuries, and we do not like the people in the South."

"I wonder why. You must have a reason for that," she said.

"What do you want, girl? What are you doing here? Go back to your village. There is nothing for you in Kalastra. Not everyone is going to be as nice to you as me," he said.

"I cannot go back. There is nothing left for me in Aseeta," she said.

"Suit yourself. I do not care," he said, walking toward his horse.

"Wait!" she said. "Can I come with you? I mean, people will not notice me if I am with a local. I will not cause any problems; I promise," she said.

"Are you crazy? You are the definition of problem. No way! You are not coming with me," he said.

"Please, I beg you. I swear you will not even notice my presence. I will shut up, not say anything," she said.

"You cannot come with me because I am not going anywhere. This is my territory."

"What do you do in your territory? You just wake the strangers up with your sword?" she asked with a smirk.

A hint of amusement cracked through his annoyance.

"No," he said, leaning forward, his breath warm against her ear, "I rob them. But since you had nothing with you, I wanted to know what kind of idiot you were."

"Oh my God! You are a thief!" she said.

"Why is it so weird? You do not have thieves in your cursed land?" he asked.

"Be careful how you talk about my village or—"

"Or what happens?" He put his hand on his sword.

"Nothing. I think I should leave. You are leaving anyway too," she said gently and tried to reach out for her bag.

She had barely taken a few steps when the man stopped and said, "Be safe!"

"I will try my best," she said.

Esther parted ways with the young man, and after riding for hours in the forest, she finally stopped. She had not eaten the whole day, and she was starving. "I am hungry, but I cannot eat fruit anymore," she said to her horse. She petted his mane. "Why have I not named you yet, huh? Let me see." She paused for a few minutes and said with a big smile, "Wind! I will call you Wind, my friend, since you run very fast, and you are just like the wind. Well, do you like your name?" The horse neighed, and Esther said, "I think that means yes. Well, now that I have named you, I should think about my next problem. I cannot eat berries anymore, and I am dying of hunger."

"Do you always talk to your horse or only when you have lost your mind because of hunger?" the young man asked. Esther looked back and saw the man from the morning.

"First of all, I think you told me you could not leave your territory, and second, who said I was hungry?" she asked.

"Do not deny it. I heard you," he replied.

"Were you following me?" she asked.

"Why would I follow you, girl? I am going to the city to sell my goods," he replied.

"You mean the things you stole from people, right?" she asked.

"Right, but I only steal from the people who can afford it," he said.

"That does not justify what you do," she said.

"I do not have to explain myself to you. You cannot judge me, little girl," he said.

"Do not call me a little girl," she said, emphasizing the *little*.

A mocking grin spread across his face.

"I am sorry. Did I offend you? What was your name again?"

"You do not offend me. You just annoy me," she said, kicking her horse to move.

"Hey, wait! Where are you going? It will be dark soon," he said.

"Where I am going does not concern you," she replied.

"Just listen to me and be a good girl. Make a fire, and I will be back soon with food."

"Why should I listen to you? I do not even know you," she said.

"Egenar," he said.

"What?" she asked.

"My name is Egenar. Now you know me. Do not go anywhere!" He started riding.

"Egenar! As if I care about his name," she said to herself, then paused for a few seconds. "What do you think, Wind? Should I wait for him? If I do not, I will sleep with an empty stomach tonight, but I do not even know him."

Egenar was in his early thirties. He had lived his whole life in Kalastra, surviving solely on robbing the rich. He was a great fighter, respected by those who knew him. He had lost his parents when he was just a boy, and since he had no one to take care of him, life forced him to learn how to live on his own. He was a caring and protective man, and he made everyone feel safe around him, yet he could be very annoying sometimes. His grayish hair and the scars on his body proved he had suffered a lot in his life, and his dark eyes always shone like a black diamond; however, one could still see frustration and disappointment in his eyes, as if he was done with life.

Esther had no choice except to trust him, so she got off her horse and started looking for firewood reluctantly. She was not sure why he had changed his mind and followed her, but whatever the reason was, she was happy she was not going to sleep hungry that night. So, she made a fire and waited for Egenar to come back. After a while, when it was almost getting dark, she saw a figure in the distance. *Is it Egenar or someone else?* she thought. The forest was completely silent, but she could still hear her heart pounding. She could not move or talk, as fear had paralyzed her. After a few seconds, she finally managed to say, "Egenar, is that you?" But there was no answer, and the figure was getting closer. She panicked and started looking for a big piece of wood or stone to use as a weapon, but before she could do anything, Egenar threw a rabbit in front of her and said, "Have you not learned anything traveling on your own? What if it was not me?"

"Are you crazy? Why did you not answer me when I called your name?" she asked with anger.

"To scare you, little girl," he replied.

"First, I told you not to call me a little girl. I am nineteen years old, and second, I think you are a lunatic because why else would you want to scare someone on purpose?" she asked.

"I scared you so you do not make the same mistake again. Things are different here. The only dangers you can find in the desert are scorpions and snakes. There are no trees or bushes to hide behind, but Elkoy's men can be anywhere in the forest, and they are very dangerous. You should always be alert and have your weapon by your side," he said.

"Who is Elkoy?" she asked.

"He is someone you do not want to see in the forest at night when you are alone. He is vicious, and he has no mercy. His men loot any village they want and kill as many as pleases them, and they can be anywhere, so you must be very careful," he said.

"Why does no one stand up to them?" she asked.

"No one dares, and no one is powerful enough to stand up to them. People are no longer fighters here. There was a time we had a great kingdom, a just king, and gallant knights, but it is all history now," he said with a big sigh.

"Are you a good fighter?" she asked.

"I am, and I am sure there are many good fighters like me in this land," he said.

"So why have you not done anything so far?" she asked.

"It is not that simple, girl. We do not have enough men, and even if we do, people have no hope to rise and fight against Elkoy. They need a leader," he said.

"All I know is that magic will not bring you a leader. You must choose one among yourselves," she said.

"You are wrong. That is not a position that can be taken by anyone. We need our queen to come back," he said.

"Who is the queen you are waiting for?" she asked.

"Queen Aphra," he said as he was skinning the rabbit.

"Why do you think she is going to come back?" she asked.

"The legend says she will rise from the sands one day, and when she does, she will unite the North and the South. She is the promised queen," he said.

Esther could not speak for a few seconds, as if the lightning had hit her. "Is Aphra the promised queen?" she murmured. *If she is the promised queen, then who am I?* she thought.

"Hey, what happened to you? Are you listening to me?" he asked.

"Yes, yes, I am, sorry. Did you say anything?" she asked.

"I said, what is your story? Why did you travel from Aseeta to Kalastra?" he asked.

"I just want to see the world. My village is tiny, and there is nothing much to explore."

"Do you expect me to believe that?" he said, looking at Esther's eyes.

"Believe what you want. I have no reason to lie," she said.

"Fine! I believe you, young lady. Our dinner will be ready in a few minutes," he said.

"Thank you for coming after me. You are a good man," she said.

"I am sure you can make it even without me, but I am going to the city anyway. Besides, I see a fighter in you," he said.

"I do not think I can fight. I have never even held a sword in my hand. I have been fortunate so far to encounter only nice people," she said.

"I am not talking about your ability to use a sword. I am talking about your spirit. You have a fighter inside you. It takes courage to travel alone from your village to a dangerous place like here for any reason it might be," he said.

"I suppose you are right. I had never thought about it before. I just knew I had to leave."

"Take it! It is ready, but be careful. It is hot," he said, handing her a piece of the rabbit.

"I hope it tastes good," she said.

"It does. You will love it. Just take a bite!" he said.

Esther closed her eyes and took a small bite.

"Well, how is it? Do you like it?" he asked.

"I like it. It is delicious," she said with a smile, then paused. "Will you tell me more about the legend? About Queen Aphra!"

"You seem very interested in her," he said.

"I think it is fascinating. I have seen many people during my journey, and some of them have helped me a lot. One of them was a woman who saved me from dying in the desert, and she told me all about the legend, about King Larko and Queen Aphra," she said.

"So, what do you want to know?" he asked.

"Why do people think she will come back?" she asked.

"People believe that, in her last breaths, she cursed those who buried her alive, and she said they would all pay for what they did to her," he said.

"Okay, but that does not mean she will come back, does it?" she asked.

"No, that alone does not," he said.

"Then what else is there to the legend?" she asked with much curiosity.

"A few years later, a group of people went to the desert to dig her up and bury her properly in Kalastra, but they could not find her bones. They searched everywhere, every inch of that desert, but there was no sign of Queen Aphra," he said.

"Maybe they did not search the right place," she said.

"They searched everywhere," he said, then paused. "Why is Queen Aphra so interesting to you?"

"No reason," she said with a smile, then wrapped her blanket tighter around herself.

"I should go grab more wood. It will be a cold night," he said.

"I will come with you," she said instantly, jumping off to accompany him.

"You do not need to, but if you say you are scared of being alone, then you can come," he said with a smirk.

"Why would I be scared? I am not scared of anything. I just wanted to help you, but since you are fine being alone, I will wait for you here by the fire," she said with a fake smile, looking into his eyes.

"Okay, I will be back soon," he said and left.

"He does it on purpose. I know it. There is nothing to fear, Esther! Nobody is in this forest except him and me. I will be fine," she said, patiently waiting for him to come back.

When Egenar got back, the fire was almost dead. He threw dry twigs into the fire and said, "That blanket is not enough to keep you warm throughout the night."

"I did not expect Kalastra to be this cold," she replied.

"What did you expect, girl? We are in the North. You should take my blanket, and I will take yours," he said.

"You do not have to do that," she said.

"Hey, girl, look at me! I have lived in this forest all my life. I will be fine," he said.

Esther wrapped the new blanket around herself, warmth seeping back into her bones.

"Thank you. You are very kind."

"Not always! I might wake you up with my sword under your throat again tomorrow morning," he said with a smile.

Esther smiled back and grabbed Egenar's blanket. The heat of the fire was pleasant, and she fell asleep soon. Egenar sat by the fire and placed his sword on his side. He was not going to sleep that night. He kept looking at Esther when she was asleep, but he could not figure her out. There was something unusual and exciting about her, and he was determined to find his answer. It was almost midnight, and he had barely closed his eyes when he heard Esther. It seemed like she was talking in her dream. He wanted to wake her up, but then she started walking. Esther was sleepwalking, and Egenar followed her. She moved away from the fire and stopped somewhere in the middle of the trees.

"Open your eyes, Esther!" a female voice said.

Esther opened her eyes, and there she was again, the woman she had seen before in Aseeta and once a few nights ago, the same woman she had seen in her dreams all her life. The bright light was everywhere, surrounding her, and she was shining like a diamond. Egenar was watching. He was mesmerized, and he could not move or say anything.

"What do you want from me? Look! I am in Kalastra. What else do you want me to do? Why do you not leave me alone?" Esther asked.

"You need to remember first," the woman said.

"Then help me remember. I have never seen you in my life before," Esther said.

"You cursed me, Esther. I have been suffering for centuries. Please forgive me so I can move on," she said with a begging voice.

"Are you dead?" Esther asked.

"I am. It was centuries ago," the woman replied.

"Why do you need me to forgive you?" Esther asked.

"Because I killed you," the woman replied.

Esther could not believe what she had just heard. It was like the whole universe was spinning around her head. The woman disappeared before she realized it, and the forest was all dark again. The sound of the thunderstorm brought Egenar back to himself. It had started raining like crazy, and Esther had passed out on the ground. He started running toward her and shouted,

"Esther! Esther!"

He took her to the fire and wrapped the blanket around her. Her body was freezing cold.

"Open your eyes, Esther! Open your eyes!" he said softly.

After a few minutes, Esther slowly opened her eyes and started crying.

"Calm down, Esther! I am here. You are safe. Do you feel better?" he asked.

She nodded and wiped the tears off her face.

"Who are you, Esther?" he asked.

"I do not know anymore. I came here to find answers for the questions that stole my whole childhood, but now I am even more confused than before," she replied.

"Are you a sorcerer?" he asked.

"I am not," she replied, crying again.

"Okay, I am sorry. Calm down! Just tell me, what was it that I saw tonight? Who was that woman? Why was she shining?" he asked.

"Believe me, I do not have an answer to your questions. I do not know who she is."

"But you know why you are here. Tell me the truth, Esther! Why did you come to Kalastra? What is it that you are looking for here?" he asked.

"Myself. I am looking for myself, my past. I no longer know who I am. I have seen that woman in my dreams for as long as I can remember, and she haunts me every time. I just want it to stop. She keeps asking me to forgive her. The first time she appeared to me like this, I was in Aseeta. I did not know where to go, but I knew I had to leave. I had to find answers to my questions," she replied.

"Why Kalastra? Why do you think your answers are here?" he asked.

"When I left, I did not know where I was going. I just wanted to leave Aseeta, but the things that happened during my journey led me here," she said.

"What kind of things?" he asked.

"I am tired, Egenar. Can we continue tomorrow?" she said.

He let out a slow, reluctant breath and placed his hand over hers.

"Of course. Try not to think of anything. Just close your eyes and sleep."

Esther did not even reply. Staring at the fire, she thought about what that woman meant by saying she had killed her. By that point, she was sure there was a connection between her, Aphra, and that woman. Maybe there were still things she did not know, the things that had happened in her past that she did not remember, and perhaps Queen Aphra was not killed that day and had given birth to her child later. Maybe Esther's ancestors were originally from Kalastra and had migrated to Aseeta centuries ago. That could be a reason she felt a connection with Queen Aphra, but if she was her ancestor, and her parents knew everything all along, why had they never told her anything?

It was a long night for both Esther and Egenar, but it was finally morning. The first rays of the sun fell on Esther's face and woke her up, yet she had barely slept. It was a cold morning, and Esther was shivering. Egenar was already up and ready, waiting for her. She was hiding something from him, and he was determined to find it out.

"We should find better clothes for you. It will only get colder from now on," he said.

"How much farther do we have to the city?" she asked.

"Two days at most," he replied.

"We should not waste any time then. I am ready," she said.

"Do you feel better?" he asked.

"I am fine. Sorry for disturbing you last night. Soon, we will part ways, and you do not need to deal with me anymore," she said, jumping on her horse.

They rode in the forest together for hours. She was silent; he did not talk either. There was just the sound of wind whistling and dry leaves crushing under their horseshoes. The forest was still enchanting, but Esther was not paying much attention to anything. Something had changed inside her since the day she had left her village, and with each passing day, she felt the burden more and more on her shoulders, like she had aged a million years in just a month. She was no longer the same girl. The dreams she kept having, the manifestation of her dreams into reality, the old man who had given her the book of knowledge, and the chief of the village who had told her she was the promised queen—all indicated she was on the right path. How could all that have no meaning and be coincidental? She kept reviewing everything that had happened the night before over and over, but she could not put the pieces of the puzzle together. What was it about Kalastra that felt so familiar? Why couldn't she remember anything? Finally, after hours of riding in the silence, Egenar said, "Not that way, Esther!"

Esther looked back and saw that the road was divided into two parts, and she was going in the opposite direction of Egenar. "I did not realize I was riding ahead of you. Where does this road lead to?" she asked.

"Both roads lead to Kalastra, but we do not go that way," he replied.

"Why?" she asked.

"No one goes to that part of the forest. It is cursed," he said.

"What happened there?" she asked.

"So many things happened there, but they were all centuries ago. That is the road they used to take Queen Aphra to Sinkaba, and that part of the forest is where Queen Aphra met King Larko," he said.

"Have you ever been there?" she asked.

"No, people who have been to that part of the forest say they hear voices there, and some have even gone crazy after spending a night there," he said.

"What kinds of voices do they hear?" she asked with curiosity.

"Whispers. No one could say for sure what they were," he said.

"I would like to go there, Egenar, and you cannot stop me," she said.

"Are you deaf? Did you not hear what I just told you?" he asked, his voice rising like a whip crack.

"I did, but I have to go there. Do not worry. I can look after myself. We should say goodbye here," she said.

"What is it that is more important than your life? I know you are hiding something from me, and it is all because of what happened last night. What is it that you are after in Kalastra?"

She shouted, "I am not after anything, and I have no secret. I am just curious. I want to hear the voices for myself."

"In that case, I am curious too. I will join you if you do not mind," he said.

"Why do you not leave me alone? What is it that you want?" she asked.

"The truth, and I will find out what you are hiding from me," he said, then kicked at his horse. "I believe I should lead the way now."

"Fine, I do not care. You can come if you want because I am not hiding anything."

"Very well. Follow me then," he said.

Esther did not care to hide anything from Egenar. The only reason she was not telling him everything was because she was sure he would not believe her. How could she convince him that she was not crazy? How could she tell him that she was the promised queen and that she was supposed to unite North and South while she did not even believe it herself? How could she answer his questions when so many things were still unknown to her? She had to find herself first, and something deep inside her told her she was close to the truth she was looking for in Kalastra. The forbidden part of the forest was the key to everything, and she could not get any closer to Aphra and Larko than in that part of the forest.

CHAPTER TWENTY-ONE

"THEY PROBABLY KNOW by now that His Majesty has escaped and is alive. We should be very cautious," Elliot said.

"We are not near the city, and no one shall find us here," Leo, one of the knights, said.

"You should eat something, Your Majesty. I know it is hard, but please try. You need to gain your strength back," Marcus, another knight, said.

"I know I should, but I cannot. The only thing that keeps me alive now is my desire to take revenge. I do not need food to keep me on my feet," Larko replied.

"We should think of a plan now and act fast before they have time to prepare," Leo said.

"That is right, Your Majesty. They must be scared now that they know you are not dead," Elliot said.

"They probably think we will come back with our army, and they are preparing for war as we speak, and that is to our advantage," Larko said.

"How can that be to our advantage, Your Majesty?" Elliot asked.

"They do not know about you. They think it was just Lord Resko who came to Sinkaba with me, and I am certain he has not said anything, even under the worst torture. Now that they know I have escaped and I am alive, the most logical thing to do is leave and come back with an army, but that is not what we will do. We will surprise them, and we must go back into the palace again. They will not be expecting us tonight," Larko said.

"Seems doable, but there are still many guards we need to pass to enter the palace," Elliot said.

"Yes, there are still guards, but chances are they will be half asleep if we enter the palace at midnight, and we should be very quiet. Once we enter the palace, we will divide into three groups. Elliot and Marcus, you will come with me to Lamia's chamber! Leo and John will have to find Jabeer's chamber and kill him, and the rest of you must go to the dungeon and free Lord Resko! I am certain he is still alive. Remember, we cannot make any mistakes! Tonight is the only chance we have," Larko said.

"Do not worry, Your Majesty. They will pay for what they did to Her Majesty. We will slay them all," Marcus said.

"I thank you all for being by my side, and I want you to know that I would give my life gladly for any of you, for you are not just my knights, you are my loyal friends, and I am sorry for accusing you of collaborating with that traitor Jasper," Larko said.

"It is we who should apologize, Your Majesty. We spent all day every day with him and never suspected a thing. We should have realized his ill desires for Her Majesty before anything happened. We deserve to die for our negligence," Elliot said.

"Nobody is going to die anymore and certainly not before we take our vengeance," Larko said.

"Then we should rest for now, so we are all fresh in a few hours," Marcus said.

When Larko and his knights got ready to move, it was completely dark, and the weather had cooled slightly, but Larko could still feel the heat in the breeze. He looked at his knights. They were all good men who were loyal to him and his father. He did not want any of them to die, but he knew they would never leave him alone, even if he commanded them. They would either all die that night or go back to Kalastra with the heads of Lamia and Jabeer in their hands. Larko grabbed a handful of sand and looked at them. Lamia, Jabeer, and the desert were all murderers to him. He hated that barren land, and he hated everything and everyone who lived there. If he could, he would wipe out Sinkaba from the face of the planet, but first, he had to kill the mother beast. He had thought so many times about how to kill Lamia in the past few days. He wanted her to suffer just as Aphra had suffered, but nothing was satisfying to him. He was gradually losing his mind. Larko could not even sleep because, as soon as he closed his eyes, he saw Aphra. He saw her choking and struggling to breathe. He saw her suffocating with her mouth open and full of sand. He saw a teardrop in the corner of her begging eyes. No, he could not sleep. His nightmares were real. He blamed himself for everything that had happened to her. He wanted to shout hard every time he thought about what she had endured, and if he could go back in time, he would listen to her that night, and he would not leave her alone. His father and Aphra had both warned him about Lamia, and they were both dead. He was all alone, and the only thing that kept him on his feet was his desire to kill Lamia.

It was past midnight, and everyone was sleeping except seven men who had nothing in their minds except revenge. The first step was passing the city gates, but as Larko had predicted, the guards were not a problem. They easily knocked down the two guards by the city gate, and after walking a short distance, they arrived at the palace. It was completely dark, no light on around the palace. The west entrance seemed to be a better choice to enter since it had fewer guards, and Larko and his knights could kill them without making any noise. They had to divide into three groups as soon as they entered the palace, and they had to do everything in absolute silence.

Inside the palace, everything seemed normal. Larko could hear occasional footsteps of guards passing through the hallways while some of them snored loudly. Last time, when Larko and Lord Resko had entered the palace, it was oddly quiet, and nothing could be heard, not even the sound of mice running around, and everything screamed that they were stepping into a trap, yet they continued. However, this time, things were different; Lamia was not expecting them.

"This is where we part ways. We shall meet each other in an hour outside the city gates. Do not come back without Lord Resko!" Larko said.

"We will, Your Majesty. We won't return without him," Leo said.

Larko and two of his knights headed to Lamia's chamber, and as he expected, only two men were guarding the door. They had to kill them quietly without drawing any attention or waking Lamia up. Two poison darts to the throat silenced them for good. Larko opened the door gently, and all three of them crawled into the chamber. He took out his sword and got closer to Lamia's bed. *Just a few more steps and everything will be over*, Larko thought. The thought of finding her bed empty or seeing all her soldiers hiding in the room did not leave him alone, but he was sure they were not expecting him that night. As he got closer, he saw a strand of hair hanging from the bed, but he could not see her face, as she had covered it with a blanket. Larko could not wait any longer. He grabbed the blanket and removed it from her face, but it was not Lamia sleeping in the bed, to his surprise. Aesha was sleeping in her queen's bed, pretending to be her. Larko was furious. He raised his sword and said, "Tell me where she is, or I will kill you!"

"I am not afraid of dying, Larko, but there is no need for aggression. I will tell you where Her Majesty is. She is waiting for you," she replied.

"Where is she? What is this game?" he asked.

"This is no game. When she realized you escaped, she knew you would come back for her, and she wanted to see you alone without your knights," she said.

"It is a trap, Your Majesty. She is playing another game," Elliot said.

"I am not lying, Larko. She is alone, and her only wish is to see you," she said.

"Fine! I will see her alone. Tell me where she is!" he said.

"She is waiting for you by the Akra Sea," she said.

Larko sheathed his sword and, stepping away from the bed, said, "I will not kill you tonight, but your time will come soon."

"You started the war, Larko, and we did what we had to do," she replied.

"I started no war. I chose the love of my life. Aphra was innocent, and your crazy queen killed her without mercy," he said.

"Maybe she is crazy, as you say, maybe she is not, but it was all because of you. You never realized how important you were in her life. Your love changed her years ago when she first met you in Kalastra, and when you took it from her, she was devastated," she said.

Larko's eyes hardened, a muscle ticking in his jaw.

"I never gave her any hope."

"You never disappointed her either," she said.

Larko had nothing in mind except killing Lamia, and he would even go to the end of the world if he had to. No one had realized their presence in the palace, and they left with no problem. They were supposed to see the rest of the knights outside the city gates in an hour, but when Larko, Elliot, and Marcus got back, there was no sign of the others. After a short wait, John and Leo came back too. Leo had Jabeer's head in his hand, but three more men were still missing, including Lord Resko. Someone could see the dead guards by Lamia's chamber at any minute, and the whole thing could be over. It was almost dawn, and the people in the palace were about to wake up. Sinkaba had already taken his love from him, and he was not going to let any other Kalastrians die in the hands of Sinkabans.

"They are coming, Your Majesty. I can see them," Marcus said.

Larko saw his men approaching them. The two of them were holding Lord Resko, who was severely injured. He could barely stand on his feet, let alone walk. Larko could not believe what they had done to him in just a few days. Nothing was left of the man he knew; he was invisible. His face was all bruised, and they had broken his hands. There were scars all over his body, and they had cut out his tongue. Larko wanted to burn the whole palace down, but he knew it was not the right time. First, he had to kill Lamia and then come back with his army. He had already killed her most trusted adviser, and the rest would be easy.

"You have nothing else to do in Sinkaba, and you can all head back to Kalastra, but I have to go to the Akra Sea. Lamia was not in her chamber. She is still alive, and she wants to see me alone," Larko said.

"Please reconsider, Your Majesty. It is dangerous to go alone," Elliot said.

"She is alone. I am certain of it. I have to do this myself," Larko replied.

"Then let us wait for you here. We came together, and we will go back together. We will not leave you to ride alone to Kalastra," Marcus said.

"Marcus is right, Your Majesty. We will go back together," Leo said.

"Fine, if that is what you want, but take care of Lord Resko! I will be back soon, and when I am, we will all leave this nasty place," Larko said.

Larko got on his horse and rode the whole day. The Akra Sea was a day's ride away from Sinkaba. It was all desert and only sand until, miraculously, a barren land met a wavy blue sea. When Larko reached the sea, the sun was almost going down. The reflection of the red sun going into the water was the most beautiful thing Larko had ever seen. He imagined Aphra for a second, holding his hand and watching the sunset with him, but his daydreaming was soon interrupted by Lamia.

"It is an epic sunset, the love affair of the desert, the sea, and the sun," Lamia said as she approached Larko.

"The sea and the sun are the two in love; the desert is the intruder," Larko replied.

"I always loved you. I loved you before Aphra, and I will always love you, yet you forgot all the beautiful memories we made together when I first saw you in Kalastra," she said.

"You do not know what being in love feels like, and I pity you even more than before, but you cannot use your love to justify your sins," he said.

"If I wanted to do so, I would not have called you here. I am ready, and I am not scared. I want your face to be the last thing I see in this world," she replied, stepping so close that their shadows merged.

"If you really love me, tell me where you buried Aphra. Let me take her bones with me to Kalastra and give her a proper burial like a queen," he said.

"That is the point, Larko. She was never a queen," she replied.

"A queen is remembered forever, even after her death. The people of Kalastra will not forget Aphra, but after I kill you here, I will wipe down your kingdom, and the people of Sinkaba will not remember you ever existed," he said.

But Lamia only smiled through the trembling light of the sunset, her eyes soft, even triumphant, as she lifted her face to his.

"But you will. No matter what, you will always remember me, and I do not care how, as long as you think of me, and that is enough for me," she said.

Larko took out his dagger and looked into her eyes long enough to see her pain and love, but nothing was going to stop him from taking her life. He touched her shoulders and stabbed her heart with the dagger as she smiled at him. She collapsed on the sand and died with her eyes open. The dagger was bloody, and so were Larko's hands, but he felt no guilt. Larko had thought about killing Lamia so many times, and he wanted her to suffer and feel the same pain Aphra had felt, but in the end, he could not do it. He pitied Lamia as much as he hated her, and killing her peacefully in his arms as she wanted was the only favor he could do to her. Lamia was finally dead, and no amount of blood spilled could bring Aphra back, but he did it to quiet the voices in his mind. He sat there by the beach, with Lamia's body by his side, and wept for hours. The gorgeous colors of sunset had disappeared, and it was all black suddenly. The waves were crashing onto the shore, and with each tide, Lamia's body was getting closer to the sea, until it finally took her. Larko was mesmerized by the sea, and the thought of leaving himself to the waves was so tempting that he could not get it out of his mind.

All he wanted was to be with Aphra again, even if he had to pay with his life, but he was not done with Sinkaba yet. His knights were waiting for him, and he had to go back to Kalastra to defeat Lord Henry and save his kingdom. Only then could he prepare his army to attack Sinkaba, and he was confident Sinkaba had no chance of surviving. He had killed the mother beast and her adviser; the rest would be easy. Sinkaba's army was not even comparable to Kalastra's, and he could easily destroy them in their time of despair. He thought about leaving at once but soon changed his mind. He was exhausted, and he had not slept even for a second in the past few days. The sand was devouring him, and he could barely move his legs. He placed his tired body on the sand and closed his eyes. Larko was all alone by the sea, and the sound of the waves was a lullaby for him, putting him to sleep and making him forget about everything.

When Larko opened his eyes, the sun was in the middle of the sky. He hated the harsh heat of the South, and all he wanted was to leave the desert behind. He rode back to Sinkaba, but when he got to his knights, he realized that Lord Resko had died in the night. Larko was devastated and furious. Sinkaba had taken away so many dear souls from him, and he was tired of being defeated. The sooner he could get to Kalastra, the faster he could gather his army and attack Sinkaba, but on the other hand, the thought of passing the city gates and facing his people empty-handed, without Aphra, shook him to the bones.

Larko and his knights buried Lord Resko in the desert, as it was not possible to carry his body to Kalastra, considering the sun's extreme heat. He hated Sinkaba, and he tried to ride as fast as he could, but the route was long and dreary, and each day was lingering as if it was going to last for eternity. Kalastra was just like Sinkaba for Larko. Nothing was beautiful anymore, and the forest was not the same without Aphra. The sun was not warm, and the chirping of the birds was not pleasant anymore. The land that was once the birthplace of his love for Aphra was now a torment for him. He had killed Lamia, and he was going to tear down her palace, but he could not feel the peace inside him yet. He was ashamed of entering his city and facing his people. He had failed to keep their queen safe, so he had to ride alone into the city.

"We have passed Mount Zaka, and we might see Lord Henry's men anywhere," Larko said.

"I still do not believe that he can defeat our army and enter the citadel," Elliot said.

"We need to be cautious, and we need to know what is going on in the city first," Larko said, then looked at Hadrian and Marcus. "You two need to ride to the city and figure out the situation. We will wait for you here, and if the castle is taken, we need to come up with a plan."

"Yes, Your Majesty. We will ride as fast as we can," Hadrian said.

Hadrian and Marcus were riding at full speed, and when they got close to the city gates, they could not believe what they were seeing. The gates were open, the Dejovian flags were torn down but still up in the air, and the sound of wailing and screaming could be heard anywhere. The city was in turmoil, but despite the horrible situation, they could not spot any rioters. They covered their faces and their cloaks so they could not be recognized and started walking in the city. Hadrian stopped an old man who was dragging his feet on the stone cobbles and asked, "What has happened here? What is going on in the city?"

"Who are you? How come you do not know anything?" the old man replied.

"My friend and I were deep in the forest for a few weeks, and we just got back," Hadrian replied.

"Lord Henry and his men attacked us, but they were not alone. They had soldiers of Sinkaba with them. They killed ruthlessly and burned down all the houses. Our knights fought back and did not let them capture the castle for days, but suddenly, yesterday all the soldiers from Sinkaba left. Lord Henry's army was down to half, and he retreated. No one knows what happened and why they left," the old man said.

"They must have heard about their queen's death," Marcus whispered.

Hadrian and Marcus were relieved to know that Lord Henry had not succeeded in capturing the city, but the people's situation was pitiful. Some of the houses were still burning, and the smell of smoke could be felt everywhere. There were dead bodies in the alleys, and women were screaming nonstop. They wanted to go to the castle and help their fellow knights, but it was more important to go back to their king and let him know that Lord Henry had fled, so they headed back and got to Larko and the rest of the knights the next day.

Larko and his knights were waiting in the meadow by Mount Zaka when they saw Hadrian and Marcus galloping toward them. When they both got to Larko, they got off their horses and knelt; then Hadrian said, "We have both good and bad news."

"I am ready for everything," Larko said.

"Lord Henry attacked in our absence, and he had Sinkaban soldiers helping him. They burned down the city and killed many people, but our fellow knights fought back and did not let them capture the castle. It seems like all the Sinkaban soldiers left yesterday after knowing their queen was dead, and so Lord Henry retreated with his army shrinking to half," Hadrian said.

"How was the city?" Larko asked.

"Disastrous! There are bodies everywhere, and the city is burned down," Marcus replied.

"We need to hurry and get to the city. My people need me," Larko said.

Larko was furious. If there was one more person that he needed to kill with his own hands, it was Lord Henry. He had betrayed his king, turned his back on his country, and allied with the enemy to take the throne. He had no sympathy or respect for his people, and he deserved to die.

Larko was finally back in Kalastra, but nothing was the same as before. The gates of the city were open, and men and women had all gathered to welcome them. They were staring at him, but he didn't dare look back. His people did not blame him, and they were just as miserable as him. The ride finally finished, and he arrived at the front steps of the castle. He got off his horse and stood there for a minute, remembering the last time he had seen Aphra; it was at this same spot. She'd been looking at him from behind the window, and he was so full of pride, thinking he was going to destroy all his enemies, and everyone would remember him as the greatest king of Kalastra. Now he was standing before the same steps, hopeless and desperate, dragging his feet up the stairs. The castle was empty and spiritless without Aphra. It was happy and alive with her, but it was nothing more than a dark dungeon without her. The knights and the people in the castle were happy to see their king alive, but they were all mourning their queen's death at the same time.

Larko headed to their chamber and opened the door. Unlike

everywhere else in the castle, he could still feel Aphra's presence there. Her scent was in the room. Larko sat on the floor and started weeping. He knew nothing was going to bring her back, but there was still one thing he had to do. He wanted to erase Sinkaba from the face of the earth. Everyone had to forget about Lamia, and he intended to do everything in his power to make that happen. Larko gave himself one night to mourn alone in their chamber, for tomorrow was a new day for him. He had to be strong so his knights would follow him to Sinkaba for revenge. He gathered all his knights in the morning, stood before them, and said, "Great knights of Kalastra! You have always been by my side, and my father before me. I thank each one of you for your loyalty and bravery. There is a reason Kalastra is the greatest kingdom in the world, and people from everywhere on this planet wish to live here. And you, my brave knights, are one of the main reasons. This kingdom is safe because of you, and Sinkaba had no chance of harming us if it were not for the battles of northern borders and our absence in the city. They infiltrated us, they lied to us, and they took our queen. She was not only the love of my life but the very face of purity and innocence in this world. I killed Queen Lamia with my own hands. I took her filthy heart out of her body, but I swear to you all, it is not over yet, and it will not be over until I eradicate Sinkaba from this world. Is there anyone among you who will join me to avenge our Queen Aphra?"

Then the knights all shouted, "Yes, Your Majesty."

Soon after, one of the knights who had served King Alger as well stepped forward and said, "We will all join you, Your Majesty, and we will not stop until we avenge Queen Aphra's death. We will destroy Sinkaba so no one even remembers there was once a kingdom there."

Then all the knights unanimously shouted, "Long live the king! Long live the king!"

Kalastra had a huge army and the best warriors in the world.

All the men and women in Kalastra were angry and vengeful, and there was no power to stop them from destroying Sinkaba. When Larko and his army arrived at Sinkaba, the city was in chaos. With Queen Lamia and her adviser dead, the palace was in absolute turmoil. Those with power who had a sword in their hands robbed the palace's jewels as much as they could, and one of the generals had even declared himself the next king of Sinkaba, but his enemies killed him shortly after taking the throne. Thieves and anarchists were robbing people and burning down their homes, and no one was safe in Sinkaba. Larko and his army were just a few miles away from the city gates, and he could see everything that was going on in the city. They were so busy stealing and killing each other that they did not even realize Kalastra's army was approaching them.

"Look at how pathetic they are! They have no mercy even for their kind," Larko said.

"It is the law that keeps the people civilized, Your Majesty; otherwise, anyone is capable of doing anything, I believe," Leo replied.

"Do you think these people deserve to live?" Larko asked.

"There are a lot of innocent people living in Sinkaba, Your Majesty. Killing them all would be a slaughter, and we are better than that," Leo replied.

"No one in Sinkaba can be innocent. These people and this land should pay for what they did to my Aphra," Larko said.

"I understand your pain, Your Majesty, and we are all here to avenge our queen, but to kill those who had no hand in that evildoing is not honorable," Leo said.

"Do you defy me, Leo?" Larko asked.

"I do not wish to, but what you ask of me now is not right, Your Majesty. This was not what we agreed upon in Kalastra," Leo said.

Larko looked at his army and shouted, "We are here to destroy the Sinkaba palace and to cut the throat of any Sinkaban who lives in this cursed land. It does not matter whether they live in the palace or the city. Show no mercy, as they did not show mercy to your queen. Anyone who disagrees with me and defies me shall bear the consequences once we get to Kalastra. This is an order!"

Few knights in Larko's army had the same opinion as Leo, but they did not dare to disagree with Larko. They remained silent, powerless to stop Larko or the other knights, but they decided not to participate in killing innocent people.

Before anyone in the city could realize it, Larko and his army arrived at the gates of Sinkaba, and they started killing people, paving their way to the palace. The smell of blood and fumes from the burning houses had filled the air in the whole city. Women and children were screaming, and everyone was looking for a refuge. Larko and his army were killing people and did not listen to their cries and pleas. The real battle started when the army reached the palace, but even the soldiers of Sinkaba did not have a chance against the knights of Kalastra. They burned down the palace and anyone who was inside. The smell of human flesh burning in the flames made Larko go crazy and vicious, and there was no stopping him. Even most of Larko's knights had lost their minds. They killed without mercy, and no one knew if they killed to avenge Queen Aphra or solely for the pleasure of spilling blood. The smoke from the palace and the burning houses in the city had turned the sky from turquoise-blue into pitch-black. The scorching sun and the heat of the flames were enough to kill anyone in the city, if Larko's knights had not already slaughtered them. It was a horrific scene. Larko and his knights were butchering people, and the constant sound of screaming and screeching was not going to stop.

Amid everything and exactly when Larko assumed he was in complete power, suddenly, there was a humongous, loud noise coming from the depths of the ground. It was so loud that it made everyone stop what they were doing, and for a few seconds, there was no sound to be heard except the loud rumbling coming from deep inside the ground. No one knew what was happening. The sound got louder and louder every second. People were all scared to death, and they started screaming again, running to find shelter. After a few seconds, the rumbling stopped, and a gigantic sandstorm in the form of a woman started to shape in front of everyone's eyes. Larko and his men had never experienced anything like that before, and they did not know what to do, and the people of Sinkaba had never seen a sandstorm with that magnitude and velocity either.

Horses neighed wildly and bolted in terror. Even the lizards and scorpions were crawling quickly to find a hiding place. There was nothing to be seen except sand in a matter of seconds, and a thick wall of brown air was approaching the city at full speed. Before anyone could run or find shelter, there was sand everywhere, piling up and burying everything and everyone in its way. All Larko could do was close his eyes and cover his face, but even then, he could feel the grains of sand penetrating the pores of his skin. Very soon, there was no screaming anymore, and all Larko could hear was the hissing sound of grains. He didn't dare move or open his eyes, so he just waited until it was all over. When he finally opened his eyes, what he saw was horrifying. There was almost nothing left of the city he had entered a few hours ago. There were small dunes everywhere as far as he could see, and people were all buried under the sand. The sand had completely covered Larko. There was sand in his hair, his eyelids, and even his mouth. He could breathe the sand everywhere, but luckily for him, he was not buried alive like the others. He started looking around for his men, for he could not believe that he was the only survivor of the sandstorm. All the burning houses were put off and buried under the sand, and even the palace was no longer burning. The sandstorm was over, but the sky was still dull and gloomy. After a few minutes, he started hearing voices, which gave him hope there were others alive like him.

The sandstorm had destroyed everything, and the city of Sinkaba was completely buried under the sand. Larko's army had slaughtered many people, and many more died in the sandstorm. Only a small group of people survived the catastrophe: a few Sinkabans, Cato, Larko, and a few knights who had not killed the innocent people. The few people of Sinkaba who had survived the sandstorm begged Larko to have mercy on them and let them live, and after everything that had happened that day, Larko had no intention of killing them anymore, so he let them go.

Larko stood there, in the middle of the desert, desperate and hopeless. He had come to Sinkaba with five hundred men, but most had perished in the sandstorm. He wanted to persuade himself that nature had helped him take his revenge against Sinkaba, but he could not find an answer for his army's death. *If I was righteous and revenge was the right thing to do, why did I lose my men in the sandstorm alongside the Sinkabans, and if the mother of the forest is angry with me, why has she not taken my life?* Larko thought. Sinkaba was destroyed as he wanted, but nothing much was left of his kingdom either. He had lost his queen and, in pursuit of revenge, all his army. He had no hope for the future and nothing to live for. How could he even go back to Kalastra? What was he supposed to tell his people? He was a failed king who could not keep his queen and his knights safe. He looked at the remainder of his army, and there were only nine men left, all angry, scared, and devastated. He had no other choice but to go back to Kalastra, even if no one in the castle wanted him back.

"Are any of you hurt?" Larko asked his men.

"No, Your Majesty. We are not," Marcus replied.

"This place is cursed. We never should've come here, and now it is too late, and we have lost so many good men," Larko said.

"It is over, Your Majesty. We cannot undo the past, but we can finally say it is over. There will be no more revenge, since Sinkaba is destroyed, as you wanted," Marcus said.

"Yes, it is destroyed, but I do not feel any joy. I have lost all my army and so many brave knights. How can I go back to Kalastra and tell their families that I lost them too on top of everything else?

The damn sandstorm defeated me. I see no victory and no reason to celebrate."

"We have triumphed, Your Majesty, but it feels bitter," he said.

Larko's heart was filled with sorrow and remorse. He headed back to Kalastra with the remainder of his knights, but each day, as they got closer to Kalastra, his heart felt heavier. He heard the screams of people begging for mercy in his nightmares each night. He even saw Aphra in his dreams. She was in the forest, standing by the lake next to the tree that they had spent the night together near once. She was not facing him. She was touching the tree with her soft, slender hands, and he was so close to her that he could touch her soft, silky hair, but as soon as he wanted to touch her, she turned back and looked at him with ice-cold eyes and said, "You did wrong, Larko. You took lives that were not yours to take. You will have to pay for your crimes. The universe will make you pay."

The nightmares and the innocent begging looks of children in his dreams were one thing, but seeing Aphra angry and upset with him was another thing. Larko was sure Aphra would never forgive him. He had lost everything, even Aphra's love and affection. His people were scared of him, and he could see the fear in their eyes, fear of him, fear of a crazy king who was capable of doing anything.

Larko sat on his throne and wore his crown, but nothing made him feel kingly anymore. Days and months passed, and with each passing day, he became more delusional. The nightmares did not stop, and the court physician could not find a cure for him either. He could neither eat well nor sleep, and his youth was fading away. He had a faraway look in his eyes that was beyond anyone's reach, and no one could save him anymore, as his soul was already dead. The news of his mental affliction soon spread everywhere, and the lords and knights were worried that Lord Henry might see that as an opportunity to attack Kalastra again.

"We cannot live in constant fear of Lord Henry. We should have killed him a long time ago," Hadrian said.

"He does not dare to attack us again. He has lost most of his men, and he has lost his ally. He is no longer a threat," Elliot said.

"He is a threat as long as he is alive. I should have found him and slit his throat the day we got back to Kalastra," Larko said.

"We should attack first before he finds a chance to gather an army," Hadrian said.

"No more military attacks! We have lost so many good men in the past few months, and my country has no more bandwidth for another war," Larko said.

"Then what do you suggest, Your Majesty?" Hadrian said.

"We will raid his camp and kill him with the minimum number of casualties," Larko said.

"He is still in the northern border, and he has less than forty men loyal to him," Elliot said.

"Infiltrating his camp should be easy. We must finish him before he finds a chance to rise again," Larko said.

"You can leave that to us, Your Majesty. We will bring you his head," Hadrian said.

"Why? Do you also think I am crazy and not capable of protecting my country?" Larko asked.

"No, Your Majesty. That is not what I meant," Hadrian said.

"Then we will leave tomorrow. He shall die with no mercy," Larko said.

The next morning, Larko and a small group of his knights rode to the northern borders. It took them two days to get to Lord Henry's camp, but when they got there, they realized the number of men in his camp was even less than what they had assumed. He knew Lord Henry had few men who were very loyal to him and did not leave him under any circumstances, including his son, so he divided his knights into three groups and sent each group to a different tent, so they all raided at the same time. Larko wanted to enter Lord Henry's tent and kill him without attracting any attention, but things did not go exactly as he had planned. When Larko entered the tent, he realized the woman who was lying next to him was awake, and as soon she saw him, she screamed. Lord Henry grabbed his sword and said, "Who are you? How did you enter my tent?"

"I am Larko Dejovian, the king of Kalastra, and I will end your nasty life tonight."

"Do you call yourself noble, entering my tent in the middle of the night?" Lord Henry replied.

"How can a traitor like you talk about nobility? You killed your people and defied your king," Larko said.

"Your father was never my king, and neither are you," Lord Henry said.

"Stand up and fight like a man. At least die with dignity!" Larko said.

The whole camp was in chaos, and the sound of swords clanking could be heard everywhere. Lord Henry was an old man, but he was a great fighter despite his age. Soon they were fighting outside the tent, and Larko had several chances of killing him, but each time, Lord Henry defused his attack. It suddenly started raining heavily, and the loud thunderstorm scared the horses, and they bolted, which distracted Larko for a second, and before he realized it, Lord Henry hopped on one of the horses and started galloping. Larko could not let him flee; he got on his horse and followed him. He was not going to let him get away. Kalastra was in danger as long as he lived, and he had to die that night. Larko finally caught up to him, and the second his horse was right next to his, he jumped on it, punched him in the face, and pushed him down. They were both on the ground and covered in mud. Larko did not hesitate, and before Lord Henry could react, he stabbed him in the heart with his dagger.

"Go to hell! I hope you are never forgiven," Larko said.

Lord Henry finally died, and Larko felt relieved knowing that he would not be a threat to Kalastra anymore. He had commanded his knights to kill anyone who was not going to surrender, and he was certain they had everything under control. It was still raining, and the two horses had run away. He was not very far from the camp, so he decided to head back on foot. After walking for ten minutes, he heard voices in the bushes. He stopped, took out his sword, and started looking around, but it was pitch-dark, and he could not see a single thing. Suddenly, he was shot with an arrow in his leg. He fell to the ground and dropped his sword.

"Who are you? Show your face!" Larko said, but there was no answer, and after a few seconds, another arrow was shot, and it hit Larko in his back. He was bleeding, and he could barely stand. "Only a coward attacks from behind. Grab your sword and fight me!"

"Only a coward raids in the middle of the night and kills without mercy," a voice said from behind.

"I killed your leader, and your mates are either dead or captured. Surrender and I will have mercy on you!" Larko said.

"Lord Henry was the greatest general of Kalastra. Neither your father nor you are worthy of Kalastra's throne, and I will never surrender to you," the man said, coming closer and showing his face.

As hard as it was, Larko stood on his feet, raised his sword, and attacked the man, but he was too weak to fight properly. The man stabbed Larko in his chest and, pushing the sword further inside, said, "I, Caledon, the son of Lord Henry, kill you tonight, and I will take over your throne."

"You are just like your father, stupid and hungry for power, but you will never have my throne," Larko mumbled, and a few seconds later, his body collapsed on the ground. Larko died, and just like that, Kalastra lost its king, with no heir to the throne. The next morning, the sun rose, the birds sang, and the river rushed like the day before, but there was no King Larko anymore. Kalastra was an orphan, and everyone knew what that meant. Dark days were ahead for its people, days of fear, days of war, days of despair and drought.

Caledon attacked Kalastra after Larko's death, as everyone feared, and he killed all the knights and lords who did not agree to obey him, but his reign did not last long either. He was betrayed by his men and killed after a few months. Kalastra saw many kings and queens over the years. So many powerful people invaded the castle, one after the other, but none lasted for even a year. People believed Kalastra was cursed, and only Queen Aphra could save them all. People told the story of Queen Aphra's unjust murder and how she had cursed Sinkaba from one generation to another, and everyone believed that only the promised queen, Queen Aphra, could bring peace and prosperity and unite the North and South. The people of Kalastra never forgot their history and what happened in the past. Every man, woman, and child in Kalastra heard the legend of Queen Aphra, and they all believed she would come back one day.

However, things in Sinkaba were different. The city was destroyed, and only a small number of people had survived the sandstorm, and those who survived took whatever they had, left the city, and never looked back. They were ashamed of what Queen Lamia had done to Queen Aphra and feared what another king in Kalastra might do to them. They tried to build their lives somewhere else in the desert and told their children about the massive sandstorm that had happened years ago in Sinkaba, which destroyed everything and made them leave their homes, but they did not speak of Queen Lamia and what she had done to Queen Aphra. They said the sandstorm was in the shape of a beautiful woman, who was angry with Sinkaba, and that she had destroyed everything with her sand hands and blown away their homes. They called their new home Aseeta. Over the years, people started moving to different parts of the desert, and some closer to Mount Zaka, but none of them ever crossed the mountain to enter Kalastra.

CHAPTER TWENTY-TWO

THE DESERT WAS harsh and cruel. Tumbleweeds were moving around everywhere with the slightest gust of wind, and the torrid heat had forced every living creature to hide in their shelters until the scorching sun had set. There was not a single sign of life in the desert, and Jasper was all alone, except for the vultures that swirled in the sky around him, waiting to finish him off. Lamia's men had taken out his eyes, and the bleeding, along with the pain and guilt, had made him very weak. They had also tortured him as much as he could tolerate. There was no life left in him, and he barely stretched his wounded body on the sand. It was blazing hot, and the sunrays beat down on his nearly perished body. The sun and the sand both wanted to torture him, and he knew he did not deserve any mercy. The guilt and the remorse were more than he could take, and all he wanted was to end his suffering.

He'd known Aphra since they were children, like she was part of his soul and identity, and now that she was gone, all that was left in his heart was a big, deep hole. All he ever wanted in his life was to be loved by Aphra, but she never saw him as a lover, and that devastated him, and the hatred and jealousy blinded his eyes and made him do what he never thought he would do. Aphra was buried under the sand, and Jasper was to blame for her destiny. He had sent the only human he truly adored in his life to her death place, and it was too late to do anything. It was all his doing, and no one was to blame, not even Lamia, because he'd wanted to be deceived by her. He had liked to believe that Larko would die, and not Aphra, as his death was the only thing Jasper thought about ever since he realized he would marry her. He hated himself for believing Queen Lamia and helping her carry out her evil plan. She would have never had Aphra in her possession if not for his help, and he'd have handed her the most precious belonging he had in the world. Jasper longed to go back in time and watch Aphra again, walking in the garden, stroking the flowers with her tender fingers, laughing, and playing with her hair open in the air, even if she was not his, but it was a dream that could never come true.

He could no longer continue. The heat had burned his arms and body, since he had stretched himself on the hot sand for days, and his feet were not strong enough to hold his body's weight; he constantly staggered as he moved along. He lay down, with his face on the hot sand, and instantly imagined what Aphra had gone through when they buried her alive. Before they started digging a hole to bury her, Queen Lamia's men had taken him farther away, tortured him, and removed his eyes. Once they were done, they told him what they would do with Aphra and left him wounded and blind and barefoot, with no food and drink, to die in the desert alone. Jasper had no reason and no hope to live for, and he wanted to die. He had spent three days in the desert, and despite his pitiful situation, he was still breathing. He knew even death would be a blessing for him. As he was lying down on the sand, he remembered the old man he had seen in the Crystal Cave the night Larko had returned to Kalastra. He had warned Jasper and told him not to take part in Queen Lamia's plan, but he was so arrogant and angry that he had completely ignored him. All he'd wanted that night was for

Larko to die so he could have Aphra, but very late, he realized that even if Larko was dead, she would still not want him, and his death would not change anything. Jasper had to let go and forget her, but instead, he'd given in to his anger and pride, and it cost him the life of his beloved Aphra.

He allowed the desert to consume him. He wanted to die the same way Aphra had died. He could feel the scorching sand particles penetrating his cells and moving toward his heart. "Take me away from here! Take me to Aphra!" he whispered. Not long after he lay on the sand, he felt a presence and a shade over his face; then a voice said, "Dying is not that easy for you, Jasper." Jasper hardly moved his head, and then he stretched his hands toward the voice and asked, "Who are you?"

"We met before in a cave in Kalastra," Zelmata replied.

"Is it you again? Are you here to torture me?" Jasper asked.

"The mother of the forest has sent me to deliver a message," Zelmata said.

"Either take my life or leave me alone," Jasper said.

"Your life is not mine to take. I am only a messenger, and I am here to tell you that you will never die. The mother of the forest has punished you with an eternal life of misery and guilt. Do not fight your fate, for you cannot change it. The sand will not take you," Zelmata said.

"They will finally take me. I will not move until I die. Either the sun, the sand, or the vultures will take me," Jasper said.

"No power in this world can take your life until the mother of the forest decides it. Your punishment is to live for eternity," Zelmata said.

"You cannot do this to me. End this torture, please; I beg you," Jasper said, trying to sit on his knees, grabbing Zelmata's cloak.

"I warned you, Jasper. I told you if you helped her kill Aphra, you would be haunted for the rest of your life. Now there is nothing I can do for you," he said.

"Talk to the mother of the forest for me. Ask her to punish me differently," Jasper said.

"I do not set the rules, and neither do you," Zelmata said.

"Look at me! Look at my body! Look into my soul! I am already dead. I will lie down here under the sun until there is no life in me anymore. Nothing can stop me from killing myself," Jasper said.

"You are making the same mistake, Jasper. You must pay for what you did. You cannot escape Karma," Zelmata said.

"I do not want to escape it. I just cannot pay for it with eternal life. Her face is carved in my mind, and I see her everywhere, even when I close my eyes, and every time she looks at me with her innocent eyes, I want to stab my own heart until I bleed to death. I am ashamed of myself, and I do not have the guts to face her," Jasper said.

"Listen to me this time! Accept your fate and take your punishment, for maybe you will be forgiven in years," Zelmata said.

"How many years? How long should I wait?" Jasper asked.

"One hundred years, two hundred years, maybe more; only the mother of the forest knows," Zelmata said, then disappeared into a bright light.

Jasper shouted, "You cannot leave me alone. I cannot wait one hundred years." Then he raised his head toward the sky, shouting with all the strength he had in his body, "Kill me now! Do you hear me? You cannot make me live without her. Tear me into pieces, turn me into a beast, but do not torment me with her memories. I cannot last even a year, let alone a century. Take my life!" But there was no response. He wept, he yelled, he hit himself with all his power, but nothing was going to change for him.

Days and weeks passed without seeing a single soul in the desert, and he did not dare return to Kalastra either. He was terrified of seeing Larko and the knights and people of Kalastra. He was not afraid of dying, as he knew no one could kill him, but he could not tolerate seeing their condemning looks. Everyone in Kalastra knew how Queen Aphra had ended up in Sinkaba and what Jasper had done to make it happen. He was ashamed of facing them, so instead of going back to Kalastra, he traveled farther south, hoping to live among the remaining Sinkabans who had survived Larko's massacre and the sandstorm, because he was certain no one knew him there.

He managed to treat his wounds, and he learned how to find his way without needing his eyes. Being blind for the rest of his life was the smallest price he had to pay for the crimes he had committed. Jasper could put up with everything except the nightmares. He kept seeing Aphra, and he could not escape her innocent eyes. The guilt he felt was more than he could handle when he realized Larko had died and what happened to Kalastra after his death. He tried to kill himself many times, but he was unsuccessful with each attempt, so he finally gave up. Years passed, and he settled in the desert somewhere close to where the Sinkabans had decided to build their new lives. He had grown old, and people knew him as the crazy blind man who lived alone in the desert and constantly screamed at night. No one knew where he had come from or who he was. People had started making stories about him, and everyone pitied and feared him. He always saw Aphra in his dreams, and for years he could not even look into her eyes in the dreams, let alone talk to her, until Aphra finally broke the spell one night and talked to him. In his dream, she wore a lavender dress, and her hair was open in the air. They were both in the Crystal Cave, and something was soothing about seeing her in that dream, something he had not felt in years. They were both young, and her face was shining with happiness as she smiled at Jasper. She was calm and sweet, and Jasper felt at ease for the first time in a long time.

"It is finally time to talk, Jasper," Aphra said.

Jasper was always ashamed and scared of looking into Aphra's eyes, but something was inviting in Aphra's voice that gave him the courage to look at her and talk.

"I do not dare to say anything, Aphra. I know I deserve all the suffering in this world and the other world," Jasper replied.

"I am not here to blame you. I am here to help you, to end your suffering," she said.

Tears welled in Jasper's eyes, streaking through the dust and grime of three hundred hopeless years.

"I do not deserve your mercy. How can I want anything from you?"

"I have forgiven you, Jasper. You will be free soon. You paid for your sins, and now it is time to leave this world behind," she said.

"There are so many things I need to tell you. You need to know that I never wanted to harm you in any way. I loved you more than anything and anyone, but I was arrogant and stupid. I was full of hatred when you rejected me, and I hated Larko for stealing you from me. I was so naive, and I was too late to save you from Lamia. I would have died for you a thousand times if I could have, but I let you down, and I have been suffering ever since," he said.

"I know your heart, and I know how remorseful you are. You will not wake up from this dream, and I will take you to the other world with me. You paid for your sins with three hundred years of solitude and suffering. Leave all your burdens in this world and take my hand!" she said, stretching her arm toward him.

"My crimes are bigger than anyone can imagine. It was not just your life I destroyed; Larko ended up losing his mind for what I did, which caused Kalastra's destruction. How can I be forgiven when I cannot forgive myself?" he said.

"We have all made mistakes in our lives, Jasper, and only the mother of the forest can judge how horrible our mistakes were. However, what differentiates us from one another is our accountability for what we did in this world. Nothing is worse than arrogance and not realizing or accepting our sins. I assure you that your heart was purer than that of most people in this world. The punishment you received was just a drop of water compared to the ocean that those who believe they are saints will experience later.

The mother of the forest has a different way of judging our actions, which is beyond our comprehension," she said.

"I believe you, and I trust you with all my heart, Aphra, and I want you to know that there has been nothing I have wanted in this world more than being forgiven in the past three hundred years, but why now?" he said.

"Now is the time the mother of the forest has chosen to manifest her will. Soon after your death, a beautiful soul will be born, and she will be the legacy of both North and South. Now take my hand, as everyone you knew in Kalastra is waiting to welcome you in the other world," she said.

Jasper walked up to Aphra, and as he took her hands, all his burdens were lifted, and he felt protected by a divine presence. His soul was finally free from years of guilt and remorse, and he was ultimately forgiven. Free from any attachment to the world of the living, he closed his eyes and walked into a bright light.

CHAPTER TWENTY-THREE

THE WEATHER WAS getting colder each day, and Esther was not used to the cold. She had seen so many peculiar things in her journey up to that point. However, seeing the snow was by far the best of them. Living in the desert her whole life, she had seen snow only a few times. When the first snowflake drifted down from the sky and landed on her hand, she was so astonished that she did not know what to do. Then, she saw the second and the third snowflake in the air, and more after that. She looked up with childish excitement and opened her mouth, trying to swallow the snowflakes as they drifted down.

"That is snow, if you are wondering," Egenar said.

"I know what it is. I had seen it in Aseeta before. It is beautiful," Esther replied.

"If we cannot find you proper clothing, you will not survive in this weather. You are shivering," he said.

"I have always wondered whether the snow is more beautiful or the rain," she said.

"Are you even listening to what I am saying, Esther? You might freeze to death," he said.

"I am sure I will not. Do you think I have been led to this place and have gone through everything to freeze to death here? The goddess of sand will protect me," she said.

"I do not know what your goddess wants for you. All I know is that I am responsible for keeping you alive until you reach your destination," he said.

"Why do you think so? You barely even know me," she said.

"I simply think you need my help, and I want to accompany you on your journey."

"If you want to help me, then please tell me how snow is shaped," she said.

Egenar smiled and said, "Leave that to some other time. We have more important things to do. It feels like a snowstorm is on the way."

"How can you tell?" she asked.

"I just can. We must find shelter. This is not good. Follow me!" he said.

"Is there a cave around here?" she asked.

"I am not sure. We do not have much time to look around. The snow is falling hard, and before we know it, it will turn into a blizzard," he said.

"What should we look for then?" she asked.

"Anything. Anything big and secure that we can fit in," he replied.

Just like Egenar had predicted, the lovely snowflakes turned into a severe blizzard in just a few minutes, and Esther was shivering hard, just looking at the white coat of snow forming on the ground and trees. The sound of powdery snow crunching under her feet was both amusing and scary at the same time. With each breath, it was like a frigid thorn was entering her lungs, cutting her throat as it went down, and each exhale warmed up her fingers a little as she placed them on her lips. Soon, her clothes and Egenar's were completely buried under the snow, and there was no color to be seen except white. The wind was howling wildly, making it almost impossible to see what was happening two feet ahead of them. She felt the numbness in her fingers and toes, and it was becoming painful to walk. She felt the freezing cold in her very bones, and all she wanted was a refuge. Esther kept her head down to avoid the flog of wind in her face, but when she brought it up, she saw something in the distance that warmed up her heart. A cabin was there in the forest, entirely covered in snow, and Esther was unsure if she was delusional or if it actually existed there. Egenar was walking a few steps ahead of her to lead the way, and Esther wanted to stop him, but she could barely even talk.

"Cabin!" she faintly said, but Egenar did not hear her, so she gathered all her strength and repeated it. "There is a cabin there, Egenar." She pointed at it in the distance. Egenar looked back and saw the cabin too. They both could not believe what they were seeing. Someone had built a cabin deep in the forest. Despite feeling numb in their toes, Esther and Egenar increased their pace to reach the cabin sooner. The roof was all white, like it had been snowing for days rather than hours, and they could not see the steps under the tons of snow. They both walked up the steps, and then Egenar reached out for the door and knocked.

"Do you think anyone lives here?" Esther asked.

"It does not seem like it," he replied, then slowly opened the door. The door creaking open echoed in the forest like the sound of a skeleton rising from the grave; then, an eerie silence followed. Egenar took the first step and carefully made his way into the cabin while Esther was waiting on the porch. After a few seconds, he shouted, "There is no one here. Come in!"

The cabin was dark and cold but still better than being buried alive in the snowstorm.

"Someone is living here. There is everything in this cabin, and nothing is dusty," Egenar said.

"What if they come back?" she asked.

"We have no choice. This cabin is our only chance of survival," he replied.

"But it is still cold here," she said.

"I will go and gather firewood now. Stay here and be careful!" he said.

"What if someone attacks me?" she said.

"Calm down, Esther! Just use the blade I gave you and cut whoever comes close to you."

"Just like that?" she asked.

"There is no one here except us. You are just tired and agitated. I will be back soon, and when I am, we will make a fire, and you will feel much better. Trust me!" he said and went out the door before Esther could say anything. Maybe he was right. Egenar had lived his whole life in the forest, moving from one village to another. He was used to sleeping on the rocks and experiencing summer and winter in the wilderness, while Esther had only lived in her village until a while ago, and the furthest she had gone was to the ruins of the palace in the desert, where she could watch the stars peacefully.

After Egenar left, Esther started looking around. The cabin was very modest, minimalistic. There was just a bed, a few books, and some pottery. She started looking into the pots, hoping to find something to eat, but all she could find was a dried piece of bread. She had not eaten the entire day, but the bread smelled so repulsive that she lost her appetite. She had endured many hardships since the beginning of her journey, but she was a tough girl, and she knew things were not going to be easy for her. She felt very close to finding the answers to her questions, yet there was a veil she could not cut through. She reached out for her bag and took out the book of knowledge the old dwarf had given her. She did not even know why she had grabbed it. She started leafing through the book, looking at the blank pages, when, suddenly, something caught her eye. There it was again: The book was communicating with her. The words were appearing on the blank page, just like what had happened a few nights ago.

Find the lake and the tree, and you will find all your answers, the words in the book said. She did not move for a few seconds. It was all real, and there was no denying the book's power. It was magical, and the book had spoken to her once again. Her heart was beating fast, and she just stared at the words while a few drops of her tears dropped on the book. The old man had told her that whenever she was confused and needed guidance, the book would show her the way, and he was right. The goddess of sand had sent her a sign she could not deny. She no longer wanted to resist, so she decided to surrender. Maybe it was all true, the legend and whatever the chief had told her. There was a lake and a tree she had to find, and she felt she was very close to the truth. If only it had not started snowing, maybe she could get there even that day, but she had to wait a little longer. She sat on the bed and reviewed everything that had happened to her since the beginning of her journey. She did not understand why she was so stubborn and did not accept that she could be the promised queen. How were others supposed to believe in her if she did not believe in herself? Then she thought of Egenar. If he believed in her, there was a chance that others would believe in her too. *I will tell him everything if he asks me again*, she thought. Then, after a few seconds, she heard footsteps getting closer to the cabin, and before she could find her blade, Egenar opened the door.

"Do not worry. It is me," Egenar said, dropping the firewood on the floor.

"You must be freezing. Sit! I will make the fire," she said.

"It is fine, Esther. I am quicker than you," he said.

"Thank you, Egenar, for everything. I am certain I could not have survived the past few days without you," she said.

"Why are you so kind to me suddenly? You have barely even spoken to me all day, and now you are thanking me," he said.

A faint smile tugged at her lips, half playful, half defensive.

"I will take it back if you are unhappy."

He huffed a quiet laugh, the corners of his mouth softening in the firelight.

"I am not unhappy, but I will be much happier if you tell me the real reason you are here. I want you to tell me the truth."

"I might tell you," she said, then paused. "Soon, maybe."

"Well, that is a good start," he said, then grabbed the firewood and threw it inside the fireplace.

"There is nothing to eat except a dried piece of bread. You can have it if you want. I am not hungry," she said.

"All I want is to make this fire and sleep. You can sleep on the bed. I will be fine on the floor," he said.

"I can sleep on the floor too. I have been through worse," she said.

"I know, but when there is a bed, the lady should take it. Do not worry about me. I am not used to sleeping on a bed anyway. I have slept on the ground or stone most of my life. I am so tired that I will fall asleep any minute now," he said, then yawned.

"Fine! Good night then," she said.

"Good night, young lady," he said.

Esther took off her boots and crawled into the bed. The woods were burning fast, and the heat of the fire was so pleasant that she could not resist keeping her eyes open any longer. The sound of fire crackling had enchanted her. She was not sure if it was a dream or a vision, but as soon as she closed her eyes, everything that had happened to her throughout her journey was right before her eyes. It was probably the best sleep she'd had in weeks, and before she knew it, it was morning. The first thing she heard when she woke up was the wind howling through the cracks in the door, and she knew nothing had changed since last night. She opened her eyes and saw Egenar sitting by the fire.

"Good morning," she said.

"I am not sure it is going to be a good morning, young lady," he said.

"Why not?" she asked.

"The blizzard has not stopped, and I do not think it will stop anytime soon," he said.

Esther rose, her bare feet pressing into the cold floor. She tugged the blanket tighter.

"What shall we do then?"

"Nothing. We should stay in the cabin until the blizzard stops. There is no place safer than here," he said.

"What if it does not stop for days?" she asked.

"What is your suggestion? Do you want to go outside in this weather? If you do, you will not survive even half a day with those clothes you have. There is nothing we can do now. We can only hope the storm passes soon," he said.

Esther was anxious. She had learned about the lake and the tree the night before, and all she could think of was finding that place sooner. She thought she had even dreamed about it.

"Why do you look so worried?" he asked.

"I am not worried. I just want to leave this place as soon as I can," she replied.

"I assume the weather will be clear by the end of the night, and hopefully, we can leave tomorrow morning, but before then, we need to eat. I do not want to starve to death here."

"Are you going to hunt in this weather?" she asked with surprise.

"I will try to be quick. We must eat. We cannot wait for the storm to pass," he said.

"Please be careful and do not go too far," she said.

"Are you worried about me? I thought you wanted to get rid of me," he said with a smile.

"I still do, but I need to eat first, so get here in one piece, please, and with food," she replied with a smirk.

"Fine! I will have to bring firewood too. Make sure the fire is not dead!" he said.

"I can collect the firewood. I will not go too far, just around the cabin. I will be fine. I am not a child," she said.

"I do not think you are, but this weather is unknown to you, and that is what worries me; otherwise, I believe you are capable of doing almost anything. You just do not know it, but if you insist, I will leave the firewood to you," he said.

Egenar was right, perhaps. Esther had many capabilities she had yet to discover, and all she needed to do was believe in herself. She put on her boots and wrapped all the blankets in the cabin around herself, and she could still feel the cold in the depth of her bones, like they were going to break at any second. As soon as she opened the door, the howling wind hit her face hard, as if a hundred needles were injected into her face at the same time, and she knew she did not have to offer to collect the firewood. The blizzard was brutal, and she could not have even imagined in her wildest dreams how angry nature could become. *There is probably a reason for this crazy weather*, she thought, trying to persuade herself. She collected as much firewood as she could carry and brought it inside the cabin. The fire was almost dead, and Egenar was not back yet. She tossed two thick pieces of wood into the fire and took off her boots and all the wet blankets, placing them by the fire to dry. She had seen the excessive heat in the desert and the brutal snowstorm, but her favorite was the rain and thunderstorm when she was on Mount Zaka. She could watch the rain for hours without getting tired. The sound of the drops falling on the ground was the most soothing thing she had ever heard in her life. Even the thunderstorm was breathtaking, not scary. She closed her eyes and imagined herself in the forest by the lake, sitting by a huge tree; it was raining, and the drops of rain were dancing and falling peacefully into the lake, creating the most magical symphony in the world. *Egenar probably knows about the lake. I should ask him when he gets back*, she thought. When Egenar got back, he was shivering, completely covered in snow, and had a rabbit in his hand.

"Sorry I could not catch you anything better. I could barely even see my surroundings."

"It is perfect. Come and sit by the fire! You are freezing," she said, then grabbed the rabbit from him. "I will prepare the food. You should get some rest."

"I do not think the storm will last long. It is a little unusual for this time of the year."

"So, do you think we can leave tomorrow?" she asked.

"Hopefully. I am not certain," he replied.

"Do you know if there is a lake in the forest?" she asked.

"Yes, there is. Why do you ask?" he asked.

"I want to go to the lake tomorrow," she replied.

"Why do you want to go to the lake? Is this also a secret you cannot tell me?" he asked.

"There is no secret, Egenar. I will tell you everything if you are willing to listen, but you might not believe me," she said, looking into his eyes.

"I have seen many crazy things in this world, young lady. Try me! There is a chance I might believe you," he said.

Esther had already decided to tell him everything if he asked again, so she did not hesitate. She sat by the fire, next to Egenar, and told him everything. She told him about her dreams since she was a little girl, the reason for her journey, the old dwarf, the book of knowledge, seeing Queen Aphra and King Larko in her dreams, and what the chief of the village had told her. When she told him everything, she felt a sudden rush of blood through her veins. She was burning up, and she did not know whether it was because of the fire or the excitement of telling her story for the first time. Then she realized she believed in everything she had told Egenar, and for the first time, she felt at peace. Egenar waited for a minute, then asked, "Was the woman in your dreams the same woman you saw in the forest a few nights ago?"

"Yes, she was. She keeps asking for my forgiveness. She has been haunting me since I was a little girl, and I was always afraid of sleeping and seeing her in my dream," she said.

"I do not know whether you are the promised queen or not, but there is only one way to figure it out. We must go to the lake and find that tree. Your goddess of sand is sending you signs to guide you for a reason," he said.

"So, you do not think I am crazy, right? You believe me?" she asked.

"I think you believe in what you told me, and that is the only thing that matters now, and I know for sure you are not crazy," he said.

"Well, that is a relief," she said, then sighed.

"Do you think I can see the book?" he asked.

"Yes, of course," she said, then grabbed it and gave it to him. Egenar looked at the book, and he could tell by the cover that it was ancient. He started leafing through it, and as Esther had told him, it was all blank, and the pages were worn out and yellow.

"When do the words show up?" he asked.

"I assume whenever I need guidance. The book itself chooses when to speak to me. Both times, I felt I had to hold the book, like a magnetic power was drawing me to it," she said.

"Amazing! This book can be either a blessing or a curse. It will help you in your journey, but it can cause you endless distress as well. You must be careful not to tell anyone about this book. If this is as ancient as I think it is, and it does what you told me, many people would long to possess it, and if they realize you have it, your life would be in huge danger," he said.

"I know. The chief had already warned me. I will not tell anyone else about this book."

"I will help you however I can. We will find the lake together, and you will know who you are," he said.

"Why do you want to help me?" she asked.

"Who knows? Maybe I am part of your goddess's plan to assist you on your journey in life. Helping you might be the only valuable thing I have done so far in my life," he said.

"I think you are underestimating yourself. You are a good person, Egenar," she said.

"Right, I am, but this fine person is famished now, and I might turn into a vicious beast if I do not devour that rabbit soon," he said with a witty smile.

"I am sorry. You are right. I forgot about the rabbit. I do not talk much, but when I do, I lose track of time," she said.

The snowstorm stopped later in the day, and the sun came out. It was not strong enough to melt the snow, but it was good enough to let them leave the cabin. After two days of staying inside, they were both ready to be on the road again and find the lake. Esther felt much happier and relieved after telling everything to Egenar. According to him, the lake was just a day's ride away from the cabin.

"Are you scared of what you will find out at the lake?" Egenar asked.

"I am not scared, but I am excited, a little anxious, maybe," she replied.

"Queen Aphra is sacred for the people of Kalastra. They worship her here. You cannot simply tell everyone that you see her in your dreams and talk to her, let alone that you claim to be the promised queen. They will rebel against you; they might even try to kill you," he said.

"Is it because I am from the South?" she asked.

"They will not accept it easily anyway, but knowing you are from the South will make it even harder," he said.

"You are right, but I should find the lake first. I can worry about the rest later."

After riding for hours, Egenar told Esther to camp for the night. The lake was close, but it was getting dark, and it was dangerous to ride. It had not snowed for a day, but the forest was still covered with fluff. They made a fire to keep themselves warm and ate the rabbit they had brought with them from the cabin. It was a peaceful night. The wind was blowing lightly, and the owls were occasionally hooting. Egenar slept early, but Esther could not close her eyes. She did not even wink; she just stared at the burning fire, thinking about what she would find at the lake. She would know once and for all the reason for all her dreams, and she would know why Queen Aphra had chosen her.

Esther did not know when she finally fell asleep, but she felt completely energized in the morning. It was a warmer day, and the sun's heat on her back was pleasant. The snow was melting, and she could hear the birds chirping. She took a deep breath and filled her lungs with the fresh breeze of the forest. Somehow, everything was more beautiful that day, as if the universe were trying to tell her a miracle was about to happen. They rode for an hour or two, and before Esther realized it, she was standing in front of the lake, turquoise-blue, with crystal clear water. The water was so transparent that she could even see all the small fishes moving around. Esther could tell everything was different about that lake. Suddenly, the whole forest was silent, not even the flap of a bird wing, and she could hear her heartbeat. She knew something extraordinary was about to happen. She hopped off her horse and started walking around. With her eyes closed, she knew the tree she was looking for would find her. After a few seconds, she heard her name. It was not Egenar; the voice belonged to a woman. Her voice was celestial, so soft and soothing. Esther followed the voice with her eyes closed. The voice was getting louder as she moved forward; then it suddenly stopped. Her heart was about to explode. She opened her eyes and saw a huge pine tree in front of her. She raised her hands and placed them both on the tree, and as she did it, she felt everything change. She felt a sudden rush of blood to her heart, and she could not open her eyes, nor did she want to. Everything was happening so fast that she was not able to react to anything. She saw herself standing in front of a massive gate, and suddenly lightning and a thunderstorm caused the gate to open, and she entered. Esther had no control over herself, nor could she say if she was alive or dead. Her body was there, but her soul was traveling through time. She saw Queen Aphra again, only, this time, she felt different. She saw herself in Queen Aphra's body, and their souls were mingled. Her body was not hers, and her face was Queen Aphra's face. Then, all her memories started pouring down on her chest like a torrent. She remembered her mother, her father, and the house she lived in with her parents. She remembered Jasper and all the days she had spent with him. She remembered the day Larko saved her from rebellions in the forest. She remembered sleeping with him for the very first time, near the lake, under the same tree she was touching. She remembered walking down the aisle and marrying him. She remembered being crowned as the queen of Kalastra, and she remembered Queen Lamia killing her in the desert.

There was no Esther in the other world. There was only one, and that was Aphra. Esther was Aphra, born again after three hundred years. The mother of the forest and the goddess of sand had given her another life. She had once lived as Queen Aphra, and Lamia had killed her, and only then, in that moment, did she realize the meaning of all her dreams. The woman who begged for her forgiveness in her dreams was Queen Lamia. She was in limbo ever since Aphra had cursed her, and after Larko killed her, she needed Aphra's forgiveness to move on to the other world. Aphra had come back to life to fulfill her destiny as the queen of Kalastra once again, and she was born in Aseeta, which, three hundred years ago, was part of Sinkaba. She was born and brought to life again in the land that had been her grave. The prophecy was true: Queen Aphra had risen from death to unite North and South.

She saw flashes of her previous life in front of her eyes, everything from childhood to the minute they killed her. Her emotions were heightened, and she had no control over her feelings. When she saw her parents playing with her at their home, she felt an unspeakable joy, a feeling so intense, she had never experienced it in her life before. She could not believe how she had forgotten everyone and everything in her previous life, like a strong power had intentionally blocked her mind to forget everything about Aphra. She missed the loving touch of her mother and how she baked her favorite bread every single morning. She saw her father teaching her how to ride a horse, how safe she felt next to him. Then she saw flashes of Jasper. She had no rage toward him, and she was happy that she had forgiven him. She saw flashes of the first time she saw him, when they were both kids, how he looked at her with love and admiration even then. She saw flashes of the good days they had spent together, riding their horses in the forest and exploring the Crystal Cave.

Then she saw Larko, the lifelong love of her life. She felt a powerful, divine bond toward him that no power in the world could break. She wanted to embrace him and hold him tight and never let him leave her again. She missed him more than words could describe. She saw herself wearing a white gown, walking slowly down the aisle to hold Larko's hands, her heart racing. It was not just love she felt; she adored him, worshipped him. His love was the reason she was born, and what they felt for each other was as divine and ancient as the moon and stars, as the oceans, as the soil itself that had created humans. Then she saw flashes of the night she was taken to Sinkaba, the night she left Kalastra forever. She saw Queen Lamia and the rage she had to kill her. She saw her men pouring the hot sand on her body and burying her alive without feeling a twinge of guilt. She was suddenly full of rage and hatred, a rage that was hidden for three hundred years, and she started screaming as loud as she could. The memory was so alive in her mind that she felt like they were burying her again. Egenar watched her from a distance the whole time, to give her privacy, but as she screamed, he ran for her and tried to wake her up.

"Wake up, Esther! Open your eyes, please!" Egenar said.

Esther opened her eyes as she cried hard.

"What happened to you? Why are you crying? Are you hurt?" he asked.

Esther did not even know how to begin and what to say. She just sat there by the tree and cried for hours. Egenar knew he had to give her time, so he did not interrupt her. Whatever she had seen, it was too much for her to take. Once she had finally calmed down a little, she sat down in front of Egenar and said, "I do not even know where to begin."

"Say whatever comes to your mind first," he said.

"I once lived here," she said, then paused, wiped down her tears, and unraveled everything, and when she finished, Egenar's face was white as ice, like he had just seen a ghost.

"I know this is all too much to take in, and you probably think I am crazy, but I did not tell you a fairy tale. I told you the story of my previous life," she said.

"Are you Queen Aphra then?" he asked.

"Yes, I am," she replied; then Egenar knelt in front of her before she could stop him.

"What are you doing? You do not need to kneel," she said.

At once, Egenar lowered his head even further, his breath leaving him in a cloud.

"I must, Your Majesty. You are my queen, and from this moment on, I will be your forever loyal servant."

"Egenar, you do not need to talk like that. You can just call me Esther, like before," she said with a smile.

"I shall never say that again, Your Majesty. I do not understand how it is possible that you are born again, and I do not know how reincarnation works, but I believe in you, and I am certain whatever you told me is the absolute truth. I always thought the legend was just a bedtime story for children, but now I see how wrong I was," he said.

"Do you think others will also believe me?" she asked.

"Those who are waiting for you will see the truth in your words and will believe you, and those with a dark heart will deny you no matter what you say and what you do, Your Majesty, so you have nothing to worry about," he said.

"Thank you for keeping me company and for being honest

with me. If it was not for your help, I would not have found this lake," she said.

"It is my honor to serve you, Your Majesty," he said.

"It is magical how everything changed in just a second, as if my memory were locked for years, and touching the tree unlocked it," she said.

"What was so special about this tree, Your Majesty?" he asked.

Esther smiled and said, "Larko rarely spent his time outside of the castle, and one time I challenged him to sleep in the forest under the sky, and he accepted. This tree was where we spent the night together, and I remember it like it was yesterday."

"Then this tree must be very ancient, probably more than a thousand years old," he said.

"Probably! It must have seen so many things in its life, so many ups and downs, kings and queens, lives and deaths, love and hatred," she said.

"You have changed, Your Majesty. You are not the same person I knew yesterday."

"I no longer feel lost. The bewildering feeling I had since childhood is finally gone. I never felt at home in Aseeta, and now I know why. I know who I am and where I come from."

"What are you planning to do now, Your Majesty?" he asked.

"I have to go back to Sinkaba, where they buried me three hundred years ago, but before doing that, I would like to go into the city and see the castle one more time," she said.

"Are you going to tell everyone who you are?" he asked.

"No, it is not time yet, and you must promise me not to talk about what you saw here today with anyone. First, I must find where I was buried alive. There is still a piece of me that is missing. I need to find my grave so I can find peace. Will you come with me, Egenar?"

"I will. It is my pleasure to be by your side, Your Majesty," he replied.

"Very well. We will leave tomorrow morning. What I went

through today is enough for one day. I need to gather all my strength to face my past tomorrow," she said.

Esther had a strange feeling, like she was born again. All her memories were gradually coming back to her, and she could vividly remember all the details of her life as Aphra. She was sure the house she was born and raised in was probably no longer there, but she still wanted to visit the hill on which her father had built their house, where she once called home. Her parents were kind and simple, and she was her father's daughter. She still remembered how her father touched her hair and how her mother cooked her favorite dish every time she asked her. For a second, she felt guilty for loving them and forgetting her parents in Aseeta. She wanted to see her mother, Esther's mother, and tell her everything about her past life. She could finally tell her the reason for her dreams and why she felt so different all the time, but she could still not believe everything that had happened to her. She'd had a strange feeling from the moment she stepped into the forest. The sun, the river, the trees, and even the animals were all trying to help her remember. Aphra had walked the forest so many times before, sometimes with Jasper as a kid, sometimes alone, and so many times with Larko. How could she forget Larko? She could not even imagine what he had gone through after her death. If only she could look into his eyes and tell him that she still loved him more than anything, despite everything he had done. She wanted to tell him to stop blaming himself because there was nothing he could do to stop Lamia's plan, and no matter what he had done in Sinkaba, she still loved him and needed him in her life, just like her need to breathe. With a big whoosh of air, the leaves started moving around, and one leaf dropped into Esther's lap. Then she felt a sudden chill, and she knew it was not because of the cold night but probably because it was Larko trying to communicate with her.

If it were not for Lamia, she would have been with Larko forever, and her life would be so different. She felt a heavy pounding on her chest every time she remembered her. How dare she come into her dreams each night and beg for forgiveness? Aphra could not forgive Lamia. As she reviewed her past life, remembering all the details, Jasper came into her mind. She could never hate him for what he did, and all she felt for him was pity. She remembered how he was begging Lamia to let her go and kill him instead, but nothing mattered anymore. Jasper had paid for what he had done, and the mother of the forest had forgiven him.

It was getting dark, and for the very first time in her life, Esther was not scared of sleeping, and even if Lamia decided to show up in her dream again, she would tell her to go to hell because she was not going to forgive her. She had haunted her for so long, but it was over, and Esther felt no more fear. Egenar kept watching her closely but left her alone at times to find herself again. It was as if she had molted that day. Esther was there with Egenar, but she did not see him or anything around her. She was in deep thought, and the occasional sparkle in her eyes proved she was thinking about a pleasant memory in her past.

In the morning, Esther and Egenar got ready to ride toward the city. It was less than half a day's ride, and they could be in the city before noon.

"We should be in the city in just a few hours, Your Majesty," Egenar said.

"I know. I remember everything now. I have been in this forest so many times before," Esther replied.

"I am sorry, Your Majesty. Please forgive my negligence," he said.

Esther smiled and said, "Egenar, you do not need to be so formal with me. I am not a queen yet."

"Once you become a queen, you will always remain a queen," he said.

"Thank you, but remember that no one knows who I am, and I do not wish anyone to know for now, so be careful when we get to the city. Do not call me 'Your Majesty' there!"

"As you wish, Your Majesty," he said with a smile.

They rode for a few hours before they got to the city gates. When they arrived, Esther stood by the gate, staring at the tall walls of the city like she was seeing it for the first time. She looked at Egenar and said, "I thought, when I figured out who I was and what my dreams meant, life would be easier for me, but the irony is that as much as I like reminiscing about good old times, there are horrible memories that still haunt me after three hundred years. I remember vividly the last time I saw these city walls. I was desperate and distressed. I thought Larko was badly wounded and not going to survive. I did not know that instead of going to Larko, I was going to my death trap."

"I cannot even imagine how it feels to live again in this world and remember your past life and everything you said and did. Life can be quite painful even if you live it once, let alone for the second time, but you are a significant being, Your Majesty. You have a mission. You are the promised queen. Your destiny is to unite North and South and build a strong empire. I believe in your vision to build a better life for these people. The mother of the forest gave you this chance because you deserved it. Although you were the queen of Kalastra for a short time, you showed wisdom and courage, and you cared for your people," Egenar said.

"There is something about you and the way you speak that motivates me to fight and continue. Thank you for coming with me," she said.

"It is my honor, Your Majesty," he said.

Esther laid her hands on the wall and touched the stones. It was the same as before, only three hundred years older. She started walking through the alleys and looked at the face of every person on her way. Before remembering her past life and what it was like living during King Alger's and King Larko's reigns, she'd assumed it was normal to be depressed and to live in constant fear, even when she was in Aseeta, but it was not. Life was beautiful in Kalastra.

The city used to be vibrant, and people were happy and prosperous. They trusted the knights and their king, but after three hundred years, the desperation and fear screamed out of their pitiful eyes. The market was still busy, but not because it was lively and spirited. People were miserable and poor and were trying to sell whatever they had to survive. Apart from the sad faces of people, everything else was the same: the streets and alleys, the fountains, the market, and the most important thing, the castle. Esther was heartbroken when she saw the castle. It was in much better condition than the Sinkaba palace, and it still existed, but half of the castle was ruined, and as Egenar had said before, anything precious in the castle was plundered years ago by looters and insurgents. Everyone in Kalastra believed the castle was cursed after the things that happened there, making it easy for Esther to roam around.

"I cannot believe I am in this castle again after three hundred years. It was hard for me to call this place home when I first married Larko, but things changed over time. Larko made me feel welcomed, and he was always patient with me," she said.

"It is amazing to hear these things from you, Your Majesty. You are both the history of this land and its future. I will leave you alone so you can check out every corner with peace."

"Thank you, Egenar. I will find you in the courtyard soon," she replied.

Standing before the steps that led to the main entrance, Esther closed her eyes and tried to remember the castle, with its glory and magnificence, again. For a second, she thought maybe she was dead, and she was experiencing everything in the other world; otherwise, how could she be in a place that she had left three hundred years ago? She looked up at the sky and said, "Why me, mother of the forest? Why did you choose me? I was a simple girl, and I never even imagined being a queen, but you made me the queen of Kalastra. You let Lamia kill me without mercy, and now you have brought me back to life again, and you have made me remember everything so that I torture myself. Why? All the people I loved and cared about are gone. I can no longer be Esther. I was never perfect as Esther before, and now you want me to be the queen, to unite all these people, but how? I do not see the strength in me. How can I carry this burden you have placed on my shoulders? How am I supposed to be a queen again?" Then, as she wanted to go up the steps, a yellow butterfly, which was very rare to see in Kalastra, sat on her arm. Esther burst into tears. She was certain the butterfly was someone she'd known in her past life. It could be her mother, her father, or maybe Larko. It was the most beautiful butterfly she had seen in her life, and as she reached out to touch it, it suddenly flew away.

When she reached the top of the steps, the door creaked open, and the sound echoed in the hallway. The sound of its opening proved no one had entered the castle for decades. As she had predicted, the castle was dark and cold, part of the castle had no roof, and spiderwebs were everywhere. She made her way to the throne room where Larko used to sit. Even with all the gloom and darkness, she could still imagine Larko sitting on his throne and wearing his crown. In her imagination, the castle was the same as before. It was still alive, with knights and soldiers at every corner and maids running up and down. When she stood by the door of her chamber, she did not think she had the courage to open the door, but she finally did. There was almost nothing left in the chamber. She sat in the middle of the cold, vacant room and burst into tears. She let herself cry as much as she wanted and as long as she needed but promised herself not to show any sign of weakness once she was out of the castle, to act like a queen as everyone expected her to do. So she cried and cried for hours, reminiscing the days and nights she had spent with Larko in that chamber. She could never repeat those good old days with Larko again, and she could never wake up next to him. They were all history. Everything was in the past, and all she could do was keep her memories alive in her mind and heart. After hours of thinking and crying, she finally left the castle, and when she did, Egenar was waiting for her in the courtyard.

"I have prepared food and drink for our journey, Your Majesty," Egenar said.

"That is perfect. Thank you, Egenar," she said.

She then hopped on her horse, and before leaving, she looked at the castle one more time and said, "I will come back, and when I do, everything will change. I will bring prosperity back to this land and smiles to the lips of these people and joy to their hearts. I will unite North and South, and I will make a kingdom that will be remembered for centuries and will be even more magnificent than what existed in Kalastra before. I will bring peace to Kalastra and Sinkaba, and I will build an empire that no one can ever forget."

CHAPTER TWENTY-FOUR

"What is SINKABA like, Your Majesty?" Egenar asked.

Esther's gaze drifted beyond the horizon, her voice carrying the faint trace of old memories.

"It is desert, barren land, with not much vegetation. It is blazing hot during the day and wintry cold at night. There is sand everywhere, as far as you can see, but one thing is truly stunning in the desert."

"What is that, Your Majesty?" he asked.

"The sky and all the stars in it. The sky is spectacular, and the stars are shinier. The only thing that made me happy when I was in Aseeta was looking up at the sky and talking with the stars," she said.

"Did you talk with them?" he asked.

"I did. I had even named them. I called my favorite star, shinier than the rest of them, *Soorehat*. I was so lonely in Aseeta," she replied.

"It is a beautiful name. What does it mean?" he asked.

"I do not know. I named it when I was only four," she said with a smile. "Maybe she was my spirit, my past life's soul in the form of a star, trying to guide me to find myself."

"At this point, I believe everything is possible, Your Majesty," he said.

"Yes, everything is possible. I have no doubt," she said.

"Do you still see Lamia in your dreams?" he asked.

"I do sometimes, but I am not scared of her anymore. My fear was feeding her to continue haunting me," she said.

"Will you forgive her?" he asked.

"Maybe I could if it was just me she had hurt, but she caused a series of events that led to Larko's death and the destruction of the Kalastrian kingdom. She ruined so many lives, not only the lives of the people in Kalastra but also those of her people. The sandstorm that killed many innocent people in Sinkaba was the direct result of her actions," she replied.

"How was she? Was she as beautiful as the legend says she was?" he asked.

"She was beautiful, there is no denying that, but she had a dark heart. I still remember the rage in her eyes when she told her men to bury me alive," she said.

"I should not have asked about her. Forgive me, Your Majesty," he said.

"It is fine. She is in my past. She cannot hurt me anymore. She is history now," she said.

"You are right. I am quite excited to see the South. I have never traveled beyond Mount Zaka in my life before," he said.

"You have the same feeling now that I had when I first started my journey; however, I was not just excited but nervous at the same time. Every particle in my body urged me to leave Aseeta, while my mind stopped me, but I chose my heart, and I am happy that I did. If I had not followed my heart, I would never have known about my past life, and that would have been horrible," she said.

"You are so brave, Your Majesty," he said.

"I believe this is all the mother of the forest's will; otherwise, I would still be in my village, trying to fit in and accepting that my dreams had no meaning, just like what my mother always used to tell me. I asked the universe for a sign, and I received it, so I knew it was time to leave," she said.

"Do you think your mother will believe you, Your Majesty?" he asked.

"I hope she does, but even if she does not, nothing will change. I have far more important things to do now," she replied.

"What do you think about camping somewhere here for the night, Your Majesty?"

"I might be a queen, but I do not have your expertise in traveling, so I will leave that to you," she replied.

"Then I think we should camp here for the night. The good thing is that we have lots of food with us, so we do not need to hunt," he said.

It was a cold night, like the other nights Esther had spent in the forest, but the heat of the fire was pleasant, and after a long day of riding, she needed to stretch her legs by the fire to keep them warm. She was hungry, and she bit into the meat Egenar had bought from the market in Kalastra. It was a beautiful night, and the moon was big and shiny in the middle of the sky, but the peace of the night was not going to last for long. First, the horses started neighing; then Egenar heard the cracking of twigs near them. Someone was there, and Esther and Egenar were no longer alone.

"Please do not panic, Your Majesty, but I think there are people around us," he said, grabbing his sword.

"Who are they?" she asked.

"I am not sure, but I hope not Elkoy's men. We are in his territory after all," he said, and before he could finish his sentence, three men jumped out of the bushes and attacked him. Esther grabbed her sword and tried to help Egenar, but she was terrified. She had never killed anyone in her life, nor had she seen battle or bloodshed, at least not in this life. She was so shocked and shaken that she did not realize when one of the men started running toward her. She had the sword in her hand, but she could not even raise it to defend herself. In just a few seconds, so many thoughts passed through her mind: her parents, Larko, her past life, and her mission in life. The man had a dark, bearded face, and he was shouting as he ran toward her. She closed her eyes, and when she opened them, a headless man collapsed at her feet. If it were not for Egenar's quick move, she could be dead.

"Are you hurt, Your Majesty?" he asked.

"I am fine," she mumbled, barely able to stand on her feet; she leaned against a tree and said, "You need to teach me how to use a sword."

"I will, Your Majesty. Things were quiet for a while, and I forgot about Elkoy. I should have been more careful," he said.

"He will not rule this territory for much longer. I will make sure of that," she said.

Egenar stepped closer, lowering his voice as if to shield her from the darkness itself.

"You are still shaking, Your Majesty. Please sit down. We are safe now. I will stand guard throughout the night. You can sleep with peace."

"I do not think I can sleep after seeing that headless man in front of me," she said.

Esther knew she had to learn how to use a sword, or she could not survive in Kalastra. She could not have Egenar protect her at all times, and most importantly, how could she rise as the promised queen and save her people from the tyranny of Elkoy if she could not even protect herself? She survived the night somehow, but the horror she experienced made her learn how to use a sword, and she was a fast learner.

They rode for days in the green lands before reaching Mount Zaka, and as they moved toward the South, the weather was slightly warming up. Each day as they traveled, Egenar taught Esther how to use the sword. Esther was no longer the scared and confused girl who could not figure out her life purpose. She had evolved in the best way a human being could. She was strong, mentally and physically. She was at peace with her past and present, and she was persistent in reaching her goal. She was unstoppable. She saw Lamia in her dreams sometimes, and each time, Lamia begged for her forgiveness, but she was no longer scary to Esther. She was just a pathetic creature suspended in limbo, trying to move on to the other world for three hundred years. To suspend Lamia for eternity was somehow Esther's form of revenge on her.

"I still cannot believe how you got through this mountain all by yourself, Your Majesty," he said.

"I just knew I had to pass. There was no other choice for me, so I faced my fear," she said.

"Is it desert right past the mountain?" he asked.

"No, it is not, but nature changes drastically. It is no longer green and lush like it is here," she replied.

Esther could not believe she was going back to Sinkaba again. Each day, as she got farther away from Kalastra, she remembered how she felt when Lamia's men had captured her and how she had spent her final days in Kalastra. They had imprisoned her in a cage, and she had lost her hope of ever seeing Larko, her parents, and Kalastra again. She never thought she could see the vast green lands and the majestic mountains again. She never thought she could see the sun rising or ride her horse in the wilderness of Kalastra. Still, everything she'd thought was impossible to happen finally did happen, only three hundred years later. When they took her to Sinkaba, right at Mount Zaka, she'd known there was no going back. The night she spent at the foothill, she said her farewell in her heart, but there she was again, looking at the same mountain, yet feeling completely different. She had a mission, and she meant to come back to fulfill her destiny. Sinkaba was not scary to her anymore. She had killed the mother beast in her visions and her mind. Lamia had no power over her, and she could no longer intimidate her.

The night Esther and Egenar stayed at the foothill of Mount Zaka, she dreamed of Larko. It was the first time she'd seen him in her dreams since remembering everything. She saw him waiting for her at the top of a hill, and he looked incredibly handsome in his armor. His hair was tidy, as always, and his eyes were shining with passion. She ran up the hill and hugged him as tight as she could. She did not want to let go, but Larko stroked her hair gently and said, "Now is your time, Aphra! Do what I failed to do! Lead your people and be their queen once again!" Then he grabbed his sword and placed it in her hands, saying, "Do not make the same mistake I made! I could not forgive Lamia, and I killed so many innocent people. Forgive and let go! If you carry the burdens of the past, you can never set yourself free." She woke up in the middle of the night, panting with exhilaration. Her hands were shaking, and her eyes were full of tears. She had seen Larko in her dream, and everything felt so real. If she could, she would make her dream a reality and freeze it for eternity. Remembering Larko and the time they had spent together was both a blessing and a torment for Esther. To know that she only had to live with his memory was an unbearable pain she could not tolerate, but she had learned to calm herself down every time the thought of Larko came into her mind.

Esther and Egenar continued their journey and passed through the mountain together. The second time was much easier for Esther since she had done it before, or maybe because she had a companion. The days got warmer as they got away from Mount Zaka and as they moved toward the desert, and if it were not for the fact that it was wintertime, they could have passed out because of the heat in the desert. After riding for a week, they were almost getting close to the village Esther had stayed at for a few days, where Hila had nursed her and where she first realized she was the promised queen.

"Soon, we will reach a village where I stayed for a few days when I was traveling north," Esther said.

"Why did you stay in that village, Your Majesty?" Egenar asked.

"I had passed out somewhere in the desert near the village, and if it were not for the woman who found me, I would be dead now. The chief of the village was an old man who first told me I was the promised queen. I did not take him seriously at that time, since many things were unknown to me," she said.

"How did he know?" he asked.

"I am not sure, but he knew more about me than I did. He begged me not to kill the people in the South when I became a queen, and I promised him not to do so," she said.

"It seems he knew everything about the past and what had happened in Sinkaba before."

"He did, but even if I had not promised him, I would never have hurt the innocent people of the South. Part of me is still attached to this barren land. These people have suffered enough. They have been living in constant fear for years, and I will put an end to all their dread after three hundred years. There has been enough bloodshed and hatred in Kalastra and Sinkaba. Uniting North and South, I will build the greatest kingdom this world has ever seen," she said.

Egenar praised Esther. When he'd first found her in the forest, she seemed helpless and lost. He felt an urge to help her out, but then he figured out a story untold behind her eyes, which made him curious to find out more about her. When Esther finally opened up to him, he knew she was different, and when she told him about her past life and that she was Queen Aphra, he believed her without even doubting for a second. Some believe with their eyes, and others with their hearts, even when there is no proof, and Egenar believed in Esther with all his heart.

After riding for another two days, they finally arrived at the village. When the people of the village realized Esther was back, they all gathered and knelt for her. They worshipped her like she was a goddess. She told them who she was and that she'd been born again after three hundred years, and she promised she would bring them peace and prosperity. She told them she was going farther south, but she would need men to join her to build an army when she was back. She told them a war would happen, and it was inevitable, and she needed help. As Egenar had predicted, all the men in the village were ready to join. They were not warriors, but they had learned how to protect themselves over the years with the lack of a central government.

Aseeta was about ten days away from the village, and the days were dragging for Esther. She could feel that somewhere along the way in the desert, they had buried her. She did not need a map or the book of knowledge to tell her where she'd been buried alive. She was sure her heart would tell her once she got there, so she carried on. They left the village and rode for days and nights, and the only thing that was still fascinating to her in the desert was watching the stars at night. She lay down on the sands at night and looked up at the sky.

The stars looked like tiny pieces of diamonds, scattered around and shining brightly, and once in a while, one of them winked, welcoming her back to the land of mysteries. Maybe the stars were her guardian angels, protecting her everywhere she went, or maybe her favorite star was her spirit born again, but this time in the form of a star thousands of years in the future, looking down on herself. A new world had opened before Esther's eyes, and there were endless possibilities in that world. She was sure she'd been born again to fulfill her destiny so her soul could thrive and be ready for the next world. She sometimes wondered where her soul was in the past three hundred years. Was it in the other world with her loved ones, or was she alone? She did not know where she was, and she did not remember anything from the other world. The only thing she remembered was her past life on earth and nothing after her death. Perhaps it was a territory no living creature could know anything about, and someone had to be either alive or dead, and perhaps some things were better kept a mystery. *A world without mystery is monotonous. If I knew everything about the other world, how could I dream or fantasize about it?* she thought.

The next few days passed in the blink of an eye, and her heart was racing fast as she got closer to Aseeta. To Egenar, the desert was just a flat piece of land with occasional dunes, but to Esther, it was the last place she had seen in her past life. Going through the same route again, she remembered all the feelings she had back then: trapped in a cage with no life left in her body, passing out because of thirst and heat as she barely kept her eyes open, and only caring for Larko, wondering how he was doing. Now, after three hundred years, she was thinking of him again, thinking about her dream and what Larko had told her. She could no longer contain her feelings. Her hands were trembling, and her heart was about to explode. A great source of power was gravitating her to itself, like a giant magnet. She was certain it was her grave calling her. She would fly if she could, but her body had turned into a solid piece of stone. Her horse neighed wildly and stopped moving. For a minute, she did not even dare to get off her horse and touch the sand, which had swallowed her down once, but she could not let her nightmares take over her soul. She had promised to be strong and to do what was needed to release herself from Lamia's tyranny. She had traveled from Aseeta to Kalastra and had faced so many dangers and fears in her journey. She had found her purpose in life, and the goddess of sand had given her a chance to live again. However, if she could not find the courage to face Lamia once and for all, it would all be for nothing, and she could never be truly free and happy.

"Aphra, whenever you feel lost and do not know what to do, listen to what your heart tells you. That is the way your guardian angels communicate with you. They are ready to light up the torches for you when your path is dark, as soon as they see you are brave enough to take the first step. Ignore what your heart tells you, and you will pay the price for it," her father used to tell her.

There was no going back for Esther. She could not forget what she had remembered, and she could not live her life in the shadow of what Lamia had done to her either, so her only choice was to do what she had already decided to do. She closed her eyes and took a deep breath. It was not hot yet at that time of year, and there was a cool breeze. The sand particles were slightly floating in the air, dancing along with her dark, silky hair. She took the first and hardest step, and took another one after that. She did not know what direction she was going, and she was just following an unexplainable feeling in her heart. The breeze suddenly stopped, and so did Esther. She looked at the sand ahead of her feet and saw the portrait of Aphra beautifully created on the sand, a masterpiece. She knew what it meant. She was standing at her grave.

She knelt and placed her hands on the sand. She was sitting by her grave, but there was no feeling of rage and hatred in her heart anymore. She was born again in the land that had taken her life once before. She grabbed a handful of sand and scattered it in the air.

"I rotted and became the sand itself in this desert. My lungs, hands, eyes, and every particle of my body have turned into sand, and the wind has taken me everywhere in the desert. You made me eternal, Lamia. Even when I die again, I still exist. You did not break me. You did not defeat me. I am still here, and I will be here forever, but you are not. I wanted so badly to torture you and to take my revenge, but I do not want to do it anymore. I cursed you three hundred years ago, but I will take it back now. I cannot say that I have forgiven you, but I will let you go; I will not hate you anymore, and I will clear you out of my mind. I will leave you to the justice of the goddess of sand, and to move on to the other world, you need to be forgiven by her, and that is not up to me," she said, then wiped down the tears that had wet her entire face. She touched the sand again with her fingertips.

"How many people can say they have visited their own grave, Aphra? Not so many, I guess. It is my destiny to become a queen. I was born to rule all this land. I was already the queen of Kalastra, but if Lamia had not killed me, Kalastra would not only be under my reign but Sinkaba as well. Farewell, my past life. I will never visit this grave again."

Esther sat by her grave for hours. There were so many things she needed to tell Lamia.

After all, she had promised herself not to revisit her grave again, and she wanted to spend as much time as she could there, or maybe a mysterious power was going to wipe out that part of her memory, and she would never find her grave again. She whispered, she screamed, and she wept, but she promised herself to never think of Lamia again and to let her go. It was nighttime, but Egenar did not dare to destroy her solitude. He was watching her from a distance but could not do anything. As much as he wanted to, he could not help Esther. She had to face her demons alone, and that's exactly what she did. She slept by her grave the whole night, and when she woke up, it was still dark, and the sun was just about to rise. Egenar was still sleeping, his cloak under his head, using it as a pillow. "Wake up, Egenar!" she said softly.

"I am sorry, Your Majesty. I do not know when I fell asleep," he said, sitting up straight.

"It is fine. We need to leave early today. We cannot waste any time," she said.

Egenar looked at her with tons of questions in his mind, but he kept quiet and said nothing. He did not dare to pry and ask her what happened. As if Esther had read his mind, she looked at him and said, "What is it you want to ask me, Egenar?"

"What happened, Your Majesty? You seem calm and confident," he said.

Esther drew a slow breath, the morning breeze catching the strands of her hair and carrying them across her face like a whisper. "I will answer all your questions today, but once we leave this place, we will never talk about it again."

"As you wish, Your Majesty," he said.

"It is my grave there, where I was buried alive. The thought of torturing Lamia did not leave me alone since we left Kalastra, but I decided not to give in. As Aphra, I had a kind heart. I was merciful, so I forgave Lamia," she said with a big sigh. "I forgave her because I needed to leave her in my past. I do not know if she will be forgiven by the goddess of sand and if she can move on to the other world, but everything is over now, and whatever happened in my past should stay in the past. It is a new dawn, and I will not drag history with me. Maybe centuries later, they will write about us or create a new legend. Who knows?" she said.

"You are braver than you think, Your Majesty. Your people are proud of you. I am proud of you," he said.

"My whole life, I thought I was a victim, and I thought I had probably done something terrible in my childhood to deserve all those nightmares. I knew I was different, but I never thought I was special. Yesterday, I decided not to be a victim anymore. I will build a kingdom that will make everyone in the future envious of what we had. I will be fair, I will be kind, I will be wise, and I will become a queen to be remembered for eternity. Will you help me on this path, Egenar?" she asked.

Without hesitation, he dropped to one knee, head bowed in solemn vow.

"There is nothing I would not do for you, Your Majesty. I will even give my life, gladly, if it paves the way for you."

Esther reached out and touched his shoulder.

"It is not your life I need. You are a brave man, and you have fought before. That is what I need, Egenar. We must hurry. My people have waited long enough for me."

"Where are we going, Your Majesty?" he asked.

A smile curved across Esther's lips, the dawn catching the gleam of determination in her eyes.

"To Kalastra, and we are going to take our land back."

ABOUT THE AUTHOR

Mona Tebyanian is a dedicated author with a profound passion for creating immersive worlds and compelling characters. Drawing inspiration from the intricacies of human connection, deep emotions, and the allure of the unknown, her work explores themes that resonate universally. *The Queen of Sands*, her debut novel, exemplifies her artistic vision and her dedication to crafting narratives that inspire and captivate.

Mona's professional background is in civil and environmental engineering, and she currently works in the semiconductor industry. She resides in Phoenix, Arizona, with her husband and twin toddler boys. When she's not writing, Mona enjoys exploring nature, reading fantasy novels, and spending time with her family.

www.ingramcontent.com/pod-product-compliance
Lightning Source LLC
LaVergne TN
LVHW091634070526
838199LV00044B/1056